Just FRIENDS

CHAPTER ONE

Carolina

High School—Sophomore Year

"I'LL PAY you fifty bucks to write my English paper."

I slam my locker shut before shifting to face the brave soul who asked that.

I don't cheat.

I don't break rules.

Everyone knows this.

He's casually leaning against the locker next to mine. A smirk is spread across his face, as if he expects me to squeal in delight that he's asking me for a favor.

Not happening, homeboy.

Homeboy is Rex Lane.

Our school's arrogant fuckboy.

A guy I'm *not* writing a paper for.

I mock his smile. "I'll *charge* you fifty bucks not to rat you out for homework bribery."

"Homework bribery?" He flashes a brighter *I'm a nice guy; do what I'm asking* grin.

I firmly nod. "Yes." I motion down the hallway. "Now, go

away. Having this stupid conversation with you is wasting my valuable study time."

I count on my rudeness to scare him off, but when his eyes brighten in amusement, I know I'm wrong.

Crap.

I have two high school goals in life:

1. Become class valedictorian.
2. Do not gain Rex's or any popular guy's attention.

Luckily, he caught me after the class bell rang, so no one is around to witness this unfortunate encounter.

"Come on, Carolina," he pleads. "Prove to me the rumors about you aren't true."

I stiffen. "Rumors?" I deliver a stern look. "What rumors?"

I mind my business. Don't gossip. Stay in my lane.

All of this to prevent rumors from circulating about me.

He licks his lips, leaning in closer, and lowers his voice. "The rumors that you have a stick up your ass and lack personality."

This jerk.

There might be a stick up my ass, but I'm going to shove my foot up his.

I narrow my eyes, and my response releases in a hiss, "Really? You want to talk about rumors? Maybe I should believe the rumors about *you*."

"The rumors that say I'm cool as fuck? A terrific lay? Fucking hilarious?"

Our high school halls flood with rumors about him.

The one that he sports an overinflated ego is officially confirmed.

"Negative," I reply. "The rumors that you're a sucky lay with a small penis."

This is a lie—a rumor I've never heard—but hey, if he wants to talk crap, so can I.

"Lies, babe, all lies. I'm more than happy to present the evidence to back up my claim." He retreats a step, dropping his hand to the crotch of his jeans, and tugs at his zipper.

I do another quick scan of the hallway before loudly snorting. "You won't do it."

He flinches, that smug smile slipping off his lips. "Huh?"

"You won't do it." I nod toward his crotch. "You won't unzip your pants and *present your evidence.*" I park my hands on my waist and kick my foot out.

He gapes at me, speechless.

"Pull it out or go away." I dismissively wave my hand. "I have a test in ten minutes, and you, standing in front of me with your hand on your junk, aren't helping me ace it. Go beg another girl to write your paper because you lack a brain … and according to the girls' locker room gossip, a decent penis size."

He drops his hand from his crotch, his smile returning. "Looks like Little Miss Innocent might not be as uptight as she leads on. There's some personality hidden underneath those awful, itchy-looking sweaters of yours." He makes a show of eyeing me up and down.

I opt out of giving him hell over the *uptight* comment. The faster he goes away, the better.

"No, she has a low annoyance tolerance."

He steeples his hands into a praying motion. "Say yes to writing my paper, and then you can go about your studying, sweater-wearing ways."

"No."

"Sixty bucks *and* a bonus of proving I'm well-endowed when we're in private."

I dramatically gag. "Gross." As much as I don't want to deal with him, I could use the cash. "Seventy-five, and I'll *help* you write the paper, but you're doing it yourself. I don't cheat." I signal to his jeans. "And keep your micropenis to yourself. I'd rather fail every class than have you prove you're *well-endowed.*"

"Paying you to *help* me write the paper defeats the point of paying you."

"*Really*? With that brilliance of yours, you shouldn't need me to write your paper."

He laughs.

"Why are you even asking me? You're in line—*behind me*—to be class valedictorian. You can easily write your own paper." I reach forward to pat his shoulder. "I have faith in you, petite-penis buddy."

"Never said I couldn't write the boring-ass paper. I'd just rather not. I'm a busy guy who doesn't give two shits about Shakespeare."

"Eighty dollars," I blurt out.

"Eighty? What the fuck? You can't up the ante like that."

"I can, and the longer you waste my time, the higher the price." I can't believe I'm agreeing to this, but hey, money talks. "Eighty dollars. Meet me at the library after school."

"The library sucks. My house."

I shake my head. "You're high if you think I'm going to your house."

"If I'm paying eighty dollars, which is fucking insane, at least give a guy the privacy of his own home."

I thrust my finger toward him. "You'd better not try any funny business."

He rubs his palms together. "This is homework, Carolina. Get your virginal mind out of the gutter."

MY LAST CLASS of the day is AP English.

It's also Rex's.

This gives him the opportunity to stalk me out of class, to

my locker, and out to the parking lot while I ignore him.

Classmates call out his name, give him head nods, and say hi as we pass them. Interest floods their faces when their eyes cut to me. It's not that I'm the class weirdo—although, as I learned today, I apparently have a stick up my ass.

High school kids are so original.

I'm more along the lines of the class do-gooder who aces every test and spends her free time volunteering.

Oh, and I'm also the preacher's daughter.

Rex definitely isn't preacher's daughter's friend material.

Hell, he doesn't even fit into his role of the mayor's son.

"Where's your car?" he asks, strolling next to me and scanning the parking lot.

I look away, embarrassment striking me. "I don't have one."

My parents gave me the option of waiting until my sister graduated and passing her car down to me or buying one myself. Considering my cash flow is zilch, waiting for hers it is.

A whiff of fresh soap and citrus hits me when he slings his arm over my shoulders.

"You ride the bus?"

I shift out of his hold. "I ride with my sister."

"Tell her you don't need a ride today." He returns his arm to my shoulders and spins us toward the opposite side of the parking lot. "Today is your lucky day, sweetheart. You get to ride with me."

"Hard pass." Surprisingly, I don't shove him away while he leads me to a newer model black Dodge Challenger.

"Come on, Lina. It'd be pretty selfish to have your sister drive you when you could ride with me."

"Don't call me that," I grumble.

His arm falls, and he ups his pace to turn around and stare at me, walking backward. "What?"

"Lina. No one calls me that." I immediately regret telling him this.

He rubs his thumb over his bottom lip. "I'm for fucking sure calling you Lina now. It'll be our thing, babe."

"Ugh, and don't call me babe either."

"Lina babe, when you tell me not to do something, it only makes me want to do it more."

"Then, it's only fair for me to give you a nickname." I tap my finger against the side of my mouth. "I'm going with … Needle Dick." There's no stopping my lips from cracking into a smile.

He points at the car. "Get your ridiculous nickname-giving ass into my car and stop insulting my dick before I really do show you."

"You've already proven you're too chicken in the hallway."

"Of course, I can't pull my dick out at school. My parents would kill me if I got caught showing off my cock like I was at the school's talent show."

I snort. "That would require you to have talent."

He smirks. "Oh, babe, I have *plenty* of talents. My first trick will be to show you how to pull that stick out of your ass."

"So I can stick it up yours?"

"I like this little attitude of yours. It's hot."

He digs out his keys from the pocket of his jeans and unlocks the car. I hop into the passenger seat with no argument. He's right. Not only would my sister bitch on the entire drive to Rex's, but she'd also charge me gas money for having to go out of her way.

I settle into the leather seat while Rex pulls out of the parking lot. He thrums his fingers on the steering wheel to the beat of a Snoop Dogg song. I use this chance to take in everything that is him.

What's fascinating about Rex is, he's not your typical popular guy—the ones you see in movies and read about in books. He's not the star athlete or the prom king or the school's notorious bad boy. His personality is what draws people to him. He's fun, cocky, and laid-back. Everyone either wants to be his friend or his girlfriend.

That is, everyone except yours truly.

I don't need that kind of distraction in my life.

Rex is also crazy smart. He spends most of his time in the computer programming lab and has even been called into the school office to fix technical issues. Rumor has it, he's also hacked into the system before.

He's tall, at least six feet, and he towered over my small frame when we walked through the parking lot. He might not play sports, but he's more toned than our quarterback. His hair is a coppery-brown and cut short. Two dimples pop out of his cheeks when he smiles, and the asymmetry of his face is flawless.

He's also rich. I'm reminded of this when he pulls into the driveway of his mansion of a home. It's the biggest in their neighborhood, and it has a giant yard and impeccable landscaping. The Lane family is considered the most affluent in our small town of Blue Beech, Iowa.

Rex shifts the car into park and steals my attention from the home when he clears his throat. "That sure was a fun ride. I've never been checked out by a preacher's daughter before."

My eyes widen.

Oh dear God.

Was I that obvious?

"That's it. Take me home," I demand. "I don't check out guys. I was simply observing the guy I'm going to be stuck with for the next few hours."

"Too late. We have a paper to write, Lina babe."

He kills the engine to the car, circles it, and opens my door as I'm debating my next move.

Go in or leave.

I smack away his waiting hand, and he moves out of the way. With a scoff, I follow him into the house. As soon as we make it through the front door, he captures my hand in his, and I nearly fall on my face when he starts pulling me up the stairs.

"My bedroom is up here," he says.

I jerk back, causing him to stop. "I'm not going into your bedroom."

He glances back at me, blinking. "Yes, you are."

"No, I'm—"

I'm cut off when he grabs my hand again, tightening his grip, and stupidly, I don't fight him this time. He steers us down a long hallway and into a bedroom.

It's a spacious room, larger than my parents' master, and surprisingly clean. Three of the walls are painted a dark red, and the other is black. Against the black wall is a sleek metal bed with a black comforter on top. It's different than any guy's room I've seen before.

Granted, I normally don't hang out in guys' bedrooms.

There's a mini fridge in the corner, a massive desk with three monitors on top, and a TV above a black console. A collection of gaming devices and games clutter the stand.

I lose his hold when he shuts the door behind us.

"Seriously?" I snap, crossing my arms. "You have no boundaries."

He grins, showing off his bright white teeth. "My mom said that can be a great trait in life."

"For who? Serial killers?"

"For guys asking girls to do their homework."

He walks around me to the mini fridge, opens it, and peeks up at me. "What's your drink of choice, Lina? Water? Pepsi? Tequila?"

I roll my eyes, pushing my black-rimmed glasses up my nose. "You don't have tequila in there." This calling-his-bluff game is fun.

"I beg to differ." He clicks his tongue against the roof of his mouth. "It's in a Gatorade bottle, tucked into the very back so no one sees it."

Yeah, right.

Today, I'm feeling gutsy.

"Give me a tequila shot then."

He squints in my direction. "You're fucking with me."

I shake my head. "I'll need it to get through an afternoon of hanging out with you."

He grins, pushing his arm into the fridge, and pulls out a bottle.

Maybe calling his bluff wasn't the smartest idea.

We're not at school where he can be expelled for doing something like this.

We're in his *bedroom.*

I gulp when I see the bottle, focusing on the amber-tinted liquid inside that's most definitely not Gatorade.

Way to call his bluff, Carolina.

Now, he's calling yours.

Time to gear up and taste tequila for the first time.

The room is quiet as he stands. His eyes are fastened on me while he slowly unscrews the orange cap and holds the bottle out to me.

I'll be damned if I let him win this ... game? Whatever it is.

Nausea cartwheels in my stomach, and I haven't even taken a drink. Lord knows how it'll feel after I do. I inhale a deep, determined breath.

I got this.

I've never drunk tequila, but I've had wine.

It can't be that different, right?

Deciding it's done doing gymnastics, my stomach tightens, as if it's preparing itself, when I snatch the bottle from him. I grip it and drag it to my lips. Right before I do anything drastic, my back stiffens, and I frown at the same time.

"How many people have taken a drink from this bottle?" I question. "I'm not about to contract some STD."

He chuckles, signaling to the bottle. "The only person

who's drunk from that bottle is me." He pauses, snaps his fingers, and points at me. "And you, in a minute."

I narrow my eyes at him. "You better not be lying."

His hands go to his chest, feigning offense. "Lina, my sweet Lina, I'm heartbroken you don't trust me."

I gulp again.

Here goes nothing.

I can do this.

Before I chicken out, I take a quick swig of the tequila. My eyes slam shut, blocking me from witnessing his reaction, and my teeth clench as I swallow down the most disgusting thing I've ever tasted. There's no stopping my body from shuddering. I hold in a deep breath out of fear of puking it up.

When I open my eyes, I immediately roll them.

A huge grin is spread across Rex's shocked face.

He whistles and leans back on his heels. "*Damn, Lina.* Either you have a secret wild side, which I'd fucking love, or I'm bringing it out of you, which I'd also fucking love."

I shrug. "You'll never know."

I inhale a deep breath, dragging up as much nerve as I can, and take another sip to prove myself. My throat burns as if it were on fire, and I smile with pride as soon as I swallow it down.

"It's your turn, Needle Dick." I extend the bottle back to him.

"Look at me, corrupting you." He grabs it, *cheers* me, and takes a gulp. "I can't wait to do it more."

Little do I know, walking into Rex's bedroom will change everything.

Rex Lane will take over my life.

He'll steal my heart.

I'll steal his.

Only we won't know what to do with what we've taken.

CHAPTER TWO

Rex

High School—Junior Year

"YO, LANE, I NEED A FAVOR," Murphy calls out, slapping me on the back while strolling past me in the guys' locker room.

I tug on my T-shirt. "What's up?"

He stops at a locker a few down from mine, opens it, and turns my way. "Put in a good word for me with Carolina." A sly grin passes over his flushed, freckled face. Dude was struggling to hit twenty push-ups in gym class earlier. "You two are tight and all, right?"

A sour taste fills my mouth. Carolina Adams has always stayed in her own withdrawn world, but little by little, I've been tugging her into mine. That tugging has shone attention on her since we spend so much time together. That's when I want to push her back into her world, away from the just-surpassed-puberty douche bags like Murphy.

"Sorry, dude. I have no good words to say," I answer with a shrug.

He groans, throwing his head back. "Come on. Do your boy a favor."

Murphy is not *my boy.* The only time I've been around him outside of school is in passing at parties. He's a lightweight who brags *and lies* about hooking up with girls. No way in hell am I letting him near Carolina.

"Why do you want me to lie to her?"

He produces an overeager smile. "I'm asking her to prom."

The fuck he is.

"No, you're not," I say with warning.

"Yes, I am," he fires back, irritation growing in his tone.

"She already has a date. *Me.* Ask someone else."

I snatch my bag from the bench and walk away without a backward glance. When I'm in the hall, I drag my phone from my back pocket, open my texts, and hit Carolina's name.

Correction: the name she changed her contact to.

Me: Meet me at my car after school. I'm taking you home.

The Smartest and Coolest Girl in the World: Okay, Mr. Bossy. What's up?

Me: It's too much to text. My fingers hurt. They had quite the workout last night.

The Smartest and Coolest Girl in the World: Gross. If you meant for that to be a sex joke, it was weak sauce.

I can't help but chuckle.

Me: See you at my car, you pain in the ass.

A YEAR HAS PASSED since Carolina *helped* me write my paper.

Help meaning, we put off writing it and hung out instead. We watched TV. I taught her how to play my favorite video games, and we ate as if we were on death row and it was our last dinner.

Day after day, we hung out with the intention of writing that dumbass paper. I ended up writing it myself in twenty minutes and still scored an A.

Who said doing shit half-assed never got anyone anywhere?

After I turned in the paper, we kept hanging out, and somehow, we became friends—which was a fucking shock to us and everyone. She introduced me to chick flicks, and I introduced her to a thing called having fun—like taking her to parties, where she wasn't allowed to leave my side. I've brought her out of her shell, and she's calmed me.

Somehow, in some-fucking-way, we click.

I'm a dude who doesn't want to get in her panties.

She's a chick who doesn't want to bang me.

There are no expectations between us.

We study. Watch movies. Go out for pizza.

She has dinner at my house at least two nights a week.

My mom fucking loves her.

Her parents, however, aren't my biggest fans, but they keep their mouths shut because my family donates a shit-ton of money to her father's church. Carolina hasn't been banned from hanging out with me yet, but that doesn't mean Pastor Adams hasn't attempted to sway her view of me.

I grin when I find her at my car with a stack of books balanced in her arms. She's wearing one of her signature sweaters, skinny jeans, and flats that tie up to her ankles. The sweater looks itchy and is ugly as hell, but I've learned to love them. A string of fake pearls lines her neck, and her deep black hair is straight, hitting her shoulders.

"What was *so* important that you had to text me *during* class?" she snaps when I reach her. "Mrs. Heath confiscated my phone in front of everyone *and* wrote me a warning."

"Screw Mrs. Heath." I grab her books from her arms. "Tell her you're my best friend next time she pulls that shit. Guarantee she'll hand it back in seconds."

"What does that mean?" She scrunches up her nose.

"Your family might be the Kennedys of Blue Beech, but I'd suggest you calm that ego down, good sir." She turns around and gets into the Charger while I toss her books into the back seat before getting into the driver's side.

"It means, Mrs. Heath *attempted* to confiscate my phone once. I made a compelling argument. She gave it back. Not to sound like a dick, but she's scared of me."

"Uh, that does make you sound like a dick."

I shrug, starting the car.

"Are you going to tell me what your *compelling* argument was?" She makes a sour face. "God, *please* tell me you didn't sleep with her. She's married and as old as your mom!"

"Hell no. Married cougars aren't my type. They tend to be too bossy. All I simply said was, I was sure her husband would love to know what her favorite after-school activity was."

"Which is?" She cocks her head to the side. "Isn't she the tennis coach?"

"She's bumping uglies with the PE teacher."

"*Gross.*" She sticks out her tongue. "Doesn't he have a wife and, like, five kids?"

I nod. "Sure does."

"How do you always know these things? You know everyone's business."

I shrug. "I watch people. I pay attention. Not to mention, I work on the school's cameras sometimes." I poke her shoulder. "Don't think I haven't seen Clint Evans stopping by your locker between periods."

Her eyes widen, a blush rising up her cheeks, and she shoves my side. "Oh my God! You spy on me?"

"Nope." I struggle to fight back a smile. "I'm making sure the school is a safe environment for my fellow peers to learn."

"I'm so sure that's where your *concern* is."

"And not to put poor little Clint on blast, *but* dude calls his mother *mommy* when they're on the phone." I exaggeratedly shudder. "Some weird shit there. I wouldn't take on that kid."

"You're seriously terrible, you know that?" Her lips twitch into a smile. "Don't pick on Clint for being a mommy's boy when I'm sure you have no problem with girls being daddy's girls."

"Oh, man, you set yourself up for this one. For your information, I do dislike chicks calling their fathers *daddy* because it's what I prefer they call me in the bedroom."

She shoves my shoulder. "I don't know why I talk to you."

"I'm your favorite person in the world, that's why." I shake my head, clapping my hands. "Now, let's step away from the daddy talk and move on to serious business. Grab your planner, sweetheart. Pencil me in to pick you up three Saturdays from now. Seven o'clock."

"Okay," she drags out. "What's up with the preplanning?"

"Prom night. Let me know the color of your dress, so we can do all that matchy-matchy bullshit."

"Excuse me?" She scowls in my direction. "You can't just *tell me* I'm going to prom with you." She throws her arms up, her voice nearing hysteria, like the boring romance movies she forces me to watch. "You didn't even ask!"

"No need for me to ask. You're going to prom with me."

"What if I don't want to go with you? You didn't even give me a promposal!"

"Tough shit. You won't find a better date. Not to mention, I'm the only guy in this school who won't try to weasel his inexperienced dick into your virginal panties." He raises his brows. "If you want a promposal, I'll get one of those banners that fly in the sky or some shit."

"You're so romantic." She crosses her arms, pouting her glossy pink lips. "Have you ever thought that I don't want my panties to stay virginal? *Maybe* I want to change that on prom night."

"Maybe you've lost your goddamn mind." I clear my throat, and my voice grows deeper. "You're my date. Your panties will remain untouched." I jerk my thumb toward her planner in the back seat. "Put it in there, circle it with a red marker, and don't forget."

She huffs. "What about Leanne, the girl you've *already* asked to prom?"

Shit. I fucking forgot about Leanne. "She can either be your sister-date or kick rocks."

"I am *not* having a sister-date!" she shrieks.

"Looks like she'll be kicking rocks then. I'll bribe her to go with someone else."

Murphy is available.

"I can't believe I speak to you."

"You. Me. Prom." I lean over and kiss her cheek. "My mom is making tacos tonight. You coming over for dinner?"

"Ugh, fine, but I'm only coming for her and the tacos."

CHAPTER THREE

Rex

High School—Senior Year

I PAUSE my game at the sound of a knock on my bedroom door.

"Come in," I call out.

When the door opens, I expect to find my mom, asking for dirty laundry or if I've decided on which college I'm going to attend.

Nope and nope.

My back straightens in my chair when Carolina walks in.

Relief settles inside me. Lately, she's been distant, blaming it on finals, scholarships, and college acceptance letters. I have no doubt she's stressed. Her parents put too much pressure on her to be perfect, and it pisses me off.

I blink, adjusting my eyes to her in the faint light coming from my desk lamp, as she shuts the door.

"Did you try to call?" I ask, tossing the controller in my hand to the side.

She shakes her head, and my stomach drops as I focus on her. She reminds me of a nervous cub who lost her mother as she fidgets with her bracelet and then her earrings and then pulls at the end of her ponytail.

The fuck?

I stand from my chair. "Is everything okay?"

Her fidgeting stops as she draws in a breath and plays with the button of her sweater. "I want you to take my virginity." The words fall from her mouth so casually, like she's asking me to watch a movie, not confiscate her fucking V-card.

There's no stopping the laughter that rolls out of me. "Good one."

She shoots me a frustrated glare. "I'm serious. I want you to take my virginity. *Tonight.*"

I pinch the bridge of my nose. "Quit fucking with me."

We've talked about her virginity—mainly me teasing and telling her to keep it forever—but she's never suggested *I* take the damn thing before. She's either messing with me or lost her mind.

Conversation change, pronto.

"Want to order a pizza? Watch a movie?"

"Screw pizza," she snaps. "I'm not going to college a virgin."

"Why not? You should stay a virgin forever."

Don't get me wrong. It's not that I haven't imagined having sex with Carolina. I've imagined sex with her a fucking lot.

In the shower with my hand on my cock.

In bed with my hand on my cock.

When we're hanging out and I have to fight to keep from getting hard.

It wasn't like that in the beginning. Sure, I thought she was cute, but I only saw her as a friend. As we grew closer and older, my attraction developed. Everything about Carolina is perfect. She has the biggest heart I've ever known, and once you cut through her shyness, she's pretty funny. She's too gorgeous for her own damn good—a one-of-a-kind beauty hiding behind her glasses and sweaters.

I've come to love those damn sweaters.

Bought her two for Christmas.

No lie, I'd love to throw her on my bed and give her what she's asking.

But I can't.

Sleeping with Carolina is a line I'll never cross.

She's my person.

She knows me better than anyone, and I'll be damned if I give that up to temporarily get my dick wet.

"I've thought about this for a while, and I've made my decision." She exhales a sharp breath. "I don't want it to be with some random guy, and I trust you more than anyone, Rex."

I clench my fists, standing only inches from her.

How can she come here and ask me that?

How can she put me in this position?

"I'm not taking your virginity." My tone is sharp. My body is tense.

"Fine." Her tone mimics mine. "I'll find someone else to take it."

I grind my teeth when she turns to leave, and I move faster than I ever have before in my life. I catch her elbow, hauling her deeper into my bedroom and away from the door.

I tilt my head down, glaring at her while my hand is still latched on to her elbow, and my lips meet her ear as I speak. "Don't do this. Don't be stupid."

"Do what I'm asking then."

"No," I bite out.

She jerks out of my hold and pushes my chest. "Why?" she hisses. "You screw girls on the regular. It's nothing out of the ordinary for you—rinse, wash, repeat. Act like I'm a random girl you've texted for a week and met up with at a party to bang."

"You're not some random girl I've texted for a week." *You're everything to me.*

She's also fucking insane. Carolina has officially lost her goddamn mind.

She quietly stares at me for a moment.

Thank fuck.

I think I've won this … talk, argument, whatever the fuck it is.

She proves me wrong when she falls back a step and starts unbuttoning her sweater.

Motherfucker.

"Carolina," I warn.

She ignores me, and the sweater falls to her feet, giving me the sight of her chest in only a plain black bra. I lose a breath, my heart beating wildly, and my stomach knots in nervousness. Just as I'm about to bend down and scoop up her sweater to hand it back, I stop.

I'm frozen in place as she unbuttons her jeans.

"Carolina," I warn again, this time harsher.

I hate that my dick twitches as I eye her. I cover my crotch with my palm, mentally telling it to calm down.

I'm not being very persuasive.

To neither it nor Carolina.

"Rex," she says, mimicking my tone again. "Do it, or I'll find someone else."

My nostrils flare at the thought of someone else *doing it.* My bedroom seems ten times smaller as we stare at each other.

Her breathing is heavy.

Mine is deep.

She's waiting for me to give her what she wants.

I'm waiting for her to change her mind.

She won't change her mind.

I know Carolina, and I know when she's determined. This is determined Carolina.

I've never seen her so determined in her life.

I'm so fucked.

She tilts her head to the side. "So … can we start now?"

Jesus.

"I don't want this to come between us," I croak out.

"It won't. We'll act like it never happened." She's so damn sure of herself.

"*Why* are we doing it then?"

She shrugs, and I scrub a hand over my face when she unzips her jeans.

Nervous of falling on my ass, I sit on the edge of my bed. My eyes fasten to her as she wiggles out of her jeans, and I gulp at the reveal of her black boy shorts. I've seen her in a bikini plenty of times when she's come over to swim. It's hard, but I've always done a decent job of not gawking at her.

It's more intimate in here than in my backyard.

We're in my bedroom. She's stripping in front of me.

And she looks fucking breathtaking.

I can't help myself from taking in every inch of her. Her skin is tan. Her straight hair is pulled into a tight ponytail, showing off the perfect angles of her face. Since the light is limited, I can't see as much as I'd like, but I see enough to want more of her. Her breasts are full, and I eye her curves, unable to stop myself from running my tongue along my bottom lip.

"*Please, Rex*," she whispers. "Do it for me."

We don't mutter a word when I stand. I keep a safe distance between us as I try to figure out a plan.

We're doing this.

Having sex.

I'm going to take my best friend's virginity.

My heart pounds as I clear my throat. "I'm not sure how to even start this."

Why do I feel like the virgin here?

"Do whatever you normally do," she says with confidence,

as if *I* were the one losing my virginity. "Part A goes into Part B." One of her hands forms an O while she sticks a finger through it with the other. "We both took sex ed."

"Okay, let's not refer to sex like we're following directions to assemble furniture." I draw in a nervous breath. "And if I do what I *normally* do, it'll get more *intimate.* I don't just stick Part A into Part B."

She flinches, her lips forming an O, similar to what her hand did. "Oh."

She takes small steps backward to my bed, throws back the comforter, and slips underneath the sheets. I'm speechless when she takes off her glasses and sets them on my nightstand.

Not exactly a compliment when a chick takes off her glasses before sex.

Please change your mind. Please change your mind.

I chew on my lower lip while shuffling my feet on the floor. My heart has never beat so hard. I'm sure I look frenzied as fuck.

She eyes me in expectation. "Get naked. Get on top of me. We'll have sex." She waves her hand through the air. "You don't have to make it special, kiss me, or any of that nonsense. Just stick your … *penis* into my vagina, pop my cherry, and we'll be all good."

"Jesus, Lina!" I run my hands through my hair. "That's not how it works."

"Uh, yes, it is. I'm a virgin, not dumb." She taps her palm against the bed. "Let's do this."

My dick twitches and is growing harder by the second. I'm shocked she hasn't mentioned the hard-on showing through my sweatpants.

I pull at the roots of my hair. "Swear to me, this won't change anything between us."

"I swear it."

I inhale deep breaths before tugging off my T-shirt and

locking my door. Her eyes are pinned to me when I drop my sweatpants, and I give myself a silent pep talk to keep my cool through this. I hesitate when my fingers hit the band of my boxer briefs, deciding to keep them on for now.

Her coffee-brown eyes meet mine as I climb onto the bed, anxiety slithering through me like a snake. The confident demeanor she's worn is melting away.

I pull back. "We can stop." *I have no damn problem with that.*

She frantically shakes her head and shifts in place. "No. Keep going."

I pull the comforter back, and she squirms underneath me as I crawl over her. A breath catches in my throat when I reach out, trailing a finger down her body and then between her legs.

She tenses, squeezing her legs together and trapping my finger. "What are you doing?"

"Getting you ready," I explain, resting my hand on her thigh.

"What? Why?" I can hear the horror lacing her questions.

"I can't just shove my dick inside you, Carolina." My voice thickens. "The wetter you are, the less it'll hurt. I want to make this comfortable for you, and that calls for foreplay."

Her chest hitches. "Oh … then I guess we can do a quick foreplay."

I shake my head, unable to fight back my smile. *Who says, we can do a quick foreplay?*

She spreads her legs wide, giving me permission, and I'm surprised my hand isn't shaking as I drag it between her legs. I rake a finger between her slit, moving it back and forth before circling it around her clit.

She gasps when I slowly push a finger inside her.

My dick aches. She's so goddamn tight.

"Relax," I whisper, waiting for her to do as I said before moving.

I hold back until her shoulders slump against the sheets

and her muscles ease before I stroke her. The more I stroke her, the more she relaxes.

"Has anyone ever done this to you?" I rasp, keeping my eyes on her.

Her eyes have been closed since the first thrust of my finger, and I've been waiting for them to open.

"Once," she whispers, her legs trembling, and a sense of satisfaction hits me when she starts moving against my hand. "It was never like this. Never *felt* like this."

My satisfaction is hit with anger.

Who the fuck did she let in her panties, and how can I find him to kick his ass?

I quicken my thrusts and hesitate before adding another finger and massaging her clit. With how tight she is, sex will be painful for her. I want to make this as comfortable as I can, to make her feel good. I don't want her to have the typical *losing my virginity sucked, hurt, and I didn't get off* experience.

My mouth waters. As badly as I want to drop my head between her legs and taste her, I hold back.

We're already crossing one fucking serious line.

That's enough.

I love the sound of her soft moans floating through my bedroom.

"You okay?" I ask around a gulp.

She nods, and her voice is scratchy when she replies, "I think I'm ready. Do you have a condom?"

I want to keep stroking her, keep playing with her, to get her off, but I only nod. I rub her clit a few more times and then carefully draw my fingers out of her. I can't hold myself back from dropping a single kiss onto her stomach. I bring my hand into a fist, release it, and reach over her, snagging a condom from my nightstand.

Her eyes dart to mine as I pull down my briefs, my cock popping free, and then she shyly looks away as I slide on the condom. She stiffens, and her eyes slam shut when I align myself at her center.

"Carolina, you have to look at me," I say. I'm as nervous as she is.

She opens one eye at a time.

"Are you sure you want to do this?" I ask. "We can back out."

"Positive," she firmly answers.

I take a deep breath. I wasn't expecting this tonight—to have this load of pressure dropped onto me. She's handing me something so precious to her, trusting me to do it right, and I don't want to let her down.

I can't believe we're doing this.

I grab her hips, tilting them up, and gently slide inside her.

I can't stop myself from groaning.

Fuck. She feels like heaven.

I slide in deeper and stop. "You good?"

She nods, forcing a small smile even though I can sense her pain.

I move again. "Still good?"

Another nod, tension clear on her face.

I halt. "Switch spots with me."

She winces. "Huh?"

"It'll be less painful if you're on top. You can control how much of me you take," I explain, slowly pulling out of her.

She reaches forward and grabs me around the back, her nails digging into my skin to stop me from moving. "I can't … get on top of you." She gestures to our connection with her free hand. "This is fine. We'll stay like this."

My voice softens. "Tell me if you change your mind or if it hurts too much."

I notice a faint smile on her lips, and her hand briefly rubs my back before dropping.

"I trust you, Rex. I trust you more than anyone."

I softly squeeze her hips and thrust all the way in, causing her back to arch and a gasp to leave her. I stop again, giving her time to adjust to my size, and I gulp as her tightness overwhelms me.

My head spins while I slowly push in and out of her. My pace is not only to lessen her pain. I'm also fighting to stop myself from busting inside her in seconds. I smile like a motherfucker when I notice it's starting to feel good for her. Her hips move up to meet mine, and she moans.

I want to run my hands up her stomach, push up her bra, and play with her breasts, but I can't. This is purely sex. Nothing more. So, I play with her clit instead.

She moans again, setting me off.

My face goes to her neck as I quicken my thrusts.

I hold back from telling her how fucking perfect she feels.

How tight she is.

How much I love being inside her.

My hips jerk, and I move faster yet also cautiously, still not wanting to hurt her. I'm close to reaching my brink, but I *need* to make her feel good. I rotate my hips and mentally give myself a high five when a high-pitched moan leaves her, and she grinds against me.

It's somewhat of an orgasm.

Not a full yell-out-my-name one, but there's more pleasure there than pain.

This is when I can't stop myself from bucking forward faster. Shocking us both, I smash my mouth to hers as I come. My lips move from hers to her ear, sprinkling kisses along the way, and I bury my face in her neck.

"*Fuck*, Lina," I groan, exploding into the condom, shivering.

My hands rest at each side of her head as I pull back, and I glance down at her, both of us catching our breaths.

Her lips tilt into a shy smile. "Thank you."

I return the smile. "It was my pleasure."

It was a bad idea, but I love that I was her first.

That she gave me that.

I also hate her for it.

Now, I know what it feels like to be inside her.

No matter what she said, our relationship will change.

Carolina has ruined other girls for me, but I have to fight it.

We can't have that type of relationship.

"Now, I can't breathe," she says with an awkward laugh, breaking me away from my thoughts.

I pull back, noticing I'm still giving her some of my weight, and rise. I grab my boxer briefs, go to my bathroom to get rid of the condom in the trash, and turn on the light when I return to my bedroom.

Carolina pulls the sheets up her chest before sitting up while I tug on my briefs.

"Oh my God!" she suddenly gasps, her hand flying to her mouth.

My attention moves to what she's looking at.

Blood on the sheets.

It's not a lot, but it's there.

"It's fine," I say gently. "I'll throw them in the wash. No big deal."

"What … what about your mom?" she stutters out.

"I'll do them myself. She won't even see, and if she does, I won't tell her it was you."

She nods.

I bend down and kiss her forehead. "Like it never happened."

"Like it never happened," she repeats.

I just took my best friend's virginity.

And now, I'm supposed to act like it wasn't the best fucking moment of my life.

CHAPTER FOUR

Carolina

College—Sophomore Year

"PRETTY, pretty please come out with me tonight," my dormmate, Margie, begs.

I open my mouth to tell her I'll pass when my phone beeps with a text from Rex.

My Main Man—I did *not* put this as his name: **Sorry, Lina babe. I've already made plans. We're going out tonight for Nigel's b-day. I can come by later if you're awake, or tomorrow night, I'm all yours.**

His response shouldn't piss me off as much as it does, but tonight's the second Friday he's had *other plans.* Sure, expecting him to hang out with me every weekend isn't fair, but damn it, he should hang out with me every weekend.

Call me codependent; I don't care.

Rex has always been my security blanket.

I was here without him for a semester last year while he deferred, undecided on his major. Undecided meaning, he spent that semester arguing with his parents. They wanted him to go into law or politics. He didn't. It'd always been the plan for the Lane boys to follow in their father's footsteps.

Kyle, his older brother, sank half of that dream when he dropped out of school to become a police officer.

His drop out pushed their pressure onto Rex.

I can't picture Rex as an attorney or in politics.

It'd bore him to death.

His parents eventually grasped there was no changing his mind, and being obsessed with their image, they found him not attending college more embarrassing than him majoring in computer science.

He now attends Iowa State with me.

Having him here has been a relief. My first semester, I was either driving home to Blue Beech regularly or he was making the two-hour trek, so we could see each other.

Him being here has helped with the loneliness of my college life.

Him being here has also fueled a spark of jealousy inside me.

The dating pond was small in our high school.

Here, it's a freaking ocean.

Panic spills through me every time I catch a girl hitting on Rex. The fear that one of them could possibly be the girl who changes his life, who steals his heart and takes him from me. Even though he denies it, one day, I'll lose him to another woman.

It's no party, being in love with your best friend, let me tell you.

Rex has been anti-relationship since the first day we hung out. His parents' dysfunctional marriage has him convinced that relationships are toxic and nothing but forced expectations. He's so afraid of failure, of ending up like his father, that he pushes away at any mention of the word *commitment*.

My friendship with Rex is the longest relationship he's ever had.

He's not a fan of relationships.

I'm not a fan of getting my heart broken.

Friends it is with us.

Even after giving him my virginity, I've never expected more from him. That night, he changed the sheets while I went to the bathroom, and we awkwardly said our good nights. The next day, we acted like it never happened. Neither one of us has muttered a word about the night I randomly walked into his room and demanded he take my V-card.

Margie snapping her fingers in front of my face breaks me away from the *I'm pissed at Rex* thoughts. "You. Me. Going out. Your sad face says you need a drink, and I will gladly help with that."

When I first met Margie—a bleached blonde wearing a miniskirt and suede knee-high boots—I thought there was no way we'd get along and that I was in for a miserable year.

I was so wrong.

Margie is a girlfriend I wish I'd had in high school.

She's popular, but she always tries to include me in everything she does.

"Hey," I argue. "I don't have a sad face." I force my lips into a smile.

"You're definitely sporting a sad face." She plops down on the side of my bed. "You know what goes well with sad faces?"

"I have a feeling you're about to tell me, and it's not going to be a proven fact," I grumble.

"Alcohol. It'll turn that frown upside down." Her tone turns into a whine. "Come on. You've gone out with me a total of three times—"

"You're keeping track?" I interrupt.

"Yes, so I can hold it against you every time you say no."

"All right." I dramatically sigh. "You talked me into it."

She tilts her head to the side, as if she didn't hear me correctly. "Huh?"

I shrug. "Having fun tonight sounds better than Netflix."

She leaps up from the bed, squealing, and then breaks into

an obnoxious dance. "Girls' night! We're going to have so much fun; you'll be begging me to go out every night!"

Doubt that.

The less people-ing in my life, the better.

I change out of my sweats into a snake-print minidress. Margie forced me to go shopping with her after we met. As soon as we walked into the boutique, my eyes went straight to this dress. She snatched it from my hands before pushing me into a dressing room and handing it back, insisting I try it on. The dress is hot—not something I'd normally wear since party attire isn't needed much in my life. When I refused to buy it, she did and hung it up in my closet *just in case.*

That *just in case* is happening tonight, apparently.

"And put these on, too," she says, shoving strappy black heels into my hands. "You're going to look so hot." She whistles when I'm finished. "*Day-um.* It looks even hotter on you now than it did in the boutique. I'm going to have the sexiest wingwoman tonight."

I run a hand down the dress with a satisfied smile. "Thank you. I still need to pay you back for it."

She waves off my response. "Consider it a dorm-warming gift. Now, put on some makeup, and let's blow this joint. Lewis, the guy with dreads down the hall, is having predrinks in his room. We'll pregame and then go party-hopping."

I nod, quickly putting in my contacts, swiping on mascara, and adding light-pink gloss to my lips. She grabs my hand as soon as I slide the lip gloss into my bag and hauls me down the hallway.

The fact that I don't break an ankle in the heels is a miracle.

I still have the rest of the night to worry about it, though.

I'm not the most coordinated person wearing flats, so fingers crossed I don't bust my ass.

"Margie, you brought a friend!" a guy calls out when we walk in.

His dreads are a sure sign he's Lewis. I've also passed him in the hall a few times since our dorm is coed.

Rex isn't a fan of my *coed* living situation and has suggested I request a transfer more times than I can count.

I notice three guys and a girl in the corner of the room, their attention glued to their phones.

Lewis shuts the door and points at me. "I've seen you before. You're in my Social Science class."

I nod and offer a friendly smile.

"For that, I'm making you a drink."

He takes the few steps to a desk covered with alcohol bottles and sodas. My eyes widen as he hurriedly pours vodka into a red Solo cup and adds a splash of Pepsi. He has a dopey smile on his face when he hands it to me.

Margie plucks it from my hand in seconds. "You're not drinking this." She gives it back to Lewis, pats my shoulder, and grabs a bottle of beer from the other desk. "Here, this is much more your style, babe."

My style is actually tequila. It's the drink Rex and I secretly and frequently sipped on in his room, straight out of Gatorade bottles.

Margie points at me. "Don't take anything from anyone while we're out tonight."

Margie reminds me of Rex.

Apparently, I have an affinity for people who like to boss me around.

"I'm a big girl," I say. "Older than you as a matter of fact."

"Is that why you go to bed at the same time as my grandma?" Her face turns serious. "Carolina, I love you and all, but you fail at the party scene. Lewis could've handed you roofied mouthwash, and you would've trusted him and drunk it."

"Okay, you're rude," I mutter.

"Stay by my side. Don't accept drinks from creeps. Steer clear of frat guys."

"I'll do my best not to drink drugged Listerine, Mom."

She kisses my cheek. "That's my girl."

THE HOUSE IS CROWDED when we walk in. A different song pounds from every room, and my shoulders bump into people when I follow Margie into the kitchen.

"You fucking suck!"

I wheel around, finding a group of people crowded around a beat-up, graffitied beer pong table. A guy at the far end grabs a red Solo cup and chugs down the remnants in seconds.

"Here, drink this," Margie says, pushing a cup in my direction.

"I'm sorry," I say, peeking up and batting my eyes at her. "My mother told me not to accept drinks from creeps."

"Good practice, babe," she says, tapping the top of my head. She tips her cup toward the table and calls out, "We've got next game!"

Oh, heck no.

"I'm *so* not playing beer pong," I hiss.

"You're *so* playing beer pong," she corrects, authority-like. "I don't care if you suck. I'll take one for the team because I know you'll have fun." She gives me a sappy grin. "Suck all you want, and I'll still be your friend. I mean, I'll be a *very drunk friend* but still a good one."

I sip on my beer as she proceeds to explain the rules of beer pong while we wait for the guys to finish up their game. I shake my head when she asks if I have any questions.

I gulp, fighting with myself on how to play this out.

"I'll go first," Margie says as we take our spots at the end of the table. "Just watch what I do, okay?"

I nod. "Got it."

"Do we have a newbie in the house?" our opponent, a guy

sporting an overgrown man bun, asks from across the table. Even though his question was directed at me, his eyes are fixed on Margie, his face masked with desire. "Does that mean you're trying to get drunk tonight, babe?"

"Shut up," Margie says, pulling her shiny hair into a ponytail before blowing them a kiss. "Prepare to lose, assholes."

She wastes no time before grabbing a white ping-pong ball and tossing it toward them, and the group yells when it lands in the cup in front of him with a *plop*.

The guy laughs and *cheers* her before downing his drink.

He takes his turn, and the ball drops into one of our cups.

Margie drinks her cup before handing me the ball. "You got this."

"I got this." I sigh to myself, drawing in the confident smirks smothered on our opponents' faces, fully expecting me to miss.

I lift my hand, gracefully sending my ball in their direction, and it sinks into their middle cup.

Margie squeals, grabbing my arm and jumping up and down before smirking at them. "Drink up, boys."

"Beginner's luck," man-bun dude yells.

"I never said I was a *beginner*," I retort. "That's what you get for *assuming*."

"Holy shit," man-bun's partner says—a scrawny guy with a shaved head. "I think I love her."

He gulps down his drink.

Makes his next shot.

I drink.

Just like with tequila, Rex is a beer pong fan—a *big* one—and he taught me how to play a mean game with him. One of our classmates always held bonfires in his field and beer pong tournaments in his parents' barn. Rex demanded I be his partner every time, and I learned the game. We were the reigning champs until we graduated.

People might think I'm a prude who doesn't have fun, but they don't know me.

I'm not me with other people, not in my comfort zone like I am with Rex.

He gets me, and when someone gets you, you're not afraid to take risks.

I'M on my fourth game of beer pong.

Margie and I have won every time, and even though we've been kicking ass, our opponents don't suck. They've hit enough cups to give me a slight buzz, which I'm thankful for.

It's clouding my thoughts about Rex ditching me.

I bring the cup to my lips … and then nearly choke when it's pulled away mid-sip.

"What the fuck are you doing here?"

My heartbeat triples in speed when I see a fuming Rex in front of me. I don't get the chance to ask what he thinks he's doing before he captures my elbow in his hand and pulls me through the crowd. He doesn't release me until we're outside and away from the madness.

"What the fuck are you doing here?" he repeats, stepping closer.

Oh, hell no.

He doesn't get to act like he can be the only one to have fun.

"I'm here for the same reason you are—to party and drink," I answer with a huff. "And screw you. How dare you drag me out of there like you're my father!"

It's dark, and the only light around us is the faint one coming from the porch light.

I can't witness the anger on his face.

I can hear it, though.

Irritation slides along every word, and tension fills his sharp breaths. "I told you, if you go to a party, I go with you."

Even though he can't see it, I scowl at him. "Weird. You don't ask for *my* permission to attend parties."

"That's different," he grumbles. "And you know it."

"How?"

"I'm a dude, and you're … well, you."

I angrily open my crossbody bag, pull out my phone, and ignore the texts he sent me an hour ago. "I'm *me*? Let me interrupt this broadcast to Google the definition of *women's rights* for you where it says I can do whatever the hell I want."

I groan when he snatches the phone, turns on the flashlight, and shines it down on me. I wince at the bright light, hating that he's putting me on display.

"I know enough about that, considering the endless documentaries you've made me watch about it," he replies.

"Obviously, I need to make you watch more."

"I do this to keep you safe, Carolina," he says. Some of his frustration slips, and a hint of gentleness comes through. "Not to be an overbearing asshole."

My eyes rise to meet his. "Safe from what? Having a good time?"

"No, safe from date-rape drugs, from dudes who take advantage of tipsy chicks, from you putting yourself in dangerous situations. I'm your best friend, and it's my job to watch over you."

"*Huh.* Maybe as your best friend, I want to keep you safe. Maybe I don't want you to get date-raped." I sigh. "If you want to be my cockblock, Lane, then I'll be yours. I'll be blocking vaginas left and right tonight." I do a show of dramatically elbowing the air on each side.

He rubs the back of his neck with his free hand. "Not funny."

"You know what isn't funny? Having a double-standard friendship." I hate that my eyes turn glossy. Normally, I'm not this sensitive, but I miss him, and I'm mad at him, and we rarely argue. "It's not fair, Rex."

"Shit," he bites out. "Don't cry."

"I'm not. My eyes are irritated from your bullshit. Seems I'm allergic."

He chuckles before holding out his hand. "Come on. I'll drive you back to your dorm."

I slap his hand away. "Nuh-uh, mister. I'm staying here and having fun, and then I'll ride back with Margie's friend."

He shakes his head. "Nice try. I'm driving you back. If you're good, I'll stop and get you an ice cream cone."

"This isn't funny," I seethe.

Rex always tries to make light of every situation because serious talks aren't his thing. I can only imagine what we look like—standing to the side of the yard at a party, arguing like a drunk couple where the girlfriend found her frat boyfriend cheating.

I snatch my phone from his hand, catching him off guard, and aim the light on him. "I'm not a child or your little sister. I'm old enough to take care of myself."

I was wrong about him being frustrated.

Now that I can see his face, every emotion shows.

He's downright pissed.

His eyes narrow as he steps closer. "You're drinking and dressed like that." He bites into his lower lip while moving his gaze down my body. "Where did you even get that dress? I've never seen it, and *trust me*, I'd remember it."

"You don't see me all the time."

"Enough times to know you haven't worn it before."

"Rex!"

I shift over to look past him and find a blonde on the porch. She yells his name again, her hand resting against her forehead as she scans the yard for him. Rex doesn't bother turning around to look at her; his intense eyes are closed in on me, as if we were the only people in this yard.

"Lina," he says softly.

"Rex!" the chick yells his name again.

I snarl in aggravation. *Why is she looking for him? Did he come with her?*

Rex might be overprotective of me, but that doesn't mean I don't want to keep an eye on him. Sometimes, I hate myself for it—like right now, when there's a girl yelling his name, wanting him to go back and hang out with her.

Hang out with her. Not with me.

I push him back. "You have a party to get to, and so do I."

He steps to the side, stopping me. "Fuck the party. You're more important."

"What will you do then?" I throw my arm out toward the porch. "Take me back to my dorm, come back, and then hook up with the chick on the porch who's looking for you?"

"I don't know," he replies, his voice on edge. "I didn't have a plan, considering I didn't know you'd be here. My biggest priority at the moment is to return you to your dorm, safe—"

I cut him off, "You're a jerk."

It's his turn to cut me off. "If you'd let me finish my goddamn sentence, I was going to say, *unless* you want me to stay and hang out with you."

"I don't want you to pity hang out with me." My voice is strained.

He looks at the sky. "*Fuck*!" His attention flickers back to me. "I don't know how much you've had to drink, but what the hell? Why are you acting like this?"

"Like what exactly?" I give him a death stare.

"Like a totally different Carolina."

"Maybe this is *me.* The new Carolina." I step to the other side of him, so he's no longer blocking me, and I walk past him, pushing the phone back into my purse without bothering to turn the flashlight off. "This Carolina is going to drink some more and maybe find a guy to look for her from the porch."

I sound like a total brat, but how dare him!

His arm circles my waist, and he pulls me back. "*This* Rex is not going to allow that shit."

I shove him away. "Jesus. Overbearing much?"

He groans. "Fine, go have fun with your friends." He shoves his finger through the air in the direction of the house. "But I'm staying here."

I scoff. "I don't need a babysitter."

"I won't be up your ass, but you're not staying here by yourself." His tone is half-calm, half-bossy. "When you're done having fun, I'll take you back to your dorm."

"Carolina!"

This time, it's my name being called out from the porch. Also, this time, Rex and I both look at the porch. Margie is standing next to the girl who has been looking for Rex.

Margie's head turns to Rex. "Rex! Piss off! I need my partner back. We had a good winning streak going on."

I use this as a quick exit plan.

"I'll talk to you later," I say, rushing away from him and scurrying up the porch steps, stumbling a bit in my heels.

Margie grins when I make it to her.

Rex calls out my name, and I don't look back while following Margie into the house.

I'M BEING WATCHED.

I *hate* being watched.

Rex's whiskey-colored eyes have been burning into me since he returned to the house with a scowl on his face and leaned back against the wall, giving him the perfect view of the kitchen. He sips on his beer while focusing on me, as if I'm his favorite show. Holey black jeans hang low on his waist, and he's sporting gray slip-on Chucks and a black leather jacket over a blue tee. A light scruff covers his cheeks and strong jaw, and his toffee-colored hair is messily pushed back.

Rex Lane doesn't look anything like a man who plays video games on the regular.

Margie and I have continued to play beer pong, but luckily, our opponents are getting drunker, so we don't have to drink as much.

I fight the urge to stare back at him and am proud of myself for only stealing quick glances every few minutes. My heart nearly stops during one of these peeks. I miss my shot, startled at the sight of the skinny blonde from the porch standing in front of him, her back to me. He's sharing his attention between her and me now, and I clench my fist around the ball. When it's my turn, I can't stop myself from hurling the ball across the room, my aim directed at him.

It lands at his feet. Blondie spins to glare at me, and I only shrug. Rex shakes his head, raising a brow, fully aware my cup miss wasn't an accident.

I look away when Margie taps my shoulder. "Carolina, stop playing dodgeball with Blondie and get your ass over there to claim your man."

I force a laugh, a sick feeling in my stomach. "He's not my man."

"He comes to our dorm enough that someone would think he's your man. He dragged you out of this party, claiming you as his."

"Or he thinks he's my father."

I grit my teeth as the girl lifts on her tiptoes to whisper in his ear, her hand caressing his jaw. He nods, as if he were listening, but his eyes are back on me.

"I say, you go punch him in the balls for even entertaining her," Margie comments.

My shoulders slump. "He's my best friend."

She scoffs. "You need to quit being blind if you think you're only friends."

My eyes water when Rex's attention leaves me longer than it has all night as he offers the girl a flirtatious smile. He's nodding, laughing at what she's saying, and she steps in closer, their bodies nearly rubbing against each other. I'm well aware

Rex has an active sex life, but when he's with me, he's with *me.*

Blondie kissing the side of his mouth is my undoing.

"I'm out of here," I say. "I'll Uber home."

I can't stop myself from looking at them again. Blondie's arm is wrapped around his neck now.

"No, I'll get Kara," Margie says. "She's the DD tonight, so she's probably ready to dip anyway. No one likes their DD nights."

I nod, tapping the side of my eyes to stop crying. Rex will probably take Blondie home tonight and screw her brains out. I shut my eyes when memories of the night he *screwed* me push through my mind. Even though I'd sworn it wouldn't change anything, I'll never forget every way he touched me and how my body responded. I'd had other guys touch me, finger me, but no one has ever made me feel as good as Rex did.

It was like he knew me in every way.

In my perfect world, I'd be kissing his mouth. He'd be taking me back to his place. We'd spend the rest of the night naked in his bed.

Too bad my world isn't perfect.

Margie takes my hand, and we walk outside.

"I told you I was taking you home, Carolina!" Rex yells behind me when we hit the sidewalk and walk toward Kara's Honda Civic.

"I told you I'm riding with my friends," I reply without looking back at him. I know him well enough to know he's following me.

Margie whips us around, and Rex is only inches away, the streetlight shining over us.

"Look, Rex, she's hanging out with her girlfriends tonight. We need to gossip about what a dumbass you're being. I promise to take good care of her."

"I know how to take care of her better than anyone," he snaps, but he's not looking at Margie. He's looking at me.

Guilt creeps through my blood at the torture on his face. I want to pull away from Margie and let Rex take me home, but I have to stop depending on him. I can't sit at home on Friday nights when he's busy and sulk about it. We're in college now, and our relationship has changed.

"Rex," I say around a sigh. "I'm going straight back to the dorm."

He shuts his eyes, defeat covering his features. "Text me when you get back then. I'll be at your doorstep if I don't hear back from you in an hour."

"Uh, stalker much?" Kara cuts in behind us.

I didn't even notice she'd stopped with us.

"Uh, best friend much?" Rex says, mocking her voice without even giving her a glance. He tips his head down and kisses my forehead. "I hope you had fun tonight, Lina babe. Text me next time you go out, but you're not wearing that fucking dress, FYI."

"Hater," Margie sings out. "Don't get mad at other guys for wanting something you're too chicken to touch."

He slams his mouth shut, fighting to control his smart-ass response. His palm falls at the base of my back as he walks us to Kara's car, and he stands in place as we pull away.

Is he going back to the party?

To Blondie?

I clench my fingers in my lap, just thinking about it.

"We need to make a quick pit stop at the grocery store," Margie demands from the front seat. "We need snacks on snacks on snacks."

"I agree!" Kara says.

"I can definitely use some ice cream," I add.

Kara drives us to the small convenience store on campus, and we get out, laughing.

"You're on ice cream duty," Margie instructs me. She points at Kara. "You're potato chips." She points at herself with her thumb. "And I'm on candy."

"Got it," I say, and we all head in the direction of our items.

My stomach growls when I hit the ice cream aisle, and I scan the endless choices. I'm in the middle of narrowing down my options to three when I jump at the sound of the masculine voice.

"You're sure out late, and by the way, you look gorgeous."

I put my hand against my chest, startled, and smile when I see the familiar man. Familiar as in I've seen him plenty of times around campus, but not familiar enough that we've had a conversation. He looks hot, wearing a green shirt and fitted black sweatpants—nothing like I've seen him in before. His short brown hair is wet as though he's just gotten out of the shower.

My cheeks blush, and I look down to hide the cheesy smile on my face. "I think it should be the other way around." I gain control of myself and meet his eyes again. They're a light blue, round, and I could stare at them forever. "I should comment that *you're* out late." I nervously laugh. "I'm a college student. It's code to stay out late."

Okay, not usually mine, but whatever.

He returns the laugh and nods toward the freezer. "Looks like we both had an ice cream craving tonight."

I nod. "Sure did. There's no better way to end the day than with ice cream."

He turns to consider his options and steps closer to me. "What's your favorite?"

"I don't think there's such a thing as a favorite ice cream. Bad question to ask someone."

He peeks down at me, his upper lip curling into a smirk, and then shoves his hands into his pockets. "It isn't a bad question. In fact, it's your typical first-date question."

"I haven't had many first dates to actually know if that's a fact or something you just made up."

"Oh, come on." He bumps his shoulder against mine. "An extremely smart and gorgeous girl like you? I doubt that."

"Eh, I prefer to study." It shocks me that I feel so comfortable in his presence. I'm normally not into small talk, and I never thought I'd be so chill talking to this man—a man I've heard so many girls on campus drool over.

"You going to tell me your favorite, or do I need to ask you out on a first date to get my answer?"

I snort. "Good one."

"I'm serious, Carolina."

This time, when I peer up at him, there's no smirk on his face.

"Are you sure …" I gulp, lowering my voice. "Are you sure that's appropriate?"

"Probably not, but I'm good at keeping secrets." He reaches across me, his arm brushing against my chest, and opens the freezer door. "Now, choose your favorite for me and tell me when you're free."

I hesitate, wondering if I'm batshit crazy. "Okay." My answer comes out in a whisper.

Why not? Maybe I need to step out of my box with other people.

I'm fighting back a smile as I dip underneath his arm, grab a mint chocolate chip, and hand it to him. I rest my back against the freezer when he shuts the door behind me. He tucks the ice cream under his armpit and leans into me, his lips close to mine.

"Carolina!"

We both pull back at Margie yelling my name from the next aisle. "What are you, milking the cow over there? Pick something, and let's go!"

"Give me your number," he rushes out, tugging his phone from his pocket.

A smile is smothered across my face as I give it to him.

"You'd better get back to your friend," he says, reaching

out and skimming his hand over my jaw. "Hopefully, I'll see you soon."

Oh my God.

Swoon.

I keep my back against the freezer door, watching him as he disappears down the aisle, and then grab the ice cream. We load up on snacks and go back to the dorm.

As soon as I change into my pajamas and take a giant bite of ice cream, my phone beeps with a text.

Unknown Number: You're right. Mint chocolate chip is the best. When are you available?

I grin, shove my spoon in the container, and hurriedly text back.

Me: Friday night?

Unknown Number: Perfect.

Maybe this girl needs to change her college life.

Try something exciting.

I almost put my phone on the charger and finish my ice cream before crashing, but then I remember I need to text Rex. There's no doubt he'll show up here if I don't.

Me: I'm home, safe and sound.

My Main Man: Good. I apologize if I was being an ass tonight.

Me: It's okay.

My Main Man: Good night, babe. Love you.

Me: Night. Love you, too.

CHAPTER FIVE

Rex

College—Sophomore Year

CAROLINA HAS BEEN the master of call-dodging lately.

Come to think of it, she's been distant all week, ever since our stupid spat at that lame-ass party.

I texted her this morning, asking her what she was doing. It's the weekend, so she doesn't have class, and I want to hang out. After receiving no response, I asked if she wanted to get pizza. An hour later, I called. My next text was asking her what the fuck her deal was. That also went ignored.

Something is up.

She never ignores me. Even when she's pissed, she always at least replies with a smart-ass GIF.

A sick feeling settles in my stomach, a heavy dread falling over me.

Is this it?

Where college drags us apart and I lose her?

I clench my fists.

I think the fuck not.

Carolina and I are lifers, friends until the end. I don't give two shits what a future boyfriend or husband or any guy I'm going to hate who comes in the picture says about it. Carolina won't have to worry about that on my end. There will never be a woman who breaks our bond, who kicks her out of my life.

Some might say that's selfish of me, but I don't care.

It's not that I've forbidden Carolina to have a boyfriend. I can't pull that shit. I just want her to hold back for as long as possible. I'm not ready to put up a fight to not lose her yet. It scares me too damn much.

When I knock on her dorm door, I don't expect her to answer dressed like every man's wet dream—or at least, my regularly scheduled wet dream … of her.

The short jean miniskirt she's wearing shows off every curve of her body, a white shirt hangs off one shoulder, and she's wearing some type of heel shit that isn't exactly a heel.

Platforms?

Shit. My sister wears them …

Wedges.

They're wedges.

Unlike my sister, Carolina isn't a frequent wedges wearer.

At least, *my* Carolina isn't.

Maybe shit has changed. She did say she was a *new* Carolina.

I just hope to fuck this *new* Carolina doesn't leave me.

"Damn, where are you going?" I bite into my lower lip.

Her dark hair is down—unlike my usual Carolina who regularly sports it in a messy bun. She's wearing makeup—her bubblegum pink lipstick drawing my attention to her plump lips—and she replaced her glasses with contacts, showing off her coffee-brown eyes. Her standing in front of me, looking sexy as hell, reminds me of her outfit of choice at the party.

Carolina's sweaters have started disappearing. I miss those ugly-ass things.

I suppress a moan, and my cock jerks in my sweats, reminding me of how much I want her … as more than a damn friend. When we had sex, when she insisted it wouldn't change anything between us, it didn't.

Well, it didn't change the dynamic of our relationship.

We still hang out, talk, and are normal around each other as if it never happened.

Emotionally, it has changed me.

I'll never forget the happiness shooting through me when she laid down on my bed and trusted me with something she'd held on to for so long. The perfect feeling of sliding in and out of her will stick with me until I take my last breath. That night, I knew Carolina would never be just a friend, but I also knew I needed to act like she was. It was the best and most awkward sex I've had in my life.

I'm a stupid guy.

Selfish at times.

I'd take her heart, sure, and I'd make her come a few times, but I could never give her everything she deserved. She's a romantic. She wants the marriage, the family, the man who knows how to be in a relationship, and that isn't me. So, I play it cool when we're together, acting as though she doesn't hold me by my heart and balls. I love her enough to never fuck her again, but that doesn't mean I don't imagine her naked and moaning my name.

But when she's dressed like *this*, fuck, it's hard not to reach out and touch her. It's hard, not telling her how amazing her body is and how I'd love to have her again.

"I'm going out with a friend," she answers with a slight shrug, like it's something she does on the regular.

"A friend?" I look around her to peek into her room, searching for this *friend.* "Is it Margie?"

God, let it please be Margie. Please fucking be Margie.

Also, God, one more request: please also don't let it be Margie dragging her to another party.

I like Margie. She's cool people, and I know her intentions of getting Carolina to enjoy college life are pure. I just wish it were going bowling or shopping, not partying with dudes who look at her with sex eyes.

"No, I have more than one friend, you know," she replies with a frown.

She turns, giving me space to walk into her room. For the first time, I feel uninvited in here.

I've lost count of how many chicks I've ditched to be with Carolina.

She knows every damn move I make.

Yet here she is, acting as though she doesn't owe me the same, that she doesn't need to explain that she's most likely going out with a guy—a stupid jackass not worthy of having her. I can't stop myself from clenching my fist.

"Then, what friend?" I question … okay, more like interrogate.

She pulls at the hem of her skirt. "A *friend*," she stresses.

"You're sure dressed up to hang out with just *a friend*. And why do you keep putting so much emphasis on the word *friend*?" My clenched fist releases to hold two fingers in the air. "You have two friends: me and Margie. So, obviously, this friend"—I cover my mouth and cough—"*douche bag*—isn't one of them."

"I have other friends from class, and I like to be cute sometimes. Sue me."

"Bullshit," I spit, unaware of how aware she is of my jealousy. "You have a date." My stomach turns.

I don't like this. I don't like this at all.

Why this is making me so sick to my stomach, I have no idea.

Oh, wait. Yes, I do.

It's because I'm fucking in love with my best fucking friend, and I never want to share her.

"It's a hangout," she says.

"A hangout with a dude?" I correct with irritation.

"*Fine*. I'm going on a date. You happy now, Daddy?"

"Hey now." I can't help my voice from turning playful. "You know how I feel about chicks calling me daddy in bed."

Oh fuck. Now, I'm thinking about her calling someone else daddy in bed. Playfulness ejected.

"Good thing all we do is *sleep* in your bed, so that's something you'll never have to worry about."

Except once, is what I want to tell her. One time, we did more than sleep in my bed.

I collapse onto her bed, making myself comfortable, and refrain from pulling her down with me. I snatch a pillow and place it behind my head. "So, who's the lucky guy?"

She pushes her phone into her purse. "Just a guy from class. No big deal."

"What class, hmm?"

"None of Your Business 101."

I snap my fingers. "How about this? Cancel your plans and hang out with me instead."

She shakes her head. "Nope."

I throw my head back. "Fine, but give me his name."

She parks her hands on her hips. "You don't need a name. You don't give me the names of all the girls you hook up with."

I perk up, my back stiffening. "Oh, so now, you're *hooking* up with him, not just going out on a date?" *What the flying fuck? No. No. I am not allowing this.*

"You're annoying," she grumbles, taking a last look in the mirror and fluffing out her hair.

"Still waiting for that name." I tap my finger against my watch.

"Still not going to give it to you."

I jump to my feet. "What if something happens to you? What if he's a serial killer or some shit? I'll need to know who you were with, so I can kill him."

"I doubt he's going to murder me," she deadpans.

"You never know." My voice turns serious, and I beat her

to her doorway, blocking her from moving into the hallway. "When you get in the car, take a picture of his driver's license and send it to me."

She holds her palm up. "Uh, no. That's not weird or anything."

"It's normal. My sister did it in college with her friends. The dude will know there's evidence you were with him, and I'll have the info to hunt him down and chop off his balls if he lays a hand on you."

"I don't badger you about your dates."

"A.) I don't date. B.) I wouldn't give a shit telling you who I was going out with."

She crosses her arms. "Move it, Rex. I need to go."

I scoot to the side, and she walks past me. I stay on her heels as we move down the hallway, down the stairwell, and out to the parking lot.

"Whoa, dude isn't even picking you up?" I say when she tugs her car key from her purse. "He already sucks."

"Oh my God," she groans, throwing her head back. "Go away."

Rushing in front of her, I turn around and walk backward while still talking. "Look, text the guy, tell him you realized I'd give you a better time than he could, and let's do something. Your choice. Anything you want." I sound close to begging.

"No, Rex," she says sternly. "Go party, like you have all the times you've ditched me lately."

I wince. "The fuck? I've never ditched you. On the *few times* I've gone to parties, I've always told you that's what I was doing. I've never made plans with you and then bailed on them."

"And I didn't make plans with you tonight, so I'm not ditching." She looks down at her phone when it beeps with a text. "I have to go."

I move to her side, keeping at her pace, my words quickly falling from my mouth—almost in desperation. I have a bad feeling about this. "Pizza sure sounds fucking killer right now, don't you think?"

She doesn't reply.

"He's not even picking you up." I snort. "Some stand-up dude."

She turns around, her face softening. "Rex, I'll be back later, okay? Don't worry about me. I'll be fine."

I swallow.

There's no changing her mind.

Just as the night we had sex, I know determined Carolina.

This is determined Carolina.

Fuck!

She gets into her car, and I knock on the window.

As soon as she rolls it down, I poke my head through. "Text me when you get home."

She nods. "I will."

"Or I'll—"

"I know," she interrupts. "Or you'll be knocking on my door."

I turn my head to kiss her on the cheek. "Have fun tonight, I guess."

My shoulders slump as I watch her pull out of the parking lot. I've never felt so fucking defeated, and I don't know why I'm *this* bothered. She's gone on a few dates before, but something doesn't seem right with this one.

It's all fun and games, dating around in college … until it's your best friend doing it.

My phone beeps with a text message from the chick I was talking with at the party. After Carolina left, I went back in for five minutes before bailing. Clarissa stopped me before I did, and we exchanged numbers.

Clarissa: Hey, want to get together? I'm still salty about you leaving the party early.

Me: Nah, not today. Rain check?

Clarissa: Rain check. Let me know if you change your mind.

I need to be available in case Carolina A.) calls me, needing a ride or to be saved or for me to beat up the dude, or B.) makes it back to her dorm, safe and sound.

When I get back to my dorm, I order a pizza, turn on the TV, flip through channels, and decide on *20/20.* It's Friday night, and I don't give two shits about being at a party. I give all the shits about wanting to be with Carolina. I can't stop myself from texting her.

Me: On a scale of 1–10, how lame is your date?

No answer. I wait fifteen minutes and text again.

Me: You must've fallen asleep because he's lame AF. I'll call you in 10 to wake you up.

She texts back a minute later.

The Smartest and Coolest Girl in the World: I can't text. It's rude!

Me: Sure you can. I do it all the time.

The pizza I ordered arrives, and I walk down to the lobby to grab it. I text her a picture of it as soon as I'm back in my room. Chicken and pepperoni—her favorite.

Me: You're really turning down this? Yum, yum. I won't save you any.

No response.

I eat my pizza, watch a few shows, and text her an hour later.

Me: The streetlights are about to come on. I expect you to be home, or you're grounded.

The Smartest and Coolest Girl in the World: You're going to ruin my date!

Me: That's my mission.

The Smartest and Coolest Girl in the World: Officially signing off.

Me: Officially waiting for you to realize the date is a bust.

Two hours later.

The Smartest and Coolest Girl in the World: Home, Daddy.

Swear to God, my heartbeat lowers a good twelve beats. *Thank God.*

Me: I might have to change my stance on that word. I like it from you.

The Smartest and Coolest Girl in the World: You're nuts.

Me: Get some rest. You're mine tomorrow.

CHAPTER SIX

Rex

College—Junior Year
Six Months Later

MY PHONE RINGING wakes me up.

Carolina.

It's after midnight.

We haven't talked today. Hell, even though we still talk almost daily, it's not like it used to be. I'm losing her to this secret douche bag she's dating, who she'll tell me nothing about. Even Margie is clueless to her new boy toy.

She put a passcode on her phone, but considering I know everything about her, I figured it out. I crossed personal boundaries and went through her text messages. His Contact was saved under *James*—like that's easy to narrow down.

I shuddered as I read through a few *sext* messages, and just as I was hitting his Contact information, Carolina walked back into the room.

I haven't gone through her phone since. It only makes me sick to my stomach, thinking about her talking to him.

"Hello?" I hurriedly answer.

"Hey," she says on the other line.

I jump out of bed the moment I hear her sobs through the phone.

"I'm outside your dorm. Can I come in?" she asks.

I don't stay at my dorm much because I fucking hate it. I like my personal space. I only have class a few days a week and normally commute back and forth from my apartment in Blue Beech, but lately—maybe because it's my worry over Carolina—I've been sleeping here the past two weeks. She's changed—ditching me, dodging my calls, even Margie said she doesn't come home some nights. Margie called last weekend and said she left with a suitcase, and no one heard from her all weekend.

"I'm coming," I rush out, pulling on a pair of shorts, not bothering with a shirt or shoes.

I run down the hallway and stairs. I throw open the door and find her standing outside in the rain.

Fuck!

She runs into my arms, and I wrap them around her while walking her inside. She's soaked and shaking as she cries in my arms in the lobby.

"What's going on?" I ask, trembling in anger and fear. "What the fuck happened? Did someone hurt you?"

She buries her face in my neck. "Not here," she whispers in my ear.

I hoist her up, and she wraps her legs around my waist while I take us upstairs. I left my door unlocked, so I walk in and set her down on my bed, keeping the light off.

"Lina babe, what's going on?" I ask, a knot in my throat. Every muscle in my body is tense. "Did someone hurt you?"

"Yes," she answers in a whisper.

"What?" The knot thickens.

"It's not like that," she says, sensing my anger. "No one … *hurt me*, hurt me." She covers her face with her hands. "This is embarrassing."

"I can take embarrassing." I reach up and move the hands

from her face, running my finger along her jaw, wiping away drops of rain and tears. "Tell me."

She sniffles, looking away from me. "You have to promise not to judge me … or get mad."

"Lina, you know I'll never judge you for shit. I'll have your back, no matter what."

She inhales a deep breath and then breaks my fucking heart.

I clench my fist, wishing I could break a motherfucker's neck.

CHAPTER SEVEN

Carolina

Six Months Later

"I NEED CHOCOLATE CHIP COOKIES, babe, and I need them stat," Rex shouts, bursting through the front door of my loft. "*Mmm* … I smell them. Perfect timing."

My gaze moves from the TV to him. "What you need is to learn how to knock."

He takes the few steps to my couch, collapses onto it, and throws his arm over the back while making himself comfortable. "I have a key." He holds up said key, grins arrogantly, and shoves it into the pocket of his jeans. "No need to knock."

I have a key to his place. He has a key to mine.

Rex claimed it was a stipulation of our friendship to have copies of each other's keys when I moved into the loft above my older sister's garage. I declared it insanity *and* an invasion of privacy when he *stole* my key, went to Home Depot, and had a copy made.

After what happened at school, I was afraid my relationship with Rex would change. I'd started pushing him away due to an outside influence putting thoughts into my head.

"You honestly think you'll stay friends?"

"He's going to leave you as soon as he finds a girlfriend."

"Push him away before he does you."

I'd stupidly listened to someone I shouldn't have.

The night I went to his dorm, I had no idea what to expect. All I knew was that I needed him, and like the best friend he is, he wrapped me in his arms, telling me everything would be okay. It was dumb of me to doubt him. We've always accepted each other wholeheartedly in our friendship. It'd take a lot for me to kick him out of my life, and I think it's the same for him with me.

As he says, we're lifers—*C&R For-fucking-ever.*

He suggested we get it tatted. I told him he was nuts.

I hadn't realized how strong our bond was until that night. He was there for me. Under all the humor and ego is one of the sincerest people I know.

I sit cross-legged, shifting in my spot, and give him my full attention. "I'll be sure to have the locks changed," I reply, knowing damn well I won't.

His signature crew haircut has grown out on the top, long and sticking up—his everyday look. He's sporting dark jeans, a black shirt, and white sneakers. Casual is Rex's style.

"What happened?" I question.

Cookies are our go-to when we're having a bad day.

Correction: us hanging out and cookies are our go-to when we're having a bad day.

"This game," he explains, blowing out a stressed breath, "it's kicking my ass. I can't be in my apartment right now, or I'll throw the console through the window."

My face softens at his admission. Rex has worked his butt off on developing this game, and it means so much to him. Not only for his own self-gratification, but to also prove wrong everyone who's doubted him for his career choice—those who claim he lazily sits at home, playing video games all day.

Eight months ago, on a whim, he sent in a demo of the game he'd been designing to one of the largest names in the industry. They loved it—which was no surprise to me. They gave him an advance and a year to finish it. Lately, he's been stressing, wanting the final product to be perfect.

"I've also missed you," he adds with a wink. "You never told me how your date with the douche bag went."

"Why do you call every guy I go on a date with a douche bag?" I ask, raising a brow. "You don't even know him."

The date was a bust. We went to dinner, had zilch in common, and haven't talked since. I only went because my sister had set it up without asking, and I would've felt bad, saying no. I'd rather have my ear bitten off Mike Tyson–style than hit the dating scene again. Technically, I've never hit the dating scene. My first serious relationship was hidden.

The sucky thing about a secret relationship?

No one knows you're heartbroken when it ends. You can't use a broken heart as an excuse to hide away in your loft or, say, drop out of college.

Okay, I didn't *exactly* drop out of college over a broken heart.

It's more complicated than that.

There are more twists and turns than my heart being shattered.

"I call them douche bags because they're lame, boring, and bad for you," Rex explains matter-of-factly.

"You're one to talk." I roll my eyes. "Who's your flavor of the week?"

Rex hasn't changed his mind about a relationship. Since we're open books to each other, I know why he runs from them. He doesn't think he's capable of having a normal relationship. He doesn't trust anyone other than his mother—he did correct himself, adding me to that list after I scowled at him for not including me—and he thinks love makes people weak. He grew up around his parents' toxic marriage, and he saw the pain his mother endured in the name of love as his father cheated.

He scratches his scruffy cheek. "Hmm … I'd say chocolate chip." Mischief flashes in his eyes. "Next week, you can whip me up some Snickerdoodle."

I can't help but laugh. "Sucks for you. All the chocolate chip have been eaten by this girl." I poke myself in the chest with my thumb.

"Lies, my dear Lina, all lies. You *always* save me cookies. It's in our friendship handbook." He squeezes my thigh, smacks a kiss onto my cheek, and rises from the couch. "You love me too much to withhold them."

He's right. I always make extra for him, *especially* chocolate chip.

They're his favorite.

He goes to my kitchenette, and I don't bother glancing back at him as I hear him opening cabinets.

After I dropped out of school, I stayed at Rex's apartment for two weeks. I was terrified to tell my parents and had to build up the guts to break the news. Rex offered to go with me, but it would've only made them angrier. They would've somehow pointed the blame at him.

My mother cried. My father threatened to cut me off. *Technically,* he did cut me off. I'm now responsible for every bill—phone, rent, car insurance. My sister, Tricia, stepped in and offered me the loft above her garage. It's roomy, with plenty of space for one person. I have a small bedroom, a living room, a bathroom, and a kitchenette. On the plus side, it's larger than my dorm room. It also came furnished with a queen-size bed, a couch, and a TV. I've added a few special touches—bright purple throw pillows, numerous photos of Rex and me, and a large bookshelf I filled with my favorite novels.

Tricia doesn't charge me rent, but I still need money to eat and for basic essentials, so I got a job waiting tables at Shirley's Diner. The money isn't great, but it will hold me over until I decide my next step, which is to eventually look into online classes.

"Uh-oh," Rex draws out, stepping into my view. A plate of cookies is in one hand, and a bottle of wine is in the other. An *empty* bottle of wine. He snags a cookie before setting the plate and wine on the table in front of the couch. "Cookies *and* wine. Who pissed my girl off today?"

"I don't want to talk about it," I grumble.

I'm not a big drinker even though I'm twenty-one now, and doing it at home isn't a normal thing for me, but it's been a day. Rex knows that I only pull out a bottle of wine when my stress level is high.

"Tough shit." He plops back down on the couch, closer to me this time, with concern etched across his face. "You force me to talk about my problems, giving my dude Dr. Phil a run for his money." He cocks his head to the side, studying me, and takes a bite of his cookie. "What's on your mind?"

I twist in my spot, snatching the glass of wine resting on the end table behind me. "You remember my cousin Faye?" I gulp down the remainder of wine. A good amount of alcohol needs to be in my system to even say her name.

He nods, swallowing down his bite before answering, "Chick who couldn't handle one beer without puking it up and then went and tattled on us for having said beers? The one who was a major bitch to you until I set her straight?"

"The one and only."

"What about her?"

"She's getting married."

He loudly whistles. "Damn, poor guy. How much did her parents pay him to put up with her evil ass?"

A laugh escapes me. Rex always adds humor to my crappy situations.

"She invited me to her wedding in Texas."

"And?" He grabs another cookie.

"And not only do I not want to attend, but I'm also lacking a date."

"Ahh … Douche Bags 'R' Us doesn't have any availability for that day, huh?"

I snatch the half-eaten cookie from his hand. "No cookies for smart-asses." I shove the entire thing into my mouth and expressively munch on it.

He chuckles. "I know you enjoy my slobber and all, but you don't have to resort to stealing my cookies. Just ask me to make out with you."

I shoot him a glare. "I'm burning our friendship bracelets."

"Good thing I have letter beads and strings to make new ones." He holds up his wrist, showing off his bracelet that matches mine. They're not beaded or cheesy, just leather bands with our initials on them. It was a Christmas gift from me. "I have plenty with your initials."

"Yeah, that's not creepy or anything."

"Oh, really?" He smirks. "Says the girl who's stolen nearly my entire wardrobe."

"Your clothes are comfy." I shrug before swatting my hand through the air. "*Anyway*, back to the wedding."

"Your sister will be there. Say you want to sit at her table. Or simple, don't go. Why are you even stressing?"

"I'm sorry, but did you forget who my parents are? They'd kill me. And my sister is friends with Faye. They'll be hanging out, sharing smiles—all that annoying stuff."

"Eh, I doubt a preacher would kill his daughter. It'd be bad for his image."

I toss my head back. "They're all about supporting your loved ones—*blah, blah*, vomit, *blah*."

I set down my empty wineglass, wishing I could pour another, but I only bought one bottle at the store. I hadn't expected my mother to spring this on me at the last minute.

Hell, I didn't even receive a personal invite. Faye couldn't care less if I showed up to her wedding. Lord knows, she won't be receiving an invite to mine. Tattletales have no room in my big day.

"Are you aware of the worst thing about attending weddings solo?"

"Nope," Rex answers, a sly smile arching on his lips. "Although I have a feeling you're about to tell me—all dramatic and shit."

"Everyone asks why I'm single!" I throw my arms in the air. "Even the kids! Shoot, even my grandmother, who suffers from dementia and doesn't remember anyone in our family, *except* her single granddaughter." I wince. "Do you know how miserable the singles table is?"

"Can't say I do. Never had to sit at one."

"Of course you haven't." I glower in annoyance. "That will change when you're eighty and you have no one because you're *so scared* of relationships and too old for a quick fling."

"Eh, I'll take my chances." He ruffles his hands through my hair, giving me a playful grin. "Who knows? We might be single at eighty together, hanging out in the nursing home, stirring up trouble. We'll have our own singles table. It'll be lit."

"Sounds like a better time than going to this godforsaken wedding."

"I'll go with you."

I narrow my eyes at him. "Funny."

Rex offering to tag along isn't surprising. We're each other's sidekicks. I'm there when he has to deal with his father, whose favorite hobby is giving Rex the third degree … and cheating on his mother.

He and Rex don't exactly see eye to eye—haven't since Rex was a teen.

"No joke," he says. "I'll go. When is it?"

"This weekend." I wrinkle my nose. "It's short notice, and I know you have a lot going on."

"I'm coming. I need a break, and you need a date."

His phone vibrates, and I see the name Megan flash across the screen when he pulls it from his pocket.

"Your skank is calling," I comment, leaning over and making a show of reading it.

"Any girl can wait when I'm with you. You know you're my favorite. My best friend comes before anyone."

He declines the call and eats another cookie.

REX GRABS my carry-on bag from me and throws it over his shoulder as we walk through the automatic glass doors. "Does my favorite girl still hate flying?"

I rode with my parents to the airport … unwillingly, and Rex met us here. My parents insisted on the carpooling, demanding we discuss my life plans, and they know I can't jump out of a moving car to avoid their overbearing questions. Car rides with them are more dreadful than having my pinkie nail ripped off, and it's turned worse now that I dropped out of college and moved back to Blue Beech.

"The preacher's daughter doesn't make reckless decisions like that."

"She doesn't have secrets."

Oh, man, if only they knew the stupid stuff this preacher's daughter did.

Nausea fills me at the thought of my parents finding out. It'd ruin them, their name, and they'd never look at me the same. To keep this from happening, I have to play someone else's game and am at his mercy. Thankfully, it hasn't been as bad lately as it was at first. I keep this secret so tucked away that Rex doesn't even know.

He's my ride or die, and I don't think he'd walk away from me if he ever were to find out. The problem is, I know Rex well enough to know he'd jump in and try to fix the situation. Him doing that would only make things worse.

"Sure do," I answer, strolling next to him through the airport.

"Good thing I upgraded you to first class." He peeks back at my parents walking behind us. "I also upgraded the 'rents. Maybe it'll convince them to like me."

"Hey, they like you," I halfway lie.

When I mentioned Rex was coming—while on the way to the airport—they weren't happy, *but* they also weren't pissed. They've been vocal about their issues with Rex and our friendship … or *dependency*, in their words. They think Rex is the reason I dropped out of school. It was the other way around. Rex had begged me to stay in school, but he supported my decision in the end.

He scoffs. "They like *my family*, so they put up with me."

"How did you even upgrade us?" I ask, walking around a group of parents yelling at their kids to hurry it up, and I take our place in the check-in line. "You don't know our ticket numbers."

"*Au contraire,* Lina. I know your email password, which led me to your ticket information because your father forwarded the info to you."

"Seriously?"

He shrugs with no shame. "You haven't changed it since senior year. You should probably do that, for security reasons and all."

When my mother finds out about her seat upgrade, she's ecstatic. My father, not so much. He argues with the attendant, then Rex, and then my mother to change it back. My mother finally rips him a new one and says it is insulting to Rex's kind gesture. Since my mom tends to make the rules in our family, he caves, shooting a glare at Rex.

"How did you know my password senior year?" I ask while my father continues to complain to my mother behind us.

Rex shrugs again. "I don't remember. I was probably bored."

"You know no boundaries." This is something I tell him on the regular.

"I do want to put in a request for you to change that password. I can't believe it's still *The_Future_Mrs_Jonas*. You know none of those guys are single anymore, right?"

I roll my eyes. "I'm concerned you know the love life of the Jonas brothers."

"I'm concerned you thought you'd marry one. If you need help, I'm a great password creator. I'm thinking ..." He fakes deep thinking, running his palm over his chin. "*Rex's_biggest_fan*. It suits you better."

If my parents weren't behind us, I'd kick my foot out and trip him.

"It's an old email and hasn't been high on my priority list. I suggest you find a new hobby because your password ideas are worse than the *Game of Thrones* finale." I rub my forehead before yawning. "It's too early for me to deal with you right now. I need coffee, snacks, and Tylenol PM to knock my ass out."

"You want something that'll keep you up but then also something that'll make you sleep? Sounds like a legit plan you thought out well. New plan: coffee, snacks. No Tylenol PM for you." He ruffles his hand through my hair, screwing up the messy bun I took a full ten minutes to perfect. "I can't be sitting next to you while you're drooling and dreaming about me. It's also a short flight. You don't want to show up all cracked out on cough meds."

I hold up a finger. "A.) I don't drool." I hold up another. "B.) Sounds like the perfect plan for me."

We get coffee, snacks, and unfortunately no Tylenol PM before heading to our terminal. Luckily, we don't have a long wait before boarding the plane. They welcome first class, and the flight attendant doesn't fail to check Rex out as we take our seats. Rex grins and winks at her as he makes himself comfortable next to me in the aisle seat.

"All right," he says after the flirty flight attendant quits giving him googly eyes and starts to actually do her job. "How are we playing this?"

I take a sip of my iced coffee, blinking. "Playing what?"

He leans into me and lowers his voice. "Am I the best friend? Boyfriend? Wedding date? What's my role here?"

His role? I pull back in confusion. "Uh, my best friend."

He draws in closer to me. "Just the best friend?"

"Just the best friend," I slowly repeat.

"Gotcha. If anything changes, let me know."

What the …?

"Do you want to act like you're someone else?" I draw out.

"No, I want to make sure you know I have your back and won't let anyone give you any shit. If they want to know why you don't have a boyfriend—which, from what you've told me, is a regular question from them—say it's me. I'm game." He tears open a bag of chips, snags one, and offers them to me.

I shake my head. "I can't lie to my family and say we're dating."

"Sure, you can. Think about it. If you change your mind, I'm all up for role-playing."

I chew on the edge of my straw. "I'm sure you're all for role-playing."

"Eh, it's usually not my kink, but I'll do it for you. I have your back if vultures come your way, talking shit." He tips his head down and takes a sip of my coffee while it's in my hand.

"AW, Carolina brought her best friend as her date. How cute," Faye, my bitch-faced cousin, announces when we walk into the banquet room.

Dread clouds my mind when she steps in front of Rex and

me, her irritating girl squad behind her. Her diarrhea-colored hair is pulled into a high ponytail, and she's wearing a white dress that hits her knees. Across that white dress is a sash that says, *Bride!*

How annoying.

Everyone here knows she's the bride, considering it's *her* wedding.

This hell wedding is a weekend affair. Tonight, we endure dinner. Tomorrow, we'll suffer through lunch and then the wedding.

I slapped Faye in the face when I was fourteen because she'd ripped apart my favorite book.

Got grounded for a month and my phone taken away.

It was worth it.

My parents added that I'd be grounded for the rest of my life if I touched her again. They said that in front of her, so Frightening Faye knew she could bully me more since being grounded for the rest of my life didn't sound like a party. Lucky for me, she moved away her freshman year.

Unlucky for me, she came back a week during the summers to visit my grandparents. One year, my parents demanded I allow her to tag along with me to Rex's house. She flirted with him the entire time and made fun of my one-piece bathing suit, so Rex kicked her out, making his mom drive her home. That was when I knew Rex would always have my back. He could've easily ditched me and hooked up with Faye, but he knew my history with her. Shoot, he hardly muttered a word to her with the exception of telling her to leave his damn house and never come back.

I stiffen, holding in a breath, while racking my brain for the perfect comeback.

"She brought her *boyfriend*," Rex abruptly corrects next to me. His arm wraps around my waist, and he pulls me in closer to him, my hip hitting his.

Faye's mouth drops open. Her eyes and finger ping back

and forth between Rex and me … between my apparent *boyfriend* and me. When she finally speaks, her words are choked out, "You two are—"

"Dating? In love? Sure fucking am," Rex says to her with no hesitation. He stares down at me, a tender smile spreading across his face. "We're much more than friends, but we do agree on one thing: we are fucking cute." His gaze turns nasty when he looks back at Faye. "I knew you'd be so happy for your cousin to find love. Maybe we'll invite you to our wedding." He makes a show of looking around the ballroom. "It'll probably be less stuffy than this shit, so it might not be your thing."

Oh my God.

I'm struggling to hold back not only my surprise, but also my laughter. *This* is why Rex mentioned pretending we're in a relationship. He knew Faye would give me shit for bringing him.

Faye stares at us, speechless, before stammering out words, "I, uh … need to find my fiancé."

"Good idea," Rex says, turning us away from her and capturing my hand in his. "I'm in desperate need of some alone time with my girlfriend."

Rex's grip is firm as he leads me out of the room and into a deserted hallway before releasing me.

I hold up my hands, my palms facing him. "*Whoa.* I thought we weren't playing the dating thing."

He tilts his head, as if he's studying me, and I do the same.

Faye's shock of us dating isn't surprising. Rex is the complete opposite of me. I'm wearing a black dress with a white collar, looking like Wednesday Addams, and my black-rimmed glasses. It was necessary for me to wear black in mourning of her husband losing his soul. I didn't shower before coming to the dinner, so my hair is half-straight, half-looking crazy.

Rex is wearing a black button-down shirt and dark jeans,

his hair perfect even though he hasn't touched it since this morning.

"We did say that," he answers, shoving his hands into his pockets. "That changed. Fuck her. No way will I listen to her talk shit about you. She would've given you hell all weekend for being solo." His dark eyes level on me. "This weekend, you're my girlfriend."

"Uh …" I draw out. "We have some issues with this game, *boyfriend*."

He arches a brow. "Which are?"

"First and foremost, we're sleeping in separate rooms."

"Easy fix," he says with a relaxed smile before it turns boyish. "I'm being a gentleman, respecting your 'rents. Your dad is a preacher. Of course we're not sleeping together." His grin moves from boyish to cocky. "I have motherfucking values, Carolina."

"They won't buy it." I shake my head and nervously walk circles around him. "This is so stupid."

He grabs my hand, spinning me around to face him. "We'll share a room then. It's not like we haven't shared a bed. Shit, I took your virginity."

I push his shoulder, feeling a deep blush ride up my cheeks, and force myself not to cover my face. "Oh my God! Shut up!" I frantically glance around the hallway, and my response comes out in a low hiss, "People can hear you!"

"We're dating, babe. They already assume we're fucking." He reaches out and runs his hand over my chin, causing me to shiver. "Now, come on, my sexy-ass girlfriend. We have a dinner to get to."

That's the first time he's brought up taking my virginity. I'm still shocked at myself for building up the courage to ask him that night. Like I told him, I didn't want to go to college, hauling around my V-card, yet I also had no interest in handing it over to a random guy.

I trusted Rex to be careful with me, to make me comfortable.

He knew I was a virgin and wouldn't make fun of me for my inexperience.

The best decision I ever made was letting Rex Lane take my virginity.

Well, the best decision for my vagina.

Not the best decision for my heart.

CHAPTER EIGHT

Rex

THIS REHEARSAL DINNER is stuck up as fuck.

I come from money. Not trying to sound like a pretentious asshole, but my family is the wealthiest in Blue Beech. I've never acted as snobby as these people, and they're not nearly as rich as my family.

My family's money isn't my money, obviously. I never take advantage of that or run to them for exuberant amounts of cash. They paid for college, but when I decided to move into my own apartment, that was on me. I make most of my income from winning video game tournaments.

But no matter how much money I have had or will ever have, I'd never look down at people like they are—with the exception of Carolina's parents. Most of the people, including good ole Faye, are treating the servers like shit, complaining about the food, and as soon as one family member turns their back, someone is already talking shit about them.

No wonder Carolina didn't want to come.

They made a show when they realized they had to move around seating arrangements to make room for me.

"We didn't think she'd have a plus-one," Faye's mother

said, her over-injected lips giving my new girlfriend a mocking smile.

Her family members are firing off question after question, as if trying to catch us on our lie. They're so desperate; it's sad. It's easy, playing this game because we know everything about each other. We've done so much boyfriend-girlfriend shit together even though we can never be boyfriend-girlfriend.

I can't cross that line because I can't lose her.

She's one of the most important people in my life.

The rehearsal dinner is in the banquet hall of the hotel we're staying in. It's also where we're having brunch in the morning, and the wedding will be held outside the hotel in the garden.

"That was dreadful," she mutters when dinner is finished and we head back to our rooms. "Thank God you came. I would've smothered myself with my napkin." She blows out a breath and loops her arm through mine. "We need to get out of here before they play another round of Twenty Questions. Swear to God, they were more interested in our love life than the bride and groom's."

Carolina isn't much of a touchy-feely person, except with me, which makes me feel so damn special. It took her a while to warm up to me and my charm. Now, she has no problem leaning into me, sticking her feet in my lap, and resting her head on my shoulder when she's tired and we're watching a movie.

Me, on the other hand? I started the whole arm-over-the-shoulders shit as soon we talked. Like she says, I have no boundaries when it comes to her—with the exception of *never, ever, ever* having sex with her again. That is the only boundary … and hurting her.

"Our love life, huh?" I ask, and she tucks her face into my chest, not wanting to have the conversation of me calling her out for her *love life* comment. "It's simple, why they paid more attention to us. The bride and groom are lame as fuck. No one cares about them."

She pulls back to playfully slap my stomach. "Rex! You're going to get us kicked out of the wedding."

We disconnect after stepping into the elevator, and I hit our floor number. Since her parents had already booked her room, I had to bribe the hotel manager to put me next to her.

"I don't think you'd have a problem with them booting us," I comment as the elevator doors close. I lean back against the wall and cross my arms, staring at her.

She looks gorgeous. It's always hard for me to keep my touches platonic, but it's fucking hell when she dresses up. Her dress hardly shows off any skin—and by hardly, I mean, the bottom of her legs, ankles, and arms. My cock twitches as I remember how perfect she looks under that dress. With every friendly touch I give her, there's not-so-clean thoughts behind it on my end. I'm proud of how strong I am for holding back.

At dinner, she pulled her black hair into a ponytail, showing off the neck I'd shoved my face in after I came inside her. All I thought about during the main course was how soft her skin would be as I kissed that neck … how she'd react to my lips on her.

She lights up every damn room she walks into, and I hate how much people give her shit for being her. She doesn't have a boyfriend because she's selective—*thank fuck*—and I respect that she's picky.

"True, *but* my parents would," she says, cutting me out of my thoughts.

She's right. Her parents are all about family and doing the right thing. They're also strict and expect Carolina to be perfect. That's one issue I have with them. Carolina was always stressed about school because they put so much pressure on her. She wasn't allowed to get a bad grade or miss homework because they were focused on her scoring a scholarship. She got a B on a paper once—a fucking *B*—and her parents lost their shit. She'd hung out with me the night before, and they blamed it on our friendship.

We shuffle out of the elevator when we hit our floor, and she digs through her clutch for her key card.

"Are you coming in and hanging out?" she asks while unlocking it.

"Only if you promise not to fall asleep in ten minutes."

She glances back at me as we walk into the room. "I can't make any promises. Stress makes me sleepy, and my stress meter is in the double red."

I flip on the light. "Stop being stressed then. Who gives a fuck what these people think?"

She sighs. "I know."

I snatch the extra key card lying on the desk. "I'm taking this."

She falls down onto the bed and drags her heels off her feet. "Huh?"

I hold up the card. "This is my copy." I open my wallet, pull out my extra key card, and drop it where hers was. "Here's my spare for you." I stick my new key into my pocket. "In case I need to get into your room or you need to get into mine."

"Gotcha." She jerks her head toward the bathroom. "Let me change first."

"Same. I'll be right back." I run to my room and change into gray sweats and a tee.

When I return to her room, she's walking out of the bathroom, wearing similar sweats and an oversize tee with our high school's logo on it.

Technically, they're *my* pajamas since both items used to belong to me. Swear to God, every time she stays over, another piece of my clothing goes missing. My attempts at getting them back have stopped because I never win.

I grin. "I'm going to have to start charging you for your theft," I say, falling down onto her bed, lying on my side, and holding my head up with my elbow. I might complain, but secretly, I love seeing her in my clothes.

She rolls her eyes. "Yeah, right." She tugs at the bottom of my shirt. "They don't make women's clothes this comfy. Therefore, your clothes are my clothes."

She makes herself comfortable next to me, her back against the headboard, and turns on the TV to *Live PD*.

It's our favorite show.

Twenty minutes later, Carolina is knocked out.

I chuckle to myself and carefully slide off the bed, not wanting to wake her. I throw the covers over her, kiss her forehead, and then go back to my room. As soon as I walk in, my phone rings.

"Hello?" I answer.

"Hey, little bro," Sierra, my older sister, says on the other line. "Are you busy tomorrow? I think my computer is on crack, and it needs you to take it to rehab. I can't access any of my clients' files."

"Sorry, sis, but I'm in Texas with Carolina all weekend," I reply.

"Oh, I like," she gushes.

Everyone in my family is Team Rex and Carolina Need to Date. There isn't one person who dislikes her. In fact, sometimes, I think they like her better than me.

"Shut up," I grumble.

My grumpiness doesn't faze her.

"What are you doing? Couples retreat?"

"Piss off. She had a family wedding and didn't want to go alone."

"I wish you two would start dating. You pretty much already act like husband and wife; it'd just have more *benefits*."

I make a gagging noise. "Gross. You're my sister."

She laughs.

I yawn. "I'm wiped. I'll look at your computer when I get home."

We say our good nights, and I notice a text from the chick I've been hanging out with lately.

I ignore it.

Ever since Carolina came to me, heartbroken, it's been hard for me to be around other women. I always want to make sure she's okay. I hate seeing her hurt, and it kills me when I think about her falling for a complete scumbag who took advantage of her.

I hate how much I care about her but can't imagine her not being in my life.

I love Carolina Adams, and there's nothing I can do about it because I wouldn't survive losing her.

CHAPTER NINE

Carolina

REX ISN'T ANSWERING my calls.

If he overslept, I'm kicking his ass.

All eyes have been on us since his relationship announcement. If we're late, there will no doubt be more gossip. I brainstorm on possible excuses for our tardiness.

We overslept.

Had wild morning sex.

Got it on in the shower.

Okay, I need to stop with the sex cop-outs.

Overslept it is.

It's boring but convincing.

Rex is a night owl and works on his video games at night. Players are most active at night, and he chats with the gamers testing his game. Last night after dinner, I set the alarm on his phone, so he wouldn't oversleep, but it wouldn't surprise me if he slept through it.

I call him again.

No answer.

I slide on my heels.

Call him again.

No answer.

I grab my clutch and check my reflection in the mirror. I woke up early to give myself enough time to get ready for brunch before the wedding. My hair is straightened and parted down the middle. I'm wearing my contacts, and I did my makeup. My dress and heels are black again.

I take both key cards from the dresser and head to Rex's room. After banging on the door six times with no answer, I shrug, unlock the door, and let myself in.

"You'd better wake your butt up!" I shout before lowering my voice in case any of his room neighbors are family. "No way am I facing these people alone, *especially* before food and coffee are in my system!"

The door slams shut behind me. His bed is empty, the blankets and sheets rustled, and I spot his phone charging on the nightstand. I toss my clutch onto the bed and move to the bathroom when I hear the shower running. The door is ajar, and just as I'm about to yell at him to hurry it up, I freeze. My mouth drops open, my fingers flying to my parted lips, and I stumble back.

Oh my freaking God.

My heart thrashes against my chest at the sight.

A slight fog is steamed over the glass shower door, but I see him. I fixate on the lean, powerful body as water cascades down his every muscle. Rex isn't only showering. No, his hand is wrapped around his hard cock, lazily stroking it. When his fingers reach the head, he turns his grip while releasing a deep, guttural groan. His free hand is flattened against the tiled shower wall, and his head is tipped down, concentrated on his stroking.

It's the hottest thing I've ever seen.

My fingers move from my lips to my throat, caressing it.

I wish I could join him.

I smack myself in the forehead.

That can't happen, Carolina.

My nipples ache when his hand speeds up and his moans

release in harsh pants. I press my thighs together, a heavy throb hitting me, and my fingertips tingle with the need to slide into my panties. Rex is so focused on his pleasure; maybe he wouldn't notice me pleasuring myself back.

I smack myself in the forehead again to knock some sense into me.

No! Bad Carolina!

No touching yourself while your best friend jacks off.

Watching him is terrible enough.

Invasion of privacy much?

What do I do?

Run out of here?

Yes. Walk away!

My heart tightens when his head drops back, and he moans out his release. His next moan snaps me out of my *Rex is jacking off in front of me* trance. I gain control of my thoughts, and my breathing is labored as I scurry to the bed. I can't stop myself from rubbing my thighs together, wishing I could run to my room and relieve myself.

I've always been attracted to Rex.

I've always wanted him.

I've never wanted him as bad as this though.

I need to pull myself together and not act like I watched him jerk off when he comes out.

Cool. Calm. Collected.

My hands shake when I collect my phone from my clutch and pretend to concentrate on the screen, not bothering to unlock it, when the shower turns off.

"Jesus, Carolina!" Rex bursts out when he strides into the bedroom. "You scared the shit out of me."

He's wearing only a towel that covers his bottom half. Water drips down his six-pack, and my eyes close in on the V that trails down to the cock I was stalking seconds ago.

My pulse races, and there's no doubt my cheeks are flushed red.

Do not look like you were just watching him jack off in the shower.

I chew on my lip and can't look him in the eye. "Uh …" I scramble for words, and they come out between rapid breaths. "I came to wake you up. I just got here. I sat down, haven't moved from this spot. Didn't realize you were in the shower … most definitely didn't see anything." I pat the bed with shaking fingers. "I've been right here, on my phone, waiting for you to get out. I didn't want to be rude and interrupt your shower. You know how rude shower interruptions are?"

He eyeballs me strangely. "What's up with you? Why are you rambling?"

He's as calm as a cucumber. The worry he caught me watching him fades. All I need to do now is act natural, so he doesn't suspect his best friend is a creep.

Now that I'm in the clear, my goal is erasing the memory of him in the shower from my mind.

Yeah, probably not happening.

My gaze flicks to his, and I fidget with my ring. "I'm a rambler. You know this."

"True, but only when you're nervous," he replies with a pointed look.

"I'm nervous about this stupid wedding."

He rakes his hand through his damp hair and nods, accepting my excuse. "Let me get dressed. I'll be ready in fifteen."

He steps forward to kiss me on top of my head, and I nearly lose my shit. Since I'm sitting, his barely covered junk is smack dab in front of my face. My mouth waters. When we had sex, I never looked at his cock. If I had *seen* the size, I would've chickened out.

I hold in a breath when he pulls back, and my eyes follow him as he travels across the room. He gathers his suit from the closet and takes it to the bathroom. Thoughts of him naked in there stay in my mind, causing me to blush.

Will I always think about him naked now?

There's no better approach to get my mind out of the gutter than to talk to my parents. I send my mom a text, saying we'll be down in twenty minutes and to save us two seats. Rex returning in his suit, looking as hot as ever, doesn't help control my desire for him. The black suit is tailored to his body. I smile. I told him I was doing all black, and he matched me.

Rex throws his arm over my shoulders. "Let's do this."

My voice is raspy when I reply, "Let's do this."

The same hand he was stroking his cock with finds my hand, and my cheeks change from a blush to bright red.

"I DON'T BELIEVE IT," my cousin, Lindsay, sneers after cornering me in the restroom.

I hit the cousin jackpot because Lindsay is just as evil as Faye. They're cousin besties. At least with Faye, I only have to see her here. Lindsay lives in Blue Beech. She's two years younger than me and gorgeous, but her attitude makes her hideous. I do my best to avoid her. Some people love living in a small town because their family is there.

Me? Not so much.

Don't get me wrong. I love my parents and sister.

And my grams—minus the whole constantly-asking-why-I'm-single thing.

That's pretty much it.

"What are you talking about?" I ask even though I have an inkling where this is going.

"I don't believe you are *dating* Rex," she practically snarls. "Unless it's been for, like, ten minutes, you're lying. He was having sleepovers with my roommate recently." She tilts her head to the side, a phony smile working over her lips. "There was *no* mention of a girlfriend."

Ugh. I have to deal with this before they've even delivered brunch to the table?

"It's new," I answer, proud of how relaxed I sound. "I know all about his past sleepovers with your roomie. It was *twice,* five months ago, when we weren't dating." I tilt my head to the side, imitating her earlier position.

She snorts. "Whatever. Everyone knows Rex will do anything for you, like, say, *pretend* to be your boyfriend because you can't get one yourself."

It's not that I *can't* get a boyfriend. Guys ask me out, but they're never anyone I see myself sharing a future with.

Why waste my time?

I clench my fists. *My parents can't ground me for smacking chicks now.*

"Piss off," I snarl. "Go back to the guy you're playing side-chick with while he shares a bed with his wife every night."

Normally, I'm not a snotty bitch, but my cousins bring out the best in me.

I push past her, leave the restroom, and order a mimosa as soon as I sit down.

Time to get buzzed in celebration of Faye's love.

CHAPTER TEN

Rex

I SQUEEZE Carolina's thigh in an attempt to stop her laughter—or at least calm it down—and I tilt my head down to whisper in her ear, "Carolina."

She snorts between laughs. "They seriously did *not* just call each other their pet names in their vows." She shoves her face into my neck to mask her giggles. "I can't. Oh my God, I can't."

"Shh …" I repeat.

Scowls turn in our direction.

"*And* terrible pet names at that," she adds.

Goose bumps rise along my skin when her wet lips brush against my neck.

"Do me a favor." She draws back to peek up at me. "If you ever hear me call a boyfriend Tubba Wubba, I give you permission to drown me in your parents' pool."

It's a struggle to hold back my chuckles. "You're going to get us kicked out."

Disapproving looks come from the people in our row, and I reply with an apologetic one.

"Good." Carolina lowers her voice. "This wedding is

lame, and the Tubba Wubba newlyweds need their alone time."

She's not wrong. This wedding has been a complete joke. The bride's walk down the aisle was a fifteen-minute affair, and their vows have been a good twenty minutes. How no one is sleeping is beyond me.

"How many mimosas have you had?" I ask.

"Not enough to let me forget those god-awful vows," she answers around a hiccup.

I grab her neck when she laughs louder and pull her face against my chest again. "I can't take you anywhere."

I've missed goofy Carolina.

She glances up at me after getting a handle on herself and taps my chest. "Technically, I brought you."

"Fine, I can't tag along with you anywhere."

While everybody is focused on the wedding, we're in our own little world.

Good thing we sat in the back.

CAROLINA TALKS a lot of shit about me flirting when she does a fair share of it herself.

Only she doesn't realize she's doing it.

Call me selfish, but I've scared off every friend who's shown interest in her.

They don't deserve her.

I left her alone for five minutes to get our drinks, and some lame dick has stolen my chair. A lame dick sporting an ill-fitting gray striped suit like he's some D-list mob boss.

I place our drinks in front of him on the table and wrap my arms around Carolina's shoulders from behind while she sits in her chair. "Hey, baby."

She smiles up at me. "Hi."

I hold my hand out for Lame Dick to shake and refrain

from ripping it off his fucking arm when he does. "I'm Rex, her boyfriend."

Lame Dick's eyes widen. "Ah, dude, I didn't know."

He knew.

He's been eye-fucking her all day, and since Carolina is my girlfriend this weekend, I've touched her and acted like her boyfriend.

"Now, you do." My attention moves to Carolina as I offer her my hand. "Dance with me."

She grins. "Oh, I guess."

I pull her to her feet and turn her around, so we're facing each other as soon as we hit the dance floor. I drag her close, my palms resting against the base of her back. Turns out, she wasn't drunk on mimosas. She was only tipsy, and I made her suck down water as soon as the wedding ceremony ended. Her tipsiness has nearly worn off.

My chest constricts as I stare down at her and release what's been on the tip of my tongue all day. "You're the most gorgeous girl here."

She's wearing her contacts, showing off her round brown eyes. Her black dress hugs every curve of her body, and curves is something Carolina has plenty of. Her heels don't bring her near to my height. She's short, which I love because it's easy to drag her head into my chest and kiss the top of her head.

It's one of my favorite things to do.

No matter what, I love my hands on her—whether it's an arm around the shoulders or hugging her face into my chest. I'm happy as hell that, on this trip, I get to do more than a simple arm draped around the shoulders, and I've been taking full advantage of that. Tonight, I'm being as handsy as I want.

I drop a hand to her waist, drawing her closer, and my other goes to her hand, weaving our fingers together as we dance.

She laughs when a sappy country song plays. "You have to say that. You're my best friend."

"And for the time being, your *boyfriend*," I correct. "I don't have to say that either. It's the truth. If I were at the singles table and looking for a girl to corrupt, I would've done what the douche bag wearing the lame suit did and came to your table to hit on you."

Her hand briefly leaves mine when she slaps my shoulder. "He was harmless."

I raise a brow. "He wasn't harmless. He was talking to *my* girlfriend."

"I wasn't interested in him." She wraps her arms around my neck, resting them on my shoulders, and laughs again—this time louder. "I don't even know *how* to flirt."

She tips her head forward, her eyes meeting mine, and I brush my lips against her forehead.

"Oh, babe," I say around a chuckle, "you most definitely know how to flirt. You just don't realize you're flirting."

She rolls her eyes. "Whatever."

"You do." My grip tightens on her hips. "When you laugh at something someone says, your face is bright and shows how real you are. When you speak, you allow every emotion to pour out of you. Your amazing heart shows in every move you make, and someone would be dumb not to want that in their life." I run my hands up and down her waist, and she shivers beneath my fingers. "I haven't seen you flirt much, but I know when you're doing it."

Lies. She's flirted with me plenty of times, but I haven't seen her do it much with other guys.

"My flirt game sucks," she mutters.

Heat creeps up my neck as she strokes the back of it with her fingers.

"Thank you for coming," she says, her voice filled with tenderness. "I would've been miserable without you."

I smile. "It's my best-friend duty. You need me? I'm there."

She laughs. "What's my best-friend duty?"

I arch a brow, considering my options. "Hmm … I'll have to get back to you on that."

"Oh God," she groans. "It's going to be video games, isn't it?"

"Possibly." I squeeze her hips. "You love my video games."

She grins up at me. "I love that you named the best woman character Carolina."

"I actually changed that. You're now the big, bad villain."

She pinches the back of my neck, and I jerk forward.

"Whatever." Her fingers rub the spot she pinched. "I thank the gods that you tried to bribe me that day. I would've been sitting miserable in the corner."

"I thank the gods you gave me shit and allowed me to corrupt you."

The music stops, and I dip her back.

"Thanks for the dance, Tubba Wubba."

She narrows her eyes at me when I drag her back up. "I'm poisoning your cookies, FYI."

MY ELBOW IS GRABBED on my way back to Carolina after a restroom break.

"Hey, handsome," a high-pitched voice purrs—trying and desperately failing at being seductive.

Lindsay, a girl from school *and* another one of Carolina's cousins, stands in front of me.

Poor Carolina was blessed with some demon-ass family members.

Lindsay brushes a strand of brown hair behind her ear and thrusts her chest forward. "It's so sweet of you to come with Carolina and play her date."

I pluck her fingers off me as if she has Ebola and glare at her. "No, I came because I'm *dating* Carolina. No playing here."

She rolls her eyes. "*Please.* Everyone knows you'll do anything for her—be her prom date, take her on pity dates, *fake* being in a relationship with her—for God knows what reason."

My jaw clenches. "I take her out on dates because I love her, not for fucking pity."

"You play the part *so well,*" she throws back, "yet not once have you kissed her … not on the lips at least." With this, she puckers her lips and kicks out her foot, showing her bare leg through the slit of her green dress. "Not to mention, you were in my roommate's bed not too long ago. Did you forget about that? Either you were cheating on Carolina *or*, as I suspect, you're lying so that she doesn't look pitiful, hence the pity date."

"Your roommate was more of a pity date than Carolina will ever be," I snarl, my nostrils flaring.

How dare she call Carolina a fucking pity.

"As for you," I go on, "you've flirted with me *how many times* and haven't managed to snag yourself a pity date?"

I hate being a dick, but fuck this.

Fuck them for treating Carolina like shit when she has a heart of gold. When Lindsay's mother was down with shingles for a month, Carolina put together a fundraiser dinner for her. She also made cookies for them countless times and dropped them off at her house.

Scorn passes over Lindsay's face, and just as she's about to speak, my name being called cuts her off.

"Hey! Rex!"

I glance back to find Carolina's father, Rick, along with two other men approaching me.

Shit!

I scan the room for Carolina and grind my teeth when I spot the group of women circled around her. All conversation is aimed in her direction, and my body turns rigid when she gulps down a glass of champagne in one swig.

Goddamn it!

Carolina is a terrible drinker.

She has a low tolerance and doesn't know her limit.

Shockingly, Carolina's parents haven't interrogated her about our dating lie, although she hasn't spent much alone time with them. No doubt they'll drill her with questions when they have her by herself.

"What do you think, Rex?"

I'm broken away from my Carolina trance when the man next to me claps.

"Huh?" I ask, sweeping my attention over to the men.

"I asked your thoughts on violence in video games." The man gestures to Rick. "He said you develop video games."

"I don't have much to say on that matter," I answer with annoyance while searching the room for Carolina when I don't see her with the women anymore.

I spot her at the bar in the corner of the room, taking a shot, and the bartender is pouring another. I don't give them another word before turning on my heel and speed-walking in her direction. Before I get the chance to confiscate her next shot, she knocks it back.

"Hey, babe," I greet, sliding my arms around her waist.

"Hey," she half-slurs, signaling to the bartender for another.

I hold up my hand, stopping him. "She's good, bro."

"She's not, *bro*," she corrects with an eye roll. "Make it a double." Her palm slaps the counter. "And get my friend one —sorry, my *boyfriend* one." She flicks her hand in the air. "Not a double for him. His job is to take care of me tonight, and one needs to be sober to do that."

I clutch her elbow and tug her away from the bar, and she's talking shit as I walk us toward the exit.

"How much have you had to drink?" I question, swinging her around to face me.

She holds two fingers apart from each other and squints one eye to focus on them. "Just a *wee* bit."

"How much is a *wee* bit?"

She wrinkles her nose, her hand dropping to her side. "I lost count at the third glass of champagne and second shot of …" Her finger goes to her lower lip, and she clicks her tongue against the roof of her mouth. "Vodka maybe? It was something in a glass."

"Jesus," I hiss. "I leave you alone for five minutes."

"Wrong. You left me alone for *fifteen* … with the sharks." The *sharks* are the overbearing women in her family.

I raise my arms, apology spilling over my face. "I was cornered on my way back!"

"People already think we're lying about being together. Let's just prove them right." Carolina also gets snarky when she drinks.

I reach out my hand. "Come on. Let's go to your room."

She smacks it away. "Let's get *me* back to the bar, and *you* can go back to chatting with my cousin."

Perfect. She saw me talking to Lindsay.

"We're not doing this here." I grip her hand, make sure she's steady, and weave us through the people.

"Bye, Rex! Call me sometime!"

Carolina halts at Lindsay's farewell. Knowing this might be a shitshow, I attempt to pull her away, but Carolina stands firm.

Lindsay is dumb enough to continue taunting Carolina, and she chirps out her words. "It was *so* nice seeing you and catching up. Want to hang out tomorrow? Grab breakfast?"

"Fuck you," Carolina snarls, startling everyone. She points at me while holding strong eye contact with Lindsay. "You look dumb, hitting on a guy who's coming to *my* room. He might've entertained your corner conversation for five minutes, but he entertains *my bed*." She holds her middle finger up. "I win."

I bite back my laughter. "Jesus, let's get you out of here."

Thankfully, she allows me to take her to the elevator, and her eyes are narrowed at me the entire ride. When we hit our floor, I take her key from my pocket and unlock the door.

"Entertain your bed, huh?" I ask as soon as we walk into the room and tilt my head toward the bed. "Is this the bed I'm doing that in?"

She falls back against the mattress and starts taking her heels off, tossing them across the room. "I have no idea what I meant, but it sounded better in my head."

"It sounded like you told her I was going to fuck you in that bed of yours." My cock hardens at the thought.

"I have no regrets. We're dating, so it's assumed we're banging, considering you're … well, *you.*"

"I won't take that as an insult." I clap my hands and rub them together. "Where are your pajamas?"

Her head jerks toward the dresser. "Folded in that thing."

"Of course they are, you organized freak, you."

"Hey," she whines. "An organized life is a happy life." She releases a heavy sigh. "When you were in the restroom, they asked me why I dropped out of school in sixteen different ways." All the playfulness and snark in her tone has dissolved, sadness clouding her features.

"What'd you say?"

She shuts her eyes, a slow breath releasing from her chest. "My mind went blank. I might've said something about joining the circus."

I stare at her in regret. "I'll never leave you with those vultures again. Promise."

"I can handle myself."

"Never said you couldn't, but tonight, you chose alcohol to help you. Replace me with alcohol next time, okay?" *Replace me with alcohol every time.*

She salutes me, a glimmer of a smile on her lips. "Got it, captain."

I sift through her drawer, and my heart jolts as I ease out an unfamiliar item. "Now, my sweet Carolina, I thought I'd seen all your pajamas. Turns out, you've been hiding these." I hold the nearly see-through blue lacy teddy in the air.

A blush covers her face before she buries it in her hands. "You're not supposed to see that! It's for bedroom eyes only!"

I hold it out, inspecting it. "Next time you spend the night, your ass had better be wearing this."

"Not happening." Her hands leave her face, and she shakes her head. "It's uncomfortable and meant to be quickly taken off. Then, it stays off."

I lean back against the dresser, crossing my ankles, and lift the teddy in the air. "Why'd you bring it? *Who* did you plan to wear it for … or take it off for?" My mouth turns dry at my question.

Did she plan on hooking up with someone here?

She sucks on her lower lip. "I don't know … in case I met someone. I didn't plan for you to play my boyfriend."

I hold a finger up. "Stop right there, young lady. You're either going to make me jealous or have my imagination running wild." *Too late.* I run my fingers over the lace while my mind starts racing of thoughts in her wearing this teddy.

She grabs a pillow and throws it at me. "Whatever. You'd see me as one of your guy friends wearing that."

"You've never been more wrong in your life," I grumble around a gulp after dodging the pillow.

"What if I wear it now?"

I snort. "Funny."

"I'm serious."

"You're drunk."

"Isn't that what a *girlfriend* would do? And this weekend, I'm your *girlfriend.*" Challenge spills along her words. "Oh, wait. You can't be my boyfriend if you were screwing Lindsay's roommate not too long ago."

I shove the teddy back into one drawer and open the one

underneath it, finding a pair of sweats and a white tank top. "That's why you're pissed?"

"Duh. My date has been screwing other women."

"Screwed. Haven't touched her roommate in months, *and* I'm not touching anyone here. Since when do you believe your cousins? What the hell?"

"Forget it," she huffs out.

I set her pajamas on the edge of the bed and rest my knee next to them, halfway crawling up the mattress until our faces are only inches apart. Cupping hers with both my hands, I run my thumb over her soft, freckle-kissed cheek and then pull myself up. "Now, stand and get your pajamas on."

"Fine," she whines, sliding off the bed, "but I need you to unzip me."

A shiver runs up my spine when I stand behind her and stare at the zipper running down the back of her dress. The room turns silent; the only sound I hear is my raging heartbeat. My fingers are tense when I grab the zipper of her dress, dragging it down, and the dress pools around her feet in what seems like slow motion. I draw in a breath, unable to stop myself from taking her in.

Jesus.

Standing in front of me is my best friend … wearing only a nude-colored thong. Her skin warms at my touch as I stupidly and bravely brush my fingers along her waist. Her breathing shudders, and she grinds back into me, rubbing her ass against the erection I shouldn't have.

"Rex," she whispers.

I fight with myself on why I'm being such an idiot when I skim my hand along the bottom of her bare breast. *Why the hell wasn't she wearing a bra?* Good thing I didn't know, or it's all I would've thought about tonight.

She tilts her head to the side. "My necklace."

As my fingers stroke the bottom of her breast, I use my other hand to sweep her hair off her shoulder and unclasp the pearl necklace I bought her for Christmas. Our connection stays when I carefully set the necklace onto the bed. Never has my heart pounded so intensely when I replace my hand resting on her neck with my lips, skimming them along her soft skin.

"Tell me to stop," I hiss. "Fuck, Lina. Tell me."

CHAPTER ELEVEN

Carolina

"TELL ME TO STOP. Fuck, Lina. Tell me."

My heart races at Rex's pleas, but I'm selfish. That word isn't leaving my lips tonight. I don't want him to stop. I want more—of his touch, of his lips, of everything that is him. The deep breaths pulling from his chest and his erection pressing against my back confirm I'm not alone in my desire.

His lips linger at the curve of my neck while he waits for me to push him away, to say *no.* When his hand grazes the underside of my breast again, I can't stop myself from grinding my ass against him.

Big mistake.

Huge.

All this in Julia Roberts's voice.

It's as if my move wakes his restraint and slaps him in the face with reality.

His hands drop from my body as if I'd caught fire, and he jerks away, fleeing to the other side of the room. I glance back over my shoulder to find him resting against the dresser, agony lining his features, and he presses a fist against his lips.

"Shit, Carolina," he finally chokes out. "I'm so damn sorry."

A brief silence passes, as if we're both battling our next move. My back stays to him while I stand by the bed. Rejection doesn't exactly make a girl want to put her boobs on display. He already has a view of my bare butt.

My gaze sharpens when he slowly eases my way and swipes the tee off the bed. A brief pause happens before he advances a step farther. I can't stop myself from laughing when he slips the shirt over my head, and as soon as the job is done, he promptly returns to his side of the room. When I turn around, there's no missing the anguish on his face.

He frowns, dragging a hand through his thick hair, and releases a long breath of frustration. "That wasn't cool. I'm sorry."

I shift from one foot to the other, pulling at the bottom of the shirt while chewing on my lower lip. "You have nothing to be sorry about, Rex." Heat creeps up my cheeks. "In fact, I highly encourage you to keep touching me. *Don't* stop."

He gapes at me. "You're drunk. Not happening."

"I'm not drunk. I'm tipsy." I smirk. "It won't be the first time I've had tipsy sex."

His upper lip snarls, and his words leave in a deep hiss. "Don't even think about going on about that shit." His tone hardens. "Conversation change, motherfucking pronto."

I gesture down my body. "I'm standing upright with no assistance from you, nor am I slurring my words or puking my guts out. I'm not drunk." To further prove my point, I hold a leg up, standing on only one while doing my best to balance myself, before repeating it with the other leg. I end my move with a ta-da gesture.

My awesome skill doesn't change his mind.

"I'm not ruining us by having sex." He rubs the nape of his neck while cursing under his breath.

"Just like with my virginity, we'll act like it never happened," I argue.

Why do I suddenly want this so much?

Is it because I spied on him while he jerked off, and I can't stop seeing it in my mind?

Or because I'm having such a good time with the boyfriend-girlfriend game we're playing, and I want it in real life?

Is it the alcohol giving me the bravery?

I'd say a mix of the three.

He stepped up and played boyfriend.

Defended me.

I love and want Rex for all those reasons and more.

Who cares if it'll change our relationship?

It might even make it stronger.

"We're not teenagers," he fires back. "There's no acting like it didn't happen. Shit has changed, and shit *will* change for the worse if we cross that line. I guarantee it."

I pout my lips. "*Please.* I promise, no changing us."

Rex has always had a weakness for my whining.

"No." His voice is stern as he pinches the bridge of his nose. "Come on. Let's get your pajamas on, so you can get some sleep. You're going to feel like shit in the morning."

Nope.

I was taught not to give up so easily.

I cross my arms. "I need a shower."

He blinks. "Excuse me?"

"I need a shower."

"Take a shower then."

"Since I'm so *drunk*, I probably need your help." My imagination flickers to watching him in the shower earlier, and my skin tingles at the thought of us sharing one.

"Shower in the morning when you're sober."

"You can stop telling me what to do now." I plow my hands into my hair before dragging the strands out. "I need to wash this hairspray out."

"Stick your head in the sink and wash it out."

"Um, negative. I might drown."

He groans. "Fine."

I grin.

He shifts to the side, making room so I can pass him, and I peek back to check that he's following me and not making a run for it.

Let him run.

I have a key to his room, and I'll just take a shower in his bathroom.

See how much he likes the idea of switching keys then.

He trails behind me … looking as though he's on the way to a torture chamber instead of a fun shower.

That's awesome.

I frown, my stomach twisting, and stop in my tracks, causing him to trip into me.

What if he truly doesn't want to sleep with me?

What if he's not attracted to me like that, and he's using our friendship as a cop-out, as a vagina block?

Oh my God.

There's no doubt I was a sucky lay when we banged, but you can't blame a girl. *I was a virgin!*

He should understand I was a sex newbie, but maybe he thinks I'll lie there like a boring starfish again.

But what the heck? I was nervous!

Surely, he's taken that into account of my suckiness.

He grabs my waist before either of us face-plants, pushes me into the bathroom, and remains in the doorway—displeasure on his face. His eyes are everywhere but on me when I pull my shirt over my head and drop it to the tiled floor. My nipples harden at my sudden nakedness. I slide down my panties, curious where this courage is coming from. His eyes stay pinned to the ceiling as if he were waiting for it to collapse on us.

I open the shower door while frowning at him for not offering the attention I'm seeking. I clear my throat and bend down to turn on the water, but *nothing.*

The ceiling is apparently more exciting than my naked body.

What does a girl have to do to get ogled around here?

"Uh … can you help me inside?" I ask.

His dark eyes *finally* cut to me, and he frowns while taking in my naked body. "It's best you shower tomorrow."

"Nope," I quip before holding out my hand and wiggling it. "Help, please and thank you."

He takes two steps forward, erasing the distance between us, catches my hand, and assists me in the shower. My shoulders relax when the warm water hits my skin. I tilt my head back, allowing the water to stream down my face. When I'm good and soaked, I wipe the water from my face, smooth back my hair, and stare at him in expectation—ready for him to join me.

The door is cracked, and he's standing outside it. His head is tipped down, his focus now on his feet, and him wearing his suit is a sure sign he's not shower ready.

"Seriously?" I groan. "How are you going to help me shower from *out there*?"

He lifts his gaze, but it still doesn't roam over my body. "You asked for help. Not for me to join you."

Don't two and two go together?

"I wasn't aware clarification was necessary." I clear my throat and deepen my voice. "This is a formal invitation for you, Rex Lane, to join me for a warm shower. Snacks will be provided, and you get a complimentary wash."

"Invitation respectively declined."

"You can't stand there with the door open!"

"Tell me when you need help, and I'll stick my hand in the shower." He shrugs. "Simple."

"*Okay,* Stretch Armstrong, that's absurd."

"Not absurd. Smart."

"All right then. I need help."

When he sticks his hand into the shower, I grab it and pull his body halfway in with me. Before he gets the opportunity to yank back, I capture his ear with two fingers.

"Get your butt in this shower right now, Rex Peyton Lane!"

This is the most awkward conversation we've ever had.

Hell, this is the most awkward conversation I've had, period.

He attempts to pull away, but I tighten my ear-hold.

"Are you seriously grabbing my damn ear right now, Carolina? This is best-friend abuse!"

"Absolutely." I press my nails into his skin before releasing him. "Now, get your butt in here. You're letting all the cold air in, and next time, I'll pinch something more sensitive than an ear."

He shakes his head, his voice strained. "I can't do that."

"You have two feet. Yes, you can."

He signals to my body. "Are you serious? You, in there, naked and wet in front of me, and you expect me to keep my hands to myself?" He repeatedly shakes his head. "I'm not taking any chances."

I grin, proud of myself.

Seduction plan working.

One point, Carolina.

"I need help with my hair, and I'm not getting out of this shower until you do it."

He's as stunned as I am that I'm being this bold.

Champagne and not being miserable at the singles table gives me courage, I see.

"Fine."

He shoves off his jacket, discards his tie, and plucks off his shoes, one by one, before removing his socks. I stand there, unmoving and shivering while he rolls his pants up.

"Scoot over," he instructs.

"Seriously?" I ask, falling back a step when his large body joins me—him wearing his pants and white button-up. "Your clothes will be soaked."

He shuts the shower door, deep breaths expelling from his

muscular chest, while we stand inches apart. "If these clothes come off, something will happen that shouldn't. This way"—he signals down his body—"there's a barrier between us, and my cock will stay to himself."

I frown and slump my shoulders. "Will something happening between us be *that* stupid?"

"Yes." There's no hesitation in his answer.

"Why?" I gulp, terrified of hearing his response.

I should've never fought for this shower party.

"You aren't someone who has sex just to have sex … only for the pleasure."

I've never seen his face or heard his tone so gentle as he continues, "It's not in your heart, in your soul, to have random sex. You want a relationship, and that's something I can't do because I'll fuck it up." His eyes squeeze shut, as if his words pained him.

"Rex," I whisper, "you're a good guy. You don't know what you're capable of. How can you knock commitment without trying it first?"

Yes, ladies and gentlemen, this convo is happening in the shower.

Me totally naked.

Him fully dressed.

His eyes drink in my face, and he presses his icy palms to my cheeks, cradling my face. If we weren't standing so close, I wouldn't make out his words. "I'm a good guy as a friend. In a relationship, not so much."

My heart aches at the pain on his face. "You don't know that."

He shakes his head. "I refuse to lose you for my stupidity. You mean too much to me. You're the first person I talk to when I wake up and the last person I talk to before I go to sleep. I called you before anyone when I got my game offer—before my family. I want to spend every damn minute with you I can. If I touched you, if I fucked you, and screw everything up—which I would—I wouldn't have that anymore. If you were some random chick, I wouldn't hold back, but I am because I love you. I hold myself back day after fucking day because I will never, ever in my goddamn life fucking hurt you."

I nod as tears slip down my cheeks alongside the water. "Okay. I'm sorry."

His lips brush the top of my head. "Nothing to be sorry about." He chuckles. "Now, turn around, so I can wash your hair, you pain in my ass."

I can't help but laugh while doing what he instructed.

"Help a guy out here," he comments from behind me. "There are four bottles of different shit in here. Which one's shampoo?"

My shoulders shake when I laugh again before handing him the shampoo.

"Mmm … this shit smells good. I'm jacking it for my next shower."

My knees weaken at the mention of him taking another shower. He massages the shampoo through my hair better than my hairdresser, and as the sound of water falling takes over the air, shame grips me. I was unfair to push him into the position I did.

"You're on your own with the body washing," he says after rinsing out my hair. "Since you're only *tipsy*, I think you can handle it."

I grab the washcloth from him, cleaning myself off, and then shriek at the sudden coldness. When I twist round, he's walking out of the shower. His clothes are dripping wet, and he snags a towel from the hook, opening it wide. Carefully, I step out of the shower, and he drapes the towel around my shivering body, drying me and being careful not to touch anything over PG-rated.

"Will you at least stay with me tonight?" I whisper as he slips my shirt back over my head before releasing the towel.

The shirt reaches my knees, and he doesn't get any glimpses of my goods.

Not that I didn't have them on display earlier.

He awkwardly wraps the towel around my hair, doing a terrible job, but I'll give him an A for effort. "Only if you keep your hands to yourself, tipsy shower girl."

I feign annoyance with a huff. "All right."

He exits the bathroom, comes back with my pajama pants, and hands them to me. When we return to the room, I hop onto the bed while he starts taking off his clothes.

"Oh, so *now*, you want to get naked," I comment, unwrapping the towel from my hair and licking my lips as his shirt falls from his broad shoulders.

He drops his pants, wearing only his boxer briefs, and then scans the room.

"You should've thought that through," I remark. "Feel free to wear the teddy you found earlier."

He chuckles. "I'm certain there're sweats of mine somewhere in here." He starts rummaging through the drawers before finding my favorite pair of his sweatpants and turning toward the bathroom.

"Wait!" I toss him the towel to take back with him and then make myself comfortable in bed as he disappears.

"You're going to feel like shit tomorrow," he says, walking back in before joining me in bed.

Facts.

I twist on my side, scoot closer, and rest my head on his shoulder. "I know, and you're going to take care of me."

He blows out a long, exaggerated breath. "Fine, but I want *two* batches of cookies when we get home."

I pat his chest as my heart warms. "I love you, best friend."

He swings his arm around me. "And I love you."

How can Rex think he'd be such a horrible boyfriend when he's been the best friend a girl could ask for?

He takes care of me, makes me feel special, and would do anything for me. He's an amazing man, and from what I experienced this weekend, he would be an amazing boyfriend.

I sigh. *One of these days, he'll realize that.*

He'll realize it with another girl and leave me in the dust.

Unless … I become that girl who wakes him up.

CHAPTER TWELVE

Rex

CAROLINA IS asleep when I wake up.

Carefully, I pull my arm off her, grab my wallet and keycard, and tiptoe out of her room. I'll come back and grab my suit later.

I'm struggling to wrap my head around last night. When I slid into bed with her, my fingers tingled as I remembered how they'd felt when running along her soft skin while I helped her undress.

I should've kept my hands to myself.

My stupidity is what started last night.

When I noticed she wasn't wearing a bra, I should've walked away.

Instead, I became a dumbass, and my dumbass move lit a fire inside Carolina … a fire I had to fight like hell to put out. It was torture, turning her down. My hands balled into fists as I kept my eyes everywhere but on her body while in the shower. When I washed her hair, there was no stopping the few quick glances I took. Her perfect, round ass was so close to my cock … warning me but also tempting me with how easily I could've bent her over and taken her from behind.

And boy, was it a motherfucking challenge.

I'm not sure what got into her last night—*definitely not me … unfortunately*—but the only other time I've seen that side of her was the night I took her virginity.

I couldn't …

I can't.

Losing Carolina scares me more than being in love with her.

My hands have to stay to myself, so she remains in my life.

Softly, I shut the door behind me, walking into the hallway, and head to my room.

"Morning."

I still at the sharp morning greeting.

Oh shit.

The air is thick as I turn on my heel to face Pastor Adams. The crease in his forehead and disapproving expression on his face confirm he thinks I'm doing the walk of shame from his daughter's room.

If he only knew.

I straighten and slap on a cheerful grin. "Good morning, Pastor Adams." I gulp, stopping myself from adding, *This isn't what it looks like.*

The shorter our conversation, the better.

Thank fuck I changed out of my suit last night.

Me wearing sweatpants looks far more believable that I slept in my room than me sneaking out in my suit.

My grin stays intact as I jerk my head toward Carolina's room. "I ran over to wake Carolina up and ask what she wanted for breakfast."

"Oh, really?" His lips press together in a grimace.

He's calling bullshit.

I look him in the eyes, establishing I'm not a rude little shit who spent all night banging his daughter. "Yes, sir."

He cocks his head to the side, his face twisting in displeasure. "What did she say?"

"She doesn't feel well."

"She's sick?"

I nod.

Carolina owes me a shit-ton of cookies.

I'm lying to a preacher.

Okay, Lord up above, it's not a full lie.

She will feel like shit when she wakes up.

He advances a step. "I should check on her."

My hand darts out as I rush closer to stop him from knocking on her door. "She went back to sleep and asked me to wake her in an hour."

He fixes a hard stare on me. "Why don't we have breakfast then? We can bring Carolina back something when we're finished. It's no fun to eat by yourself, and my wife is at the spa this morning."

I jerk back, a sudden headache slamming into me.

Oh, man.

Not a coffee date with my fake girlfriend's father.

How do I get out of this?

"Uh, yeah, sure," I mutter, knowing I can't decline without looking like an asshole. "Let me get dressed."

"Good idea," he deadpans and stops me as I whip around. "I suggest you refrain from roaming public hallways shirtless in the future ... especially on a Sunday morning. It's disrespectful."

I peek back at him. "Appreciate the advice."

I shuffle into my room, change into jeans and a shirt, brush my teeth, and hurry back into the hallway where he's waiting. I was hoping he'd bailed on me. We make small talk while taking the elevator downstairs to the restaurant. Lucky for me, we have plenty of time for this coffee chat since our flight doesn't depart until this afternoon.

"For someone who's been close to my daughter for years and is now *dating her*, you sure don't come around often," he says as we sit down at the two-person table, and he smooths a napkin over his lap. "We've never shared a one-on-one conversation."

He's right.

Even in high school, Carolina came to my house when we hung out. Sometimes, her parents knew of her whereabouts, and other times, she told them she was studying at the library.

Carolina's exact words about hanging out at her house after I suggested it was, "We'll have to sit in the living room on different couches and watch a documentary about the sins of having sex before marriage."

The preacher is an old-school man. He's around my father's age, but unlike my father, his age shows. He's slender, a man who wears loafers on the regular, and his brown hair is peppered with gray strands. He's been the preacher of the town church for as long as I can remember. They're a religious family with strict rules and deep values. He's a good man who'd probably be more welcoming to me had Carolina and I not been such great friends … and boyfriend and girlfriend now.

How are we going to fake break up without me looking like an ass?

With my reputation, everyone will assume it was my fault, and I'll look like an even bigger asshole for breaking the heart of the preacher's daughter.

"We haven't, sir," I answer to his one-on-one time comment and pause, allowing him to take lead on this torturous chat.

"You don't frequent church," he sternly adds. "And no need to call me sir. I'm Rick."

"I've been busy with my job and school—"

He cuts me off, "You never attended when you were in your teens either with the exception of holidays."

"You're right." No need to dispute facts. It'll only make me look dumb.

Our waiter, Bobby, arrives at our table to save me from

this awkwardness and takes our order. As soon as Bobby leaves, Rick is back to his interrogation.

"Is there a reason for that?"

"No."

Bobby comes back with Rick's coffee and my espresso—because I'm extra—and sets them in front of us. "Your order was put in and will be out shortly."

We both thank him.

"How are your parents doing?" Rick asks, pouring creamer into his coffee.

I'm unsure of which conversation I want to avoid more—me and Carolina or my shitshow of a family.

"Good." I take a long sip of my espresso, wishing I'd declined his breakfast offer. I should've told him I was sick, too. I'd planned to take the morning to digest what had happened with Carolina. Now, I'll be digesting last night and this conversation with Rick.

"How are you coping with their divorce?"

I never asked for this counseling session.

"Coping perfectly fine," I reply at the reminder of what an asshole my father is. "My mother is a strong woman and did the right thing." She should've divorced him a long-ass time ago.

"You think that's the right decision to make?" He raises a brow. "Giving everything up?"

I focus on my drink, avoiding eye contact to shield my annoyance. "When someone hurts you as much as my father did my mother … *my family*, then yes, I excuse her for leaving him. He cheated and hid secrets too large to heal from."

He waits until I look at him again before replying, "You know, I counseled them before she made the final decision to proceed with the divorce. I tried to help them reconcile."

Why is he telling me this shit?

Shouldn't he have to keep that confidential?

"Marriage is sacred," he goes on.

My hand clenches around the handle of my mug. "I agree."

"Do you plan to marry my daughter?"

I choke on my drink, and it takes me a moment to swallow and clear my throat before I can reply, "What?"

"You are dating my daughter now, correct?" His face tightens, as if the thought pains him.

"Yes." *And I love her.*

"What are your intentions with her? Marriage? A quick fling?"

My pulse races as I work my answer through my mind before relaying it. "I care about Carolina. She's been my best friend for years."

"Best friend? What about girlfriend?"

"It's new. We're trying it out. We've had feelings for each other for years, and we decided it was dumb to keep holding ourselves back from happiness."

Uh-oh. This fake relationship will definitely be following us home to Blue Beech.

"Do you plan on breaking her heart?" Worry is etched along every feature on his face. This interrogation isn't him being an asshole; it's him protecting his daughter's heart.

I repeatedly shake my head. "No, of course not. It's never my intention to hurt Carolina—*ever.*"

"She's in love with you." There's no bullshit in his tone.

I go quiet for a moment. I know she loves me, but I pretend to be blind about it.

"This is typically the part where boyfriends say they love their girlfriend back."

I stutter for the right words. "I love Carolina. She's the most amazing person I know."

My answer doesn't satisfy him. "I'll ask again, what are your intentions with my daughter?"

"For us to be happy."

He leans back in his chair, his eyes suspicious, and points

at me, moving his finger back and forth. "Guys like you, they don't date the preacher's daughter."

I can't help but scowl. "Carolina is more than just a preacher's daughter, and I don't think it's fair to put that label on her."

Bobby becomes my favorite person when he interrupts us again with our food. Dude is getting a good-ass tip from me this morning.

Hopefully, Rick worries more about his food than talking to me.

I splash hot sauce onto my Spanish omelet and take a large bite.

"Tell me why Carolina dropped out of school," Rick urges, not even giving his pancakes a glance.

I swallow down my bite. "She didn't feel it was right for her."

"She had no issues her freshman year." He takes a drink of coffee and wipes his mouth. "Out of nowhere, she decided to drop out and move home. Was it for you? Did something happen to her?"

I understand his concern. I had one hundred questions for Carolina. She answered some, lied about some, and refused to answer the others.

"Carolina hasn't told me the entire truth on why she moved home," I honestly answer. "Whatever she's going through, I hope she'll open up to us when she's ready."

He frowns. "Don't break my daughter's heart, Rex."

"I won't." *I'll try not to.*

"And I expect the next time I catch you sneaking out of her room, it's after you're married," he says, giving me a pointed look. "My daughter has values."

With that, he pours an excessive amount of syrup on his pancakes and takes a large bite.

I HAVE a doughnut in one hand and a coffee in the other as I stroll into Carolina's hotel room.

"Rise and shine," I call out.

After my wonderful and not-at-all-awkward breakfast with her father, I ran to my room and showered.

Carolina yawns while sitting up in the bed. "Quit being so perky." Another yawn. "It's too early for that." Her hair is a tangled mess, there's dried slobber on the side of her mouth, and even with the shower, there're still blotches of mascara under one eye. She's a gorgeous, hot mess.

I hold the doughnut bag and coffee up. "I brought food for your hungover self. I'd be nice to this perky dude."

"All right," she groans. "Thank you. Carbs is just what the doctor ordered."

"Or what the preacher ordered." I hand her the bag and a napkin before placing the coffee on the nightstand next to her. "Your dad picked it out for you."

She stills, just as she's about to take a bite of the doughnut. "My dad?"

I plop down on the edge of the bed by her feet. "Yep. We had breakfast."

"You had breakfast with my dad," she drags out.

"Sure did. It was quite a blast, let me tell you. We drank mimosas and took tequila shots. He sure enjoyed the hair of the dog."

She stretches her leg out to kick me. "You're such a liar."

"About the shots, yes. About us having breakfast, no. He wanted to have coffee with his daughter's new boyfriend to tell him not to break your heart." I leave out the questions about future marriage and why she left school.

Her eyes widen, the doughnut falling onto the bag in her lap, and her hand cups her mouth. "Oh my God! I forgot about our boyfriend-girlfriend game. What happens when we get home? How are we going to break up?"

I poke her foot. "Let's say you cheated on me."

"What? No! You're not blaming the breakup on *me.*"

"Oh, and I'm supposed to take the blame?" I point at myself and shake my head. "I'm not being the bad guy." I scratch my cheek. "There are reasons other than cheating. We can say you joined a nunnery. You join, no one suspects anything, and all will be right in the world."

"You need to stop suggesting I join a nunnery. Not happening." She shoves a bite of the doughnut into her mouth.

"Why? Your father probably has some great connections."

She rolls her eyes, chewing. "You just want me to stay single and non-sexually active for the rest of my life."

"Fine, no cheating or nunnery. We'll say we're better off as friends."

She throws her head back. "It's way too early to discuss our fake breakup for our fake relationship."

I nod in agreement. "Your head hurt?"

I'm acting as normal as I can.

Does she remember what happened last night?

She wasn't drunk. I definitely won't be bringing that shit up, though.

"Nope." She finishes off her doughnut.

"Liar."

"Ibuprofen, please." She points at her bag. "Left pocket."

I snatch her bag, grab the ibuprofen, snag a bottle of water from the mini fridge, and hand them to her.

"Thank you," she says, swallowing the pills down.

She hands me the water, and I set it on the nightstand next to her coffee.

"Our flight leaves in a few hours," I inform her, sitting back down on the side of the bed. "I'm shocked you're not packed and ready to go yet."

"Last night drained all the life out of me. I can't wait to go home."

"BACK TO REALITY," Carolina says after we land and stroll through the airport. "I never thought I'd be so excited to be home from a vacation." She holds up her hand to correct herself. "Technically, it was a *hell-cation.*"

We took an Uber to the airport with her parents this morning, and Carolina tried her hardest not to appear hungover. The disapproving glances her father shot her way proved her convincing skills sucked ass.

I bump my shoulder against hers. "Rude to say that to the person who accompanied you on the trip."

"Fine." She bumps my shoulder back. "It would've been a *hell-cation* had you not been there. Seriously, thank you for coming, Rex."

"I'll always have your back … until you break up with me later." I press my hand to my heart. "I'm already putting together a broken-heart playlist."

She rolls her eyes. "You're breaking up with me. I've been brainstorming for the perfect story."

"Too late. I've already made the decision. You're into some kinky shit in the bedroom that's *way* out of my comfort zone." I struggle to hold in a laugh. "I refuse to let you spank me with whips and give you a golden shower."

"Oh my God," she gasps, slapping my arm, and she casts a glance at her sister walking a few feet behind us. "What is wrong with you? My sister is right there, and you know how much of a tattletale she is. I can't have my parents thinking I want you to pee on me!"

I chuckle. "I highly doubt your parents know what a golden shower is."

"Uh … you ever heard of Google?"

"Google?" I stroke my chin. "What is this Google you speak of?"

She hitches her bag up higher on her shoulder. "I like your

idea, but it needs to be switched around. *I* was the one who refused the peeing thing."

"I see we're having some creative differences here. Time to find a better approach. You riding home with me? We can talk about the best way to break up."

"Duh. My parents already know." She blows out a long breath. "I'm definitely not sharing another ride with them."

"How did you know I'd let you ride home with me? Maybe your boyfriend needs some alone time."

"Don't care. I'm riding with you. Get over it."

I chuckle. "I love it when you're bossy."

There might've been some awkward times during our trip—like, say, when she got naked and asked me to shower with her—but I'm sad it's over. Not that I won't be spending more time with Carolina back home, but it was nice to be able to touch her without it appearing weird. I was her boyfriend in Texas. It was my job to be all touchy-feely. If only I could do it here in Blue Beech.

Our vacation is over.

Our fake relationship will end.

Our lives will go back to normal.

Neither of us has muttered a word about the shower incident, and I'm hoping it stays that way. I already felt bad enough about turning her down. Carolina doesn't put herself out there like that; it's not in her nature. It was rough to say no, but it was also satisfying to know she trusts me enough to pull herself out of her comfort zone. Sure, she was drunk, but had I been some random dude, she would've never dropped her panties in front of me.

At least, I hope not.

We grab our luggage, and Carolina turns her parents down for a ride four times before we finally say good-bye and walk to my car in the parking garage.

"Have I mentioned how much I love this car?" she says after we throw our luggage in the trunk and get in. "It's so much fancier than mine. You just keep getting more tech savvy."

"An electric car is not tech savvy," I argue from the driver's side as we pull out of the parking spot.

She stretches out her legs. "In our small town, anything above a gas-hogging truck, Jeep, or minivan is tech savvy."

"Which is why, Lina babe, I don't suggest it. Finding charging stations is a bitch."

I fucking love my Tesla. It took me a while to finally make the plunge and buy it, but it'd been my dream car for years. After I signed my contract with the development company for my game, I sold the Charger and bought the Tesla. The next item on my list is purchasing a home after my lease ends.

"I'm too poor to buy a new car anyway," she says with a frown. "I might stay poor for the rest of my life since I dropped out of school … says my parents."

I gulp, gripping the steering wheel as I glance over at her. "Do you think you'll ever tell them the truth?" *Do you think you'll ever tell me the entire truth?*

"Who knows?" She wrinkles her nose. "Maybe in thirty years." She shakes her head while turning her attention out the window. "It's embarrassing. I'm stupid."

"Hey," I say softly. "You're not stupid. You were taken advantage of."

"My stupidity is more than just him." She casts me a nervous glance. "It's him, what happened with Margie, *all* of it. I feel stupid, weak, and wish I could go back in time."

My stomach sinks at the heartbreak in her voice, and I wish I could wrap her in my arms, hold her tight, and let her know it'll be okay … as I've done so many damn times since that bastard did what he did.

"My parents wouldn't understand *being taken advantage of* because I made that stupid choice," she continues. "It was a consequence of my decision. None of this would've happened had I not been irresponsible … had I not been too scared to tell the truth and stopped hiding it."

Yet she's still hiding it.

"Has living at your sister's improved?"

At first, Tricia gave her shit for dropping out, which is bullshit. Tricia didn't go to college. She married her high school sweetheart right out of school and started a family. Her parents approved of that, but they don't approve of Carolina waitressing and getting her shit together. Her sister hasn't failed to remind her how much work and money their parents put into Carolina's education.

"A little," she replies. "I stay in the loft as much as I can when I'm there. When she makes her surprise visits *for girl talk*, I agree with her, so she'll go." She shrugs. "What can I do? I'm not going to be a bitch. She's giving me free rent, for goodness' sake, and losing money by not renting it to anyone else. I can handle a little lecturing for that."

"The offer to move in with me is still open," I say.

She shakes her head. "Hearing my sister's lectures is better than being around you and your women."

"Oh, come on." I crack a smile. "You act like I'm with a different woman every night. Hell, I spend nearly half of my time hanging out with you and the other working on my fame."

She laughs when I glance her way and smirk.

"You're at my apartment more than your own anyway," I add. "It'd be no different."

I've offered the spare bedroom in my apartment to her several times. I'd love for her to be my roommate, for me to be able to watch over her and hang out with her more.

"On the days we're not together, you're with another chick, not working on your fame—unless it's to be Blue Beech's biggest man-whore even though you've already won the title." She waggles her finger in my direction. "Don't forget, I've been there on numerous occasions when random chicks show up at your doorstep."

"I didn't know *numerous* meant twice," I correct. "And I made them leave."

My other nickname for Carolina is the Exaggerator Queen. She always multiplies everything I do by at least five. Two chicks show up, and she'll say it's ten. I tell her I've had sex with one chick, and she says I've had sex with five.

"Are you going home or to my place?" I ask when the *Welcome to Blue Beech, Iowa* sign comes into view.

"Home for now," she replies. "I might come by later. I need to unpack, do laundry, take a long bath, and get over this stupid hangover."

I nod and head toward her sister's house. "Text me in a bit … with a breakup text."

She sighs. "Not happening, homeboy."

A playful groan leaves my throat. "At least send your boyfriend a picture of you in the bath." I slam my mouth shut as soon as I say the words, and I want to slap myself.

Teasing Carolina whenever she said she was taking a bath was one of my favorite pastimes, but now, after the shower incident, bath sexting references are a terrible idea.

Her face pales, confirming she no doubt remembers what happened last night. "Not …" she stutters. "Not happening."

I force myself to sound as playful as I can. "Kidding, my sweet girlfriend."

CHAPTER THIRTEEN

Carolina

HANGOVERS ARE A BITCH.

Turns out, while around distant relatives you don't like, drinking helps you tolerate them. It also turns out that drinking will convince you that attempting to seduce your best friend in a hotel room is a fantastic idea.

Damn you, alcohol. You're the best friend who's also a bad influence.

Good for the mind but bad for the hormones.

Rex was thankfully smart enough not to mention last night. He knows I'd die of embarrassment, and he'd lose his favorite cookie-maker. As much as I'd like to forget last night, I can't. All I'm doing while taking my bath is asking myself, *Why?*

Why did I enjoy our boyfriend-girlfriend game so much?

Why, even as awkward as I feel now, wouldn't I mind if he came barging in here, asking me to share my bath?

Why? Why? Why?

These past few months have been hard on me and on my heart, but Rex has been by my side every step of the way. He goes beyond the best-friend title, and sometimes, I wish he'd move into the boyfriend title.

I love him so damn much.

If only things were different.

If only he believed in love.

I understand he doesn't want to break my heart. I've seen him struggle with women—struggle when they begged him to give them more than a quick screw, struggle to cut them off, struggle to put himself out there. As much as I love him rejecting them, I wish he hadn't turned me down the same way.

When I get out of the bathtub, I drop my towel and get dressed into my pajamas. On my way back to my bedroom, I snatch my phone and hop into my comfy bed. As soon as I glance at the screen, nausea fills my stomach more than this damn hangover.

Margie: Hey! My birthday is next week. We're having a dinner at El Pacinos! Tacos and margaritas are calling our names. Please come!

So many emotions flood through me as I stare at her text message—envy, guilt, and sadness. A tear slides down my cheek as I contemplate whether to reply. Some days, I do. Some days, I don't.

Me: I have plans. Sorry.

Seconds later, my phone vibrates.

Margie: Come on, Carolina. Talk to me. You said I didn't do anything to piss you off, but all you do is blow me off. You left the dorm without even saying good-bye!

She's right. Rex and his roommate, Josh, went to my dorm and packed up my things, and I haven't been back.

Me: I've been busy working, and campus is such a long drive.

Margie: I can come there. Girls' night this weekend?

Me: Not this weekend. I'll get back with you.

Margie: Whatever. I'll just stop reaching out.

I sigh, wishing I had the guts to say more.

I haven't talked to Margie since I dropped out. When I disappeared from my dorm, she called and texted every day. I never answer her calls, but I text back, telling her I am busy or have a lot going on. I blow her off every time she asks to hang out.

After plugging my phone into the charger, I tuck myself into bed. My head might feel better after sixteen hours of sleep.

"GOOD MORNING, honey! How was your trip?" Shirley asks, her voice cheerful and loud when I walk into the diner bright and early.

Shirley is the owner of the diner I work for and waitressed here for years before her mother passed it down to her. She's a dark-skinned woman in her sixties who's a kind soul full of wisdom. I frequently studied here for hours in high school while eating slices of her famous pie. She never complained about me taking up a table, nor did she fail to slide a free slice in front of me—cherry, my favorite. She attends my father's church regularly and is a frequent donor of everything sweet.

"I think I'm in need of a vacation from that vacation," I grumble, grabbing an apron and tying it around my waist.

She laughs. "Oh, family weddings. They're always so fun."

"And also depressing," I add with a frown.

When I moved back to Blue Beech, my father offered me a job at the church, but I declined. Working for him is a bad idea. I'd hear his lecturing forty hours a week, and he'd watch every move I made. I still volunteer for functions at the church on my time off, but I can pick and choose those dates. They're normally when my father is busy or in a public place.

Shirley's Diner has been a staple in our town for decades. It has cute '50s-themed décor—complete with classic red booths, black-and-white-checkered floors, and bright teal walls. The most popular part of the diner is the silver counter in the front with a glass case filled with slices of pie in every flavor imaginable. Shirley makes them herself every night, and I stay over to help sometimes. It's the least I can do for her since she gave me a job and donates so many of them to the charity dinners I throw.

"Your boyfriend is in your booth," Candy, another waitress, sings while skipping into the kitchen.

Rex and his family have always been regulars at the diner, but he's here nearly half of my shifts and sits in the same booth in my section every time. On these days, he wakes up earlier than usual, brings his laptop to work, and eats. He also leaves me crazy tips, to which I try to shove back into his hand, pockets, shirt—wherever there's a crevice on him—but he won't allow it. He knows how hard up for cash I am. He also knows I won't take any money from him, so this is his way of helping me out.

"He's not my boyfriend," I reply.

Candy rolls her eyes while Shirley laughs in the background. "He's *so* your boyfriend."

"Sweetie, sooner or later, that boy will be your *husband*," Shirley gushes. "You two need to do some growing up." A grin takes over her wrinkled face. "You wait and see."

"Shirley, I'm beginning to think you're crazy," I remark, shaking my head.

"Not crazy, honey, just wise." She squeezes my shoulder.

I push my notepad into my apron, drag my hair into a ponytail, and rub at my tired eyes.

"Good morning, Lina babe," Rex greets as soon as I come into his view. He's wearing a black baseball hat that covers his bedhead and a loose gray sweatshirt. "I'm a little offended you told them I wasn't your boyfriend."

Thankfully, since the diner only opened an hour ago, nearly all the booths are empty, and no one is hearing this boyfriend talk. Rex is sprawled out in his booth, his closed laptop on the other side of the table. An elderly couple—Candy's grandparents—are situated in a booth in her section, and a few police officers are immersed in conversation at the counter.

"What?" I ask when I reach him. "How'd you hear that?"

"I not only like this booth because it's in your section, but I can also hear *all* the kitchen talk. You ladies are loud as hell when you gossip about me." He arches a brow. "It seems to be your favorite subject back there. Wait until they find out I was granted the role of being your boyfriend over the weekend and we have still yet to break up."

"Oh God, get over yourself," I grumble.

I'm clueless on how to tell my parents we broke up. We should've thought about this following us home when we started the stupid charade. No matter what, when I tell my parents we broke up, they'll blame it on Rex. Even if I say it was my decision, there will be no changing their mind. They've seen Rex as a bad influence all these years and me as their innocent little princess—except for the whole dropping out of school. My innocence status dropped a few notches after that.

He stretches his legs out and smiles. "Have I mentioned how much I love you in that uniform?"

"Yes," I say with a groan. "Every day I serve you."

Our uniforms stay with the '50s theme—red-and-white-striped dress with a white apron and white shoes. We all sport them with the exception of Shirley, who's retired from the outfit and wears a tee sporting the diner's logo. Last week, we jokingly started a petition to change our uniforms, and she said she'd consider the change.

"I'll have my usual, my hot candy cane-striped waitress." He doesn't even bother to open his menu. "And a coffee."

I leave to start his order, and when I return to his booth, his laptop is open in front of him. I drop a handful of sugar packets onto the table before setting his coffee down. Rex has a sweet tooth—hence why he loves my cookies.

"Aunt Lina!"

I glance back to see my nephew, Henry, barreling my way, and I nearly stumble back when he hugs my legs, peeking up at me with a bright smile. A Superman cape is tied around his neck, and his sneakers light up with every move he makes.

"We came to see you for breakfast!" he beams. "Grammy said I can get smiley-face pancakes!"

I bend to squeeze him into a hug and see my sister coming our way with my two-year-old niece, Addy, on her hip.

Tricia's gaze pings from me to Rex in the booth, her eyes widening in interest. "Oh, hey, your boyfriend came to see you this morning. How cute."

I can't tell if her comment is a compliment or a dig. My sister is a hard person to read and isn't a Rex fan. He hooked up with one of her friends in high school and then never called her back after the sixteen voicemails said friend left. She needs to get over it. She's married with children now.

Tricia and I weren't close growing up. My parents were strict with every move I made but not with Tricia. She had more freedom and could get away with mediocre grades, and my parents accepted her choice not to attend college. After I moved into her loft, our relationship has improved, but we're definitely not best friends. She's also taken on the hobby of finding me a man to marry.

Trailing Tricia is my mother, the expression on her face even more unreadable than Tricia's tone.

"Did you say boyfriend?" Candy squeals, rushing our way. She is nearly jumping up and down when she reaches us. "Carolina keeps denying it!"

"Oh, they're together all right," Tricia confirms. "They made it official over the weekend at our cousin's wedding."

My eyes flash to Rex's in a *help me* look.

"Isn't that right?" my sister adds skeptically, her gaze pointed at Rex as if this is a test.

"That's right," Rex answers, shutting his laptop and sliding it away from him. "We've been keeping it on the down-low for this very reason—to stop people from gossiping and making a big deal about it. It's new, and no matter what, we'll always be best friends first."

What the heck did we get ourselves into?

"Mom! Pancakes!" Henry squeals, interrupting this awful moment and stealing everyone's attention.

Kiddo is getting extra pancakes today.

Henry rushes toward the booth, sliding down to the wall, and Shirley already has a high chair ready to go for Addy when Tricia sits down next to him.

"Hi, sweetie," my mom says, giving me a peck on the cheek before moving her attention to Rex and giving him a wholesome smile. "Good morning, Rex."

"Morning, Mrs. Adams," he says with a grin before gesturing to his booth. "You guys are more than welcome to join me."

"You're so sweet," she replies. "We have a handful over there that might be too noisy for you this early in the morning. I can't promise that you wouldn't be wearing Henry's pancakes by the end of the meal."

Rex chuckles.

"Be over in a minute to take your order," I rush out to her before this gets weirder.

"Perfect, honey."

"Holy shit," I hiss to Rex as soon as she's out of earshot. "We need a plan, *pronto*, to break up this relationship."

Rex taps his fingers against the table. "We should've thought about the post-wedding aftermath."

I squeeze into the seat across from him and lean in closer, lowering my voice. "It's simple. You broke up with me."

He rests his elbows on the table. "The fuck it is. I'm not being the bad guy in this fake breakup. *You*"—he points at me—"broke up with"—he thrusts his thumb toward him—"me."

"Fine," I groan, throwing my hands up while he relaxes back against the booth and grabs his coffee. "I'll say it's because you couldn't sexually please me. I can work with that."

He tilts his mug toward me. "Yeah, go tell your preacher father that I couldn't sexually please you. No one in this town will believe you."

I scoff. "Why?" I do a sweeping gesture of the diner. "Because all the women here know what it feels like to be sexually pleased by you since you've slept with everyone in this town with a vagina?"

"Nope." He takes a loud sip of his coffee. "I haven't slept with Candy or Shirley—"

I cut him off. "Really?"

"What? You insinuated I've slept with all the women in town. I haven't slept with your sister—"

I interrupt again, "Thank God for that."

"Or your mother."

I snatch the knife from his side of the table. "I'm going to stab you and get fired from this job."

He stretches his arms along the booth. "There isn't one person in here who I've slept with." He pauses and lifts a finger. "Well, except for you." He clicks his tongue against the roof of his mouth. "I've also never shared a shower with any of them." He does the same motion as before. "*Except for you.*"

I cross my arms, heat creeping up my cheeks. *Oh no. He's not bringing this up for the first time here.* "Oh, you mean the shower where you were too wimpy to get naked?"

"Not a wimp. I was the only smart one in that shower," he says, his voice thick.

"Wimp," I snap back.

His dark brows furrow. "Drunk ass."

I jump up from my seat. "I need to get back to work. I'll be sure to spit on your waffles."

He licks his lips. "I love your spit."

I roll my eyes. "Quit the flirting. It's been made known that your flirting leads to nothing but boring showers."

He tenses. "That shower was definitely not boring."

"It was for me. You couldn't even look at me." I'm struggling to keep my voice low. I'm also struggling not to bop him in the head with the menu on the side of his table.

"Trust me, my dick got hard with every peek I made. When I saw your ass in the shower in front of me, I nearly died." He holds up his coffee. "Can I get a refill, please?"

I blink at him, ready to see my heart fall at my feet as it rages against my chest.

"Extra cream," he adds, licking his lips and thrusting the cup closer my way.

Just as I'm struggling to come up with a reply, Henry calls my name. I pivot on my heel, trying to catch my breath, and look at him.

"We're ready to order!" he calls out. "I need lots and lots of syrup with my pancakes, please!"

"Sugar-free syrup," Tricia adds.

"You'd better go help them," Rex adds with an annoying chuckle.

I slide his coffee mug along his table, leaving it there, and stroll over to take their order. On my way back to the kitchen, I swipe Rex's mug from his table without saying a word.

"I'm so jealous," Candy squeals after I call out my orders to the cooks. "Why would you want to hide being in a relationship with *Rex Lane*? He's so hot."

I went to high school with Candy. She was part of the popular crowd and wasn't that nice then, but she's been cool since I started here. I *somewhat* think of her as a friend. She only irks me when it comes to Rex and how she makes a big deal about him being here.

The rest of my shift goes smoothly. I bring Rex his coffee refill and breakfast, and he thankfully doesn't mention our shower party of no fun again.

CHAPTER FOURTEEN

Rex

"THANK GOD YOU'RE HERE," Maliki comments when he answers the door.

It's late. I've been up, working on my game, and then Sierra texted me, reminding me about her computer. She instructed me to text Maliki when I was here and not to knock since Molly would most likely be sleeping.

Their house was recently remodeled and looks awesome. Sierra is an interior designer, so she had the most say in the changes. Maliki stepped to the side, letting her create her dream home for them.

"She's been whining about her computer nonstop," he adds as I follow him into the living room.

Sierra is on the couch, and next to her is a sleeping Molly, her head resting on Sierra's lap.

"Oh, shut it," Sierra chimes in. "I have not."

Maliki nods toward Molly. "I'll put her to bed."

Sierra nods and plants a kiss on Molly's forehead before Maliki scoops his daughter up in his arms and carries her down the long hallway.

"Let me grab my laptop," Sierra says, pulling herself up

and plodding barefoot to the kitchen while I relax on the couch.

Maliki returns at the same time she hands it over to me. He's cool as shit, and he owns the only bar in our town—Down Home Pub. He took it over years back when his father nearly went bankrupt and then moved to Florida. My sister works with him, bartending a few nights a week, but now that her interior design company has taken off, she's cut down on her hours.

"How was your lovers' trip?" Sierra asks, her and Maliki sitting next to each other. She turns, resting her back to his side, and he tucks his arm around her waist.

It's time like these when I wonder in the back of my mind if I'm capable of having that. Sure, Carolina and I *snuggle* sometimes, but this is more than snuggling. There's a certain intimacy, and the love they have for each other bleeds off them. Briefly, I wonder what it looks like when Carolina lies against me like that. Does our … *friendship* … *our love* bleed off us?

"It wasn't a lovers' trip," I scold, opening her laptop and powering it on.

Sierra tilts her back and smiles up at Maliki. "Aw, babe, do you remember when we were friends and tried to hide that we were in love with each other?"

Maliki's arm tightens around her, and he brushes his thumb against her cheek with his free hand. "Yep, and what a waste. Imagine all the extra time we could've had if we had stopped pussyfooting around."

Sierra lifts her head while they look at me with expectation.

I switch my attention to the laptop, hitting keys. "No pussyfooting around. I don't get what no one understands about us being only friends."

Fuck. Why is this all I've been hearing about lately?

Maliki chuckles, shaking his head. "Quit giving him shit,

babe. He'll figure it out eventually."

Sierra groans. "Hopefully, it doesn't take him too long. Remember what happened when you didn't step up?"

He frowns. "Don't remind me."

"I got *married.*" She stresses every syllable as the words leave her mouth before focusing on me. "Do you want Carolina to marry someone else, Rex?"

I rub at the sudden tension in my neck, the thought hitting me like a headache. "Carolina isn't getting married."

I fucking hope not.

"How do you know?" Sierra continues, as if her mission tonight is to piss me off. "*I* got married."

"She won't," I grind out, contemplating whether to change her password and the language to Chinese in revenge for her taunting.

I love my sister, and I know she means well. We've always been the closest, but she's a pain in the ass.

"Are you saying that because you don't want her to get married?"

"Jesus, babe," Maliki cuts in, shooting me a sympathetic stare while giving her a gentle squeeze. "You're going to make his head explode."

She sighs. "I want to see my baby bro happy, and he needs to stop being dumb."

I hold up her computer, arching a brow. "The one who can't figure out her computer is calling me dumb?"

"Learn from my mistakes, little bro." She skims her fingers along Maliki's arm. "Don't you think they'd be cute, babe?"

"So cute," Maliki says, mocking her voice. "Fucking adorable."

"Funny," she deadpans. "Remember who you sleep next to at night."

Their relationship story is pretty damn entertaining. Maliki used to kick my sister out of his bar whenever she was underage and tried to sneak in. It became a thing to them.

They're so opposite—my sister being the rebellious sorority princess and Maliki being the bartending bad boy who hated commitment. I admire their relationship so damn much.

Maliki smacks a kiss against the top of her head. "The best damn woman in the world is who I sleep next to at night."

I gag. "Gross. You two save your flirtfest for later." I drop the laptop onto the couch and stand. "Computer is fixed."

"OH, SWEET CAROLINA, BA, BA, BA!" Josh sings when Carolina walks into our apartment.

He does it every damn time.

"Shut up and leave her alone," I grumble in annoyance, pausing my game.

Josh is cool. We shared a few classes together at Iowa State and were partners on a project. He's a few years older than me, clean, not *that much* of a pain in the ass, and he pays rent on time. The only times I consider kicking him out is when it comes to Carolina. He—along with every-fucking-body else—gives me shit about our relationship and has threatened to ask her out one too many times. He won't. There would be an eviction notice on his bedroom door as soon as the words left his mouth.

He's your typical hipster who wears beanies over his shoulder-length hair that he pulls into a man bun most of the time, he sports a scruffy beard, and his closet is packed with flannels in every color.

"Damn," he grumbles, attempting to fight back a smug smile. "Can't a man say hi?"

"You didn't say hi." I divert my attention to Carolina. "You hungry? I ordered a pizza."

She worked a double today and is always hangry when she gets off work.

She licks her lips. "Yum. You da best."

I grin. "Well aware of that, babe."

She looks damn adorable when she strolls into the living room—wearing a loose, flower-patterned dress that isn't made to look as sexy as it does on her. It shows a hint of cleavage, causing me to gulp as I remember the night in the hotel room.

Fuck. Will I ever forget that night?

She kicks off her white flip-flops on her way to the couch and takes the open seat next to me, tucking her legs underneath her ass. "How many levels do you need to finish? Are you still stuck?"

I love that she asks this. Hardly anyone—except for her, my mother, my sister, and Josh—asks about my game. They're the only ones who take it seriously and understand how important it is to me, how much I love it. Carolina has been on this game's journey since nearly day one—hearing me throw out idea after idea, change shit, work on levels, and beg gamers to give it a try.

She listens, understands, and offers advice about my game. Not too many chicks are comfortable with hanging out with a guy who plays video games as much as I do. Either that or they *fake* being into it, not even knowing the difference between my game and Fortnight.

Carolina does because she genuinely cares.

"I'm slowly getting out of my slump," I reply, unpausing it and hitting buttons on the controller. "It was too easy, breaking through a few levels. I needed to make it harder." I've been working nonstop for twelve hours, only taking bathroom and food breaks.

Thank fuck Josh isn't a big TV watcher. I like testing in the living room rather than my bedroom.

"Attaboy! I'm so proud of you!" She gestures to the screen. "How you do all this—create, design, code. It's so amazing."

I fasten my free arm around her back and drag her closer to my side. "Thanks, Mom."

She shoves my shoulder, causing my character to die. "Shut up and take my compliment."

"Looks like it's easy to die when a chick is touching you," Josh says from the chair next to me. "You have that going for you. Include a hot girl to distract them in every game."

I flip him off.

He laughs. "You fools coming out tonight?"

"No way," Carolina answers around a yawn. "I'm beat, and I work the morning shift tomorrow."

"Losers," he teases, winking at Carolina.

I narrow my eyes at him and hold up the controller—a silent warning that it'll hit him in the face if he continues his annoying-ass flirting.

I turn my attention to Carolina. "Looks like it's you and me tonight."

Josh jumps up from his chair, snaps his fingers, and pings his finger back and forth between me and Carolina. "Good. You two kids do something bad."

I flip him off again as he walks away, his laughter booming through the apartment.

CHAPTER FIFTEEN

Carolina

I TUG my phone from my apron when it vibrates, and my heart sinks when I read the text from the last person I want to talk to. He's the man I hate and who's made my life a living hell.

James: You can't keep ignoring me.

My fingers are close to shaking as I hit the reply button.

Me: I'm not ignoring you.

James: Let me correct myself. You can't keep avoiding me.

I roll my eyes. He didn't correct himself. *Avoiding* and *ignoring* are the same thing.

Me: Whatever. What do you want?

James: Don't forget who has the upper hand here.

My jaw hurts as I grit my teeth at his threat, and I wish I were brave enough to do something. Call me weak … a coward … but fighting him on this will lead to serious consequences.

I've found there are two ways to appease him:

1. Agree.
2. Stroke his ego.

My phone beeps again.

James: I want to see you.

Me: I've been swamped with work.

James: Yet you had time to fly to Texas.

Me: Are you following me?

I glance around my surroundings in the diner's kitchen even though there's no way he's in here. From now on, I'll be looking over my shoulder with every move I make. I came home with the thought he'd never make the drive here. Hopefully, I wasn't wrong.

James: No. I saw your little boyfriend posted it on Instagram.

He's following Rex?

He hates Rex.

Me.

That's why he's following Rex.

To follow me since I blocked him.

Just as I'm about to reply with expletives that'll piss him off more, I'm saved by a text from Rex.

My Main Man: Going to Down Home tonight. Come with?

Me: Sounds good to me.

My problems slip from my thoughts when I'm with Rex. I also feel safe with him.

My Main Man: You want me to scoop you up?

Me: 9:00?

My Main Man: See you then.

I untie my apron, drop my phone into my purse, and head back to the loft without replying to James's message. My guess is he's drinking, in a mood and feeling sorry for himself, or having girl problems. He reaches out whenever one of those problems happens, bugs me for a day, and then disappears for a while … and then the cycle starts over a few weeks later.

Whenever possible, I have Rex pick me up when we go out —because I'm selfish. That way, he can't bring another woman home with him. Sure, she could always go to his house after, but I tend to invite myself over and hang out with him. Not that he's ever said no. Not once has he ever brought home a woman when he's with me.

Rex is seen around town as the rebellious, rich kid.

His reputation always makes me laugh. Hell, I believed it, too, before we became friends.

He's considered *rebellious* because he does what he wants, he has never had a serious girlfriend, nor has he been interested in one, and he defies his father with every move.

Rex doesn't care about that rep and hardly shows anyone who he really is. We've learned each other's secrets, flaws, skeletons, and secret traits.

Which is why we're in love with each other.

Rex knows this.

I know it.

It's just easier for us to play pretend.

"DAMN, LINA," Rex says, strolling into my living room. "You look hot."

I lower my gaze to my white summer dress and strappy brown sandals. Summer dresses are my go-to outfit. They're comfy, cute, and effortless to pull together—my style. I've never been one to keep up with trends, and my parents were strict with what I wore growing up.

My contacts are in, my hair halfway up, halfway down, and I have a hint of makeup on.

I shyly grin.

Rex complimenting me isn't new.

My dress could be a paper bag, and he'd still flatter me.

Having a best friend who pumps up your ego on the regular is fun.

"Thank you." I snatch my pink sweater from the edge of

the couch and drag it over my shoulders. "You don't look so bad yourself."

His walnut-colored hair is messy. Envy hits me of how simple his hair routine is. All he does is run gel through it, spiking it up, and he's all set. A gray moto jacket fits his muscular shoulders perfectly, a thin white tee underneath it, and his black jeans have rips down the front.

He playfully pops the collar of his jacket. "Yeah, I know."

I snort and smack his stomach on my way to grab my crossbody bag. "Geesh, how has your head not exploded from all that ego you carry in there? Must be because your brain is so puny."

"Weird." He chuckles. "You sure have no problem taking compliments that boost your ego."

"That's different."

"Do explain how it's different."

"I don't pop my collar like a 2002 rap song and say, 'I know.'" I mimic his collar-popping gesture. "I politely say thanks without letting it go to my fat, smug head."

He's laughing as he opens the door, and he follows me down the outside stairs to the driveway.

This week was a rough one. A drink will help dim my problems … dim my secrets. I duck into his car after he opens the door for me, and then he goes to his side. The ride to Down Home is short, and the parking lot is packed when we pull in. The pub is the place to go for a good time and to relax. Even when it's a full house, the setting unwinds you. Sierra remodeled the bar and made it her goal for the customers to feel like they're at home, sharing drinks with friends.

Music playing from the live band hits us when we walk in, and Rex's hand finds mine before he leads us to a crowded table in the center of the room. He steals two unoccupied stools from another table and brings them to ours, gesturing for me to sit in one while taking the other. When I sit, he tugs me closer, and I settle back while doing a once-over of our table.

Rex's brother, Kyle, is across from me with his arm slung over his girlfriend, Chloe's, shoulders while he sips on a beer. Their history has always fascinated me. They hated each other in high school, became neighbors, and are now in a serious relationship. It's been a rough ride for them with Chloe being involved in their family drama. I'll never forget the night Rex called me, ignited with a fury I'd never heard from him before, when he found Chloe's secret. It was some soap-opera, Jerry Springer drama.

Chloe is chatting it up with Lauren Barnes, who's sitting next to her. I've admired Lauren for years. Her family has never failed to help me with any charity or benefit dinner I bring to them. The Barnes family is one of the kindest families in Blue Beech. Her fiancé and Kyle's best friend, Gage, is next to her. They were high school sweethearts, and everyone was waiting for their marriage announcement, but instead, Lauren broke his heart. He returned a few years later with no intention of rekindling with Lauren. That didn't last long, considering they have a baby girl together.

Lately, Rex prefers to hang out with his family and brother's friends than the people we went to school with. Since they're chill and always accepting of me, I have no issue with that.

"Hey, Carolina," Sierra greets from the other side of me, a friendly smirk on her face.

I smile at her. "Hey!" I signal to the crowd. "It's a full house tonight."

She nods. "Sure is."

"No hey for your little bro?" Rex asks her.

Sierra wiggles her fingers in an exaggerated wave. "Hello, my pain-in-the-ass brother."

"Carolina," Kyle says, setting his beer down. The

resemblance between him and Rex is crazy. "I love when you come with my brother. You tame him."

"Fake news," Rex argues. "I tame her."

Kyle snorts. Sierra scoffs. Gage laughs.

I pat Rex's head. "I keep him in line like a good little boy."

The waitress stopping by to take our order interrupts our conversation. Rex and I order two Jack and Cokes, and he adds in an order of nachos supreme for us to share—my favorite.

"You're not working tonight?" I ask Sierra.

She shakes her head. "Nope. I've been overloaded with work, so Maliki hired a part-time bartender to cover for me."

She shoves a hand through her blonde hair before pulling it into a high ponytail.

Sierra is gorgeous. She was nicknamed the Pageant Queen of Blue Beech, growing up. Okay, the *rebellious* Pageant Queen of Blue Beech, since she acted out like it was her job. After becoming single, she took a job working at the pub with Maliki before starting her own interior design business.

Her gaze moves past my shoulders, and I shift in my chair, following her attention to Maliki pouring a beer behind the bar. Maliki is hot—there's no denying that—with his dark hair, muscles, and facial scruff. He's older, in his thirties, and he was known as a ladies' man who'd never settle down. Word was, he swore serious relationships weren't his thing, but Sierra came into his life. He changed for her, going from a ladies' man to one of the best boyfriends I've seen.

I love their love, but it also scares the shit out of me.

It proves people who think they're not capable of love are.

What happens when Rex finds the woman to change him?

His heart is big enough for commitment, for him to be someone's everything and make her his everything. That fear just needs to be broken.

"Is it hard for him to relax when he owns the place?" I ask, turning back to Sierra.

"Definitely," she answers. "It's better now that we don't live above the bar anymore. It's not as easy as running downstairs to check on things."

She sips on her pink cocktail. Down Home was never big on cocktails. It was more of a beer and hard liquor establishment until Sierra came into the picture.

I nod in understanding. "I get that. It was difficult for my father to separate family and work with us living next door to the church."

We spent more time there than at home since my father was the preacher and my mother ran the after-school program.

The waitress comes back with our nachos and drinks, and Rex has her start a tab for us. Rex was a huge partier since high school, and it only worsened his first year of college, but now that he's doing so well with his game, he's cut down on the drinking. A hungover brain isn't a productive brain. It's frustrating that people don't notice the change in him—the maturity evolution is what I've named it, to which he always responds with an eye roll.

One of those people being his father, Michael Lane. He lives his life with the belief that all Rex does is party and waste his life away. Since Rex avoids as much contact with him as possible, he doesn't bother correcting him. Michael has always been friendly with me, but he's a jackass to Rex, which pisses me off. I force smiles but never go out of my way to start a conversation with him when I attend dinners at Rex's house.

Call it rude. Whatever.

Anyone who treats Rex like crap is a sucky person in my book.

Rex takes a swig of his beer before peering at me. "I'mma run to the restroom. Save me some nachos." His hand brushes along my shoulders as he walks away.

Chloe updates everyone on her and Kyle's adoption

journey and reveals they're considering becoming foster parents while waiting for approval.

I'm mid-nacho-chomp when Rex is walking back from the restroom, and I nearly choke on the chip when a woman stands in front of him, blocking his way. I pinch my lips together, nausea swirling inside my stomach, and shove the nacho basket up the table.

"Don't worry about her," Sierra comments, bumping her shoulder against mine as I painfully gawk at Rex and Blockzilla. "He doesn't want her."

My eyes narrow when the girl slides her hand up his arm. "Rex wants any woman who looks in his direction."

Flirty women are a constant when we go out. They attempt to force themselves onto him while I play indifferent and fake that it doesn't hurt my heart. Rex never entertains it, but that still doesn't stop my envy.

"No, babe, he wants you." Sierra releases a heavy sigh. "He's scared. Maliki was like that. He just needed a little convincing."

I transfer my attention to Sierra. "Convincing how?"

I halfway know the answer to my question. She and Maliki played a cat-and-mouse game for years, ever since she was eighteen and snuck into his bar.

She nudges her head toward where Rex is standing, but I stop myself from looking back. "Call him out on his bullshit. Call him a chickenshit until he stops acting like a chickenshit. And if all else fails, date someone else. Scare him into getting his head out of his ass."

"You and Maliki are different than me and Rex. We've been friends for years. Plus, you're bolder than I am. I'm pretty much a chickenshit, too."

"You're a total badass, and my brother is head over heels for you. He's just too stupid to admit it."

She throws her arm out, motioning toward Rex, and I

brace myself to be upset as I peek over at him. He's ditched the girl and dodging bodies while heading in our direction.

"See!" she cries out. "Y-O-U!"

Rex takes his place by my side again, interrupting our conversation, and Sierra glances up at Maliki with a grin when he joins us and says hi to everyone. He kisses Sierra, whispering words against her mouth, and they become disgustingly cute.

"Another one of your women?" I question Rex, a frown on my face before I shove a nacho into my mouth.

"Nope," he replies with a straight face.

I narrow my eyes at him.

"What?" He shrugs. "She asked if I'd buy her a drink. I said no. She then asked if she could buy me a drink. I respectively declined like the gentleman I am and walked away." He shrugs again. "No biggie."

"I'm amazed you didn't take her up on her offer," I grumble.

"Not interested. I'd never ditch you for another chick."

"Oh. My. Freaking. God!"

Her shrill voice hits me right before Candy comes into our view. She halts at our table, as if someone hit the brakes on her legs.

I dip my head down and cover half my face with my hand, fully aware she's about to make a scene.

"If it's not the happy couple making it official!" she shrieks. She pouts out her lower lip when her green eyes cut to Rex. "It sucks you're off the market, but I'm happy someone nice like Carolina snagged you!" Her words come out in a slight slur. "She's a keeper. Don't you go breaking her heart, or I'll break your thumbs! And it's hard to play video games without thumbs."

This is not happening.

Out of all places, she announces it in front of a crowd of people.

Every muscle in my body stiffens, my heart clamoring against my chest while I struggle not to freak the hell out. Rex's hand sweeps underneath the table, settling on my thigh, and he tenderly squeezes it.

"What?" nearly everybody at the table asks in their own manner.

It takes me a moment to uncover my face, and my gaze swiftly darts around the table, taking in everyone's response. Excitement. Happiness. Curiosity. Not one person appears pissed as their attention bounces back and forth from me to Rex.

"Whoa, did I miss something?" Kyle asks. "Is it finally happening?" He gestures between me and Rex. "Did you two finally get your heads out of your asses and admit you're in love?"

"Sure did!" Candy answers for us with extra pep in her voice. "You should've seen them at the diner." She folds her hands over her chest. "*Swoon*!"

We were so not swoon.

Sierra eagerly focuses on me. "Tell me everything."

"Details!" Chloe adds.

"How'd this happen?" Lauren yelps.

I stare at Rex in horror.

Oh my God. Oh my God.

How are we getting out of this?

It's not only my parents we have to create a breakup story for. It's now pretty much the entire town. And when it happens, most of them will give Rex hell for it, placing all the blame on him.

Rex's hand stays on my thigh as he speaks, "This is why we kept it on the down-low." He motions toward the table. "We didn't want this shit to happen—you clowns making a big deal about it." His hand leaves my thigh, and he curves his arm around my shoulders, dragging me closer to him. "Yes, we're trying something new."

"I love it." Sierra beams.

"Kiss!" Candy yells. "Now that the cat is out of the bag, you should totally kiss!"

I want to kill Candy.

No more picking up any extra shifts for her.

Her voice rises as she starts pumping her fist into the air. "Kiss! Kiss! Kiss!"

Kyle joins in on her chanting … then Chloe … then Lauren … and then the rest of the damn bar.

My mind goes blank when Rex cups the back of my head.

"Might as well make the crowd happy." His mouth crashes against mine.

Screams erupt across the bar, and clapping ensues.

Rex doesn't give me a quick peck. No, his soft lips part, and his tongue plunges into my mouth, teasingly stroking against mine. He tastes like beer and salt. His hand knots into my hair, and he yanks me closer, his mouth claiming me as his girlfriend.

My cheeks are on fire.

I'm making out with Rex in front of everyone.

And it doesn't feel pretend.

The. Best. Kiss. Ever.

It's life-changing.

Friendship-changing.

We're so screwed.

All the commotion around us is drowned out as he devours my mouth.

I'm clueless as to how much time passes before he tears away from me.

He tenderly kisses the tip of my nose.

I shiver when his cheek touches mine, and he whispers in my ear, "FYI, I'm not ending this. Figure out how you're going to break my heart." His tongue runs along the edge of my lobe, and I tighten my thighs. "You taste delicious, by the way."

This friendship just got a lot more complicated.

REX DOESN'T ASK if I want to go home as he drives to his apartment.

He knows me well enough to know the answer.

Hanging out with him is more enjoyable than hanging out in the loft solo.

Tonight was a shitshow, to say the least. I'd expected a simple night out of having drinks, not for every resident of Blue Beech to believe we're dating.

Rex stuck to water the rest of the night since he was driving. Like at the wedding, he played the boyfriend role perfectly—further confirmation he's capable of commitment even if he doesn't believe it himself. It was as if Candy hit a switch in him tonight. His hand never left me after our kiss—whether it was on my hip, my shoulder, or my thigh. He kissed my cheek a few times, but there was no more mouth action.

Thank God.

Had it been like the first one, there would have been a decent chance I'd lose my mind and straddle him in front of everyone because I was so turned on.

I toss my sweater on the back of the couch and kick my sandals off when we walk into his apartment. His three-bedroom place screams total bachelor pad. Rex has the master bedroom with an attached bathroom, Josh has the second bedroom, and the third is empty for a new roommate. Rex is picky about who he rents to.

He tosses his keys onto the coffee table while I run to his bathroom. I glance around his room on the way there. It matches his personality perfectly. One wall is painted a deep red while the other three are black. A black-and-white canvas painting is hung over his bed along with video game and cinema posters. I grin when I pass the picture of us from graduation on his nightstand.

When I leave the bathroom, Rex is in the kitchen, standing in front of the open fridge.

"Yo, drink?" he shouts over his back while snagging a bottle of water.

"H2O, please!" I join him in the kitchen while he grabs another bottle and shuts the fridge.

His jacket is off, his feet bare, and his thin white tee shows off his muscular arms. Just because Rex isn't built like a bodybuilder with bulging arms doesn't mean he isn't fit. He's tall and lean. I love how he towers over me.

When he comes closer, my pulse races as I remember our kiss, him touching me at the bar, and of him in the shower, stroking himself.

"Are you still worried about your game?" I ask when he hands me the water.

He leans back against the counter, his forehead scrunching. "Every damn day."

My heart breaks at the stress on his face. "I'm sorry. Anything I can do to help?"

The offer grants me a smile.

"You help me every time we hang out—calming me and shit," he says.

"I'm your personal Xanax, huh?" My words come out in a laugh.

"Pretty much." He chugs down half his water.

"Let me check it out." I stroll into the living room, him lagging behind me, and drop my water onto the floor before grabbing a gaming remote. "It's been a hot minute since I've played, but my amazing skills haven't been forgotten." *Hopefully.* I pop a squat onto the carpeted floor and stretch my legs out in front of me.

Rex powers on the TV and game console.

I beam with pride when the game's home screen pops up

on the TV, displaying the characters, and I point at the TV with the remote. "That princess had still better be me."

"You think I'd risk you kicking my ass if I changed it?"

"You'd never change it anyway."

He cocks his head to the side, smirking. "I might when you break up with me."

I roll my eyes. "You'd better not when *you* break up with *me*. You can make the character dudes hotter in case my character wants to date one of them."

"Hotter character dudes, huh?"

"Damn straight," I answer with a firm nod.

His hand rests over his heart. "Ouch. You're already breaking my heart."

Shock storms through me when he sits behind me, spreading his legs to each side of my body, and he slowly drags me between them until my back hits his solid chest.

I peek back at him, struggling to remain confident. "Nope. I told you I wouldn't be the heartbreaker. You made it worse with that kiss of yours." My gaze swings back to the TV. "What was up with that?"

He pushes my hair behind my shoulder and runs his fingers through the strands. "They were fucking chanting for us to. How suspect would it look for a happy couple to be that reluctant to kiss?"

"Why do you care if it's believable?" I question. "You refused to touch me at the hotel, but now, you're making out with me in public?" The game beeps when I touch the start button, and I shake my head as my level begins. "Mixed signals alert."

"Confused best-friend alert," he grumbles.

Whoa.

"What?" My fingers freeze, causing my character to die. "What are you saying?"

"I struggle daily to protect our friendship, but why do I crave to kiss you now that I've had a taste? I want to touch you." He blows out a ragged breath. "*Fuck*, Carolina. You have no idea how badly I want to touch you ... to tell you I love us playing boyfriend and girlfriend."

"Then do it," I dare.

He buries his nose in my hair. "It's not that simple, Lina."

Rejection is the third party in this friendship of ours.

Sierra's advice from the bar zips through my thoughts

I hold the controller in my sweaty palm and am proud of myself for staying composed. "It's okay. You're not my type anyway."

His chest moves behind me as he laughs. "Oh, really? I'm not your type now, huh?"

"Nope. To be honest, you never have been."

"You begging to share a shower and for me to touch you sure screamed I was your type."

"Desperation. My vagina gets needy when I drink."

"Mmhmm. Tell me then, what's your type?"

"A guy not scared to share showers." I pause, drawing in a gutsy breath. "A guy who isn't afraid to touch me."

His chest presses against my back, and his hand slips from my hair to my thigh, inching underneath the hem of my dress. He does this silently, not a word being muttered out of his mouth.

Tonight, I will be bold.

"Someone who isn't afraid of taking chances," I continue around a gulp.

His free hand drops to my other thigh.

"Someonc who isn't afraid to slide their hand higher."

His voice is raspy when he speaks, "We're playing with fire, Carolina."

Yes—a fire that has the capacity to not only incinerate our friendship, but also our hearts.

But I'm done with not taking risks.

Done searching for a guy who'll never compare to what I feel for Rex.

"If we're going to fake a relationship, might as well take advantage of the relationship perks."

A wave of pleasure smacks into me when I rub the bottom of my butt against him, feeling his growing erection. He's turned on *by me.*

He steals the remote, hits the start button, and hands it back to me while the game loads. "Play."

"What?"

I'm offering sex on the table, and he wants me to play a damn video game?

I know he loves it and all, but *what the heck?*

"Play. The. Game." His hand eases underneath my dress. "Don't die, and I won't stop."

I clutch the controller in my hands and stare at the screen. *How does he expect me to play while he's doing that?*

My fingers shake while he caresses my bare skin. The game hasn't changed much, and I'm on the first level, so this shouldn't be so hard. I'm playing at a slow pace and still alive.

I spread my legs wider, a silent plea for more, and he takes the hint—skimming his hand higher while the other stays rested. My eyes are heavy, and I fight not to shut them while he explores me—this time dipping between my thighs but not going where I need him.

I stop when his thumb slips underneath my panties.

A combination of a chuckle and a groan escapes him. "Keep playing, baby."

I shake my head while reluctantly doing what he demanded. "Are you serious? Not possible."

"Pass this level. Get an orgasm."

What a reward … if only it wasn't freaking impossible.

I spare my character from dying at the last minute. "Pass a level, and you have sex with me?"

His lips brush my ear, and I can feel his heart thumping wildly against my back. "Three levels."

To give me more incentive to pass the damn level, he slips

his hand into my panties and cups me between my legs, the heel of his hand brushing against my clit.

My fingers slam against the remote buttons as I buck my hips forward. "Jesus, you're making a girl beg and play video games all for the D?"

"Sure am." He sinks a finger inside me, and my back arches against him. "You're so wet for me."

"Don't get too cocky. It might be for the guy in the game."

"Keep playing." He adds another finger.

"There's no way," I moan while he slowly strokes me.

"I'll make you come so hard if you beat the level. I promise."

I groan in defeat when my character dies and toss the controller to the side.

"Game over," he says, dragging his fingers out of me.

My hand shoots between my legs to stop him, and I press it tighter against me. I've never been so turned on in my life. I jerk my hips forward while using his hand to manipulate how I want it while moaning, and I hope he doesn't pull away when I release him.

He doesn't.

He groans in my ear, pressing a palm against my stomach, and roughly drags me into him, thrusting against me.

He balls up my dress in his fist and hoists it up until my butt is showing.

"Holy fuck," he hisses around a low groan, shoving another finger inside me, and my nails dig into his hand. "Move up."

I relax my hold on him and moan at the loss of his fingers … and then again when I'm pushed forward on my hands and knees in front of him.

I moan, my head dropping, as he smooths his hand over my ass before massaging it.

"So much for my strong willpower," he says, sliding my

panties to the side before sinking two hard fingers back into my wet core.

I rake my nails against the carpet, and he situates himself behind me.

I'm close.

So close.

I match his every thrust. "Oh my God!" I cry out. "I'm about to come!"

"Yeah," he says. "I feel you tightening around my fingers."

The pleasure amplifies when he finds my clit again.

"The motherfucking party is here!"

My heart stops so quick that I don't know how I'm not dead when Josh barges into the apartment with a flock of people behind him. Rex's fingers slide out of me in seconds, and he falls down, pulling me onto his lap. The controller is shoved back into my hand, and he starts the game back up.

Our breathing doesn't match people who were innocently playing video games.

More along the lines of Zumba … or *sex*.

Josh freezes, taking in the scene. "Oh fuck." His eyes widen before he turns on his heel to face the group. "Let's grab some grub. I'm fucking starving."

"What?" a woman whines. "Order a pizza here or something. I'm not paying for another Uber."

Josh snaps his fingers and creates a zipping noise before pointing at the kitchen. "Let's do shots in the kitchen then! I have some grade-A tequila in there, and we can order a pizza."

Luckily, they follow him into the kitchen, and Rex pulls us up as soon as they disappear. I'm silent when he takes my hand, and we scurry down the hall to his bedroom. He releases me as soon as the door shuts behind us. When I turn around to face him, he's resting his back against the door, his hand to his chest as he catches his breath.

"I declare myself a winner since we were interrupted," I comment.

Technically, I died before they showed up, but this argument sounds better for a possible orgasm.

"How about I be the winner as I give you the best orgasm you've ever had?" He doesn't give me time to answer as he stalks forward, his face covered with need, and crushes his mouth against mine.

CHAPTER SIXTEEN

Rex

BAD IDEA. *Bad fucking idea.*

That is what my brain is telling me.

Keep kissing her.

That's what my dick is telling me.

Love her.

That is what my heart is telling me.

Will we regret this tomorrow?

We're at our breaking point—putting it all on the line for this attraction we've fought for too many years.

Heat rushes through my veins as I cup her soft cheeks and devour her mouth in a way I've never kissed a woman. But then again, I've never wanted anyone so damn much in my life.

Our kiss is impulsive. Heated. Urgent.

Our desire is finally being freed from its cage.

I tune out the music blasting in the living room—most likely a courtesy from Josh to drown out any noise that might escape my bedroom. He deserves a thank you later. No doubt he'll demand my gratitude be rewarded with details on what he walked into. That's not fucking happening. Convincing him nothing happened will be a bitch, though, considering

Carolina was on her hands and knees, her dress shoved up to her waist, while my fingers were inside her.

Pretty fucking hard to dispute that.

I snarl at the thought of him seeing her so exposed and sink my teeth into her lower lip. Carolina moans in response, and I hiss as she returns the favor, her bite sharper than mine. I wouldn't be surprised if she drew blood. It's a fucking struggle to breathe when I break our connection to retreat a step.

Her cheeks are flushed, her lips swollen, as she stands in front of me. Our eyes lock—hers overflowing with anticipation and hunger, matching mine.

I squeeze my eyes shut, coming to grips with what's about to happen. "What do you want, Carolina?"

"You," she breathes out. "I want you." She reaches down, grabs the hem of her dress, and pulls it over her head. She stares at me with confidence while providing the view of the woman who means everything to me.

Every ounce of tension in my body releases, all my fucks fly out the window, and I rub the tip of my thumb along my lower lip. There's no stopping my hand from dropping to my crotch to adjust my erection through my jeans even though there's no hiding how hard I am.

A beam of satisfaction floods her features. Her lips part as she reaches behind her back to unsnap her bra, and she tosses it to the side. I stifle a groan when her next move is to shimmy out of her soft pink panties.

Carolina is standing in the middle of my bedroom with her perfect, petite body on full display for me. Her breasts are fuller than they were in high school, and I gulp at the thought of tasting them. Her hips are curvier. It blows my mind that she's offering me something so damn precious.

I don't deserve it.

I've never deserved Carolina.

Yet here I am, jeopardizing it all.

My eyes cut to the limited view of her pussy, and my mouth waters.

"I keep making all the moves." Her words snap me out of imagining all the things I want to do to her. "It's your turn, Rex."

Whoa. She's making the moves?

I'm certain I was the one with my fingers shoved inside her pussy, but if making a move is what she needs from me, I'll make a goddamn move—a move that'll have her moaning and squirming underneath me.

She raises a brow in challenge, a daring smile dancing on her moist lips.

I wipe out the small distance dividing us, my hands finding her hips, and tip my head down. "You know I'm not one to turn down a challenge."

She grins deviously. "I know."

My lips crash into hers again and never separate as I walk us to my bed. She squeals when I bend my arms, my hands cupping her armpits, and I playfully toss her onto the bed. She wastes no time sliding up the bed, making room for me to join her, and rises to her knees. I join her, my pulse pounding with every move, and fall to mine.

As soon as I'm settled, she frantically pulls my shirt over my head and flings it across the room. "All of it." Her fingers start fumbling with the zipper of my jeans. "Right now."

I curl my fingers around her wrist, nudging her hand away, and do the job for her. I drop my pants along with my boxer briefs down and kick them off my feet. Her beautiful brown eyes widen when it's her turn to eye-fuck me, her gaze lingering on my cock.

She leans forward, her ass coming off the bed a few inches, to circle her arms around my neck and tug me closer. We make out slowly, and I take my sweet time kissing her—nipping at her lips, sucking on the tip of her tongue—all while she grinds against my thigh, panting.

This is it.

Our lips stay connected as I settle her onto her back, her dark hair nearly blending with my black pillow, and I crawl up the bed. I use my legs to spread hers and slip between them. A quiet moan escapes her when I bury my head in the crook of her neck, kissing my way down it. I cup her breast with my large palm while my mouth continues its journey. My lips replace my hand the moment it reaches her nipple, drawing the tiny bud into my mouth, twirling my tongue around it, and then sucking hard.

"Holy crap," she releases in a loud hiss while writhing underneath me. "More. *Please.*"

With no warning, I give her what she's demanding and thrust two fingers inside her warmth. Her pussy is soaked, which makes it easier to glide my fingers in and out of her tightness because, Lord … she's so fucking tight that I can barely fit the two in. Satisfaction hits me of how turned on she is.

Because of me.

Her pussy is this wet in response to how much she wants me.

Fuck, if this isn't about to make me come already.

I tilt my head and gently suck on her swollen clit. Her legs rise at the knees to each side of me, and her body quivers as I brush my tongue into her slit, licking it alongside my fingers. Her back arches, a desperate cry escaping her when I withdraw my fingers. Her cries change from desperate to strained when I replace them with my tongue, pushing it deep inside her.

"Jesus," she bursts out, bucking against my face. "Don't stop."

Curses fly out of my mouth as I lick and suck her pussy, my thumb climbing to her clit and massaging it in gentle circles.

"More," she urges.

I eat her pussy harder, and her hand falls to my hair when

I add my fingers to the mix again. It fucking hurts, the way she's clutching at the roots, but I'll handle it. I'll deal with anything to give her the best orgasm of her life.

"Please," she begs breathlessly. "Quit holding back and have sex with me already."

It kills me, but I ignore her pleas.

Her moans grow louder, and the hard breaths knocking from her lungs tell me she's close to reaching her brink.

I briefly pull away to peek up at her before going back to work. "Come on my tongue, baby."

As if my words set her off, her back flies off the bed, and she holds my head in place. Her legs tremble as she lets herself go, and I deliver a simple kiss on her clit before lifting my head.

"Holy wow," she gasps, catching her breath. "Now, have sex with me."

I jerk back, stupidly shocked at her words momentarily. She was begging me to fuck her only minutes ago.

I chuckle, shaking my head, and suck on the fingers that were inside her before responding, "Not happening tonight. I got you off. Don't be selfish."

"*You're* the one being selfish," she argues with a hint of a frown as she points her chin toward my hard-as-a-rock cock pressed against her thigh. "If anything, you need this more than I do."

My knees nearly buckle when she wraps her fist around my dick, and I can't stop myself from jerking forward.

"I'm not fucking you with a house full of people," I grit out, throwing my head back as she starts stroking me.

"I'll be quiet," she whispers. "You can cover my mouth with the same hand that was in my vagina."

Holy hell.

Where did this Carolina come from?

As much as I crave to push her down and fuck her hard, we're not ready for that step.

My hand swoops down, wrapping around her wrist to stop her. "It's okay. This was for you."

"Trust me," she says around a snort, stroking me faster. "This will most definitely be for me, too."

My cock twitches, begging me to give her the go-ahead, and my mouth drops open as I move closer to offer better access. She seizes that opportunity to rise to her knees and shove me onto my back. I don't have time to argue before she wraps her warm lips around my hard dick and sucks on the tip, and I nearly bust when she takes my entire length into her mouth. It's my turn to thrust my hips up, feeding my cock to her as she draws it in and out of her mouth, swirling her tongue around my tip.

It doesn't take long before a surge of pleasure zips through me, and my balls tighten.

"I'm about to come," I warn in case she isn't a swallower.

She only sucks harder as if she can't wait to taste me.

My hips jerk forward, every nerve in my cock awakened as I explode in her mouth.

"Holy fuck," I seethe, still coming down from the high of the best damn blow job ever. "That was amazing."

She sits back, her butt hitting the back of her legs, and affection spills over her features. "When can we do it again?"

My lips tilt up in a grin, and I give her a raspy laugh.

Maybe this is what we were destined to be.

Best friends.

Temporary lovers.

Then, I'll lose her.

Our lives will never be the same.

We're risking it all for sex.

FOR THE FIRST TIME EVER, I'm awake before Carolina.

The morning sun shines through my bedroom blinds,

offering me the view of her tucked comfortably at my side. I'm on my back, and she's on her stomach. One of her legs is slung over my hips, and her arm is draped across my bare chest.

We've shared a bed plenty of times, but it's different this morning.

We gave each other oral last night.

One of my old high school T-shirts is bunched up at her waist, granting me a peek of her white boy shorts and the bottom cheeks of her plump ass. She grabbed a pair last night from the drawer in my dresser she assigned to herself, which is now overflowing with panties and bralettes.

She stirs, showing off more of her ass, and her body shifts more on top of me. My dick hardens as I recall what took place in this bed—her shoving me onto my back and sucking my cock as if her life depended on it. The taste of her is on my tongue.

There's no going back from this.

We weren't drunk.

There's no blaming it on the alcohol or pretending it didn't happen.

All morning, I've stressed over what this means for our relationship.

I need to know where Carolina's head is.

After her mind-blowing blow job, I kissed her and jumped out of bed. Otherwise, I would've ended up fucking her. She joined me in getting dressed, stealing another one of my tees, and swapped her contacts for glasses.

Josh's guests usually spend the night, and my door was locked, but I wasn't risking anyone seeing her naked.

There's no containing my cheesy smile when she wakes up, and her eyes soften when they see me.

"Good morning, sunshine," I chime.

"Morning," she says sleepily, not alarmed at our position.

"How'd you sleep?"

"Wonderful actually." She grins. "It's been a while since I slept over."

"A while as in a few days ago at the hotel."

"Since I've slept *over*, not shared a bed with you."

"I guess it missed you."

She repositions herself and props her chin on my chest, staring up at me. "Want to talk about the elephant in the room?"

"Here, I considered you the shy one."

"I am … except around you." She pokes me in the chest. "It's your fault, making me hang out with you all the time."

"Hey, this isn't a one-way street. Somehow, you know every detail of my life, you force me to watch shows about desperate housewives banging their lawn boys, and you insisted you teach me how to bake."

She laughs. "I'm an evil woman."

"Damn straight you are."

Thank fuck we're comfortable. Normally, I don't do sleepovers in fear of suffering through the morning after. If I ever do stay over, I leave early without breakfast or conversation.

"What will we be walking into when we leave the room?" she asks.

"Huh?"

"Josh and his friends were sure having fun last night."

"More fun than us?"

A blush rides up her forehead. "Eh, doubt that."

I wrap a strand of her hair around my finger. "Like me, Josh is picky about our houseguests. One guy is his cousin, the other is a girl he's steadily dating, and then her friend."

"Josh has been steadily dating someone?"

"Shocking, huh? They've been off and on for a minute and are *on* right now. She and her friend are cool."

A silence passes as she gawks at me. "Do you … ever hang out with her friend?"

"No." I tuck the strand of hair I've been playing with behind her ear. "I haven't slept with her."

"How'd you know that's what I was thinking?"

"I always know what's going on in that pretty head of yours."

She slaps my chest. "I hate you."

"You love me." I roll us over, settling her on her back and staring down at her. "Is this real life right now?" My gaze travels down her body.

She pinches me. "You feel that?"

I flinch. "Uh … yeah?"

"Then, yes, it's real life." She briefly looks away before she frowns, her eyes meeting mine. "Why wouldn't you have sex with me? Was last night a one-time thing?" She smacks her forehead. "I'm so confused."

"That makes two of us."

"You wouldn't have sex with me last night, though. Why? You don't give other girls a hard time about it."

"You're not any other girl, Carolina."

"What are we then? Friends with benefits?"

"We're way beyond friends with benefits. I can nine thousand percent confirm that."

"Super-best friends with oral benefits?"

"Wrong again."

"Is it because you think I suck at sex?"

"What? Why would you think that'd crossed my mind? As a matter of fact, you're pretty damn hot in bed."

"I was boring when we had sex in high school."

"You mean, when you were a *virgin*?" I stroke her jaw with my free hand. "I didn't expect you to be a pro at sex or for it not to be awkward. We were teenagers."

"Still, no doubt it sucked for you."

I scoff. "Did you forget I came? I was worried it'd sucked for you."

"Yes, it was painful, but you were gentle with me."

I'll always be gentle with you.

We're interrupted by her stomach grumbling.

"Breakfast?" I ask, pulling away from her.

"I'm starving."

"Do you work today?"

She shakes her head. "I have the spaghetti dinner fundraiser to raise money for the after-school program at church." She motions back and forth between us. "*We* have the fundraiser dinner. I told you to mark it in your calendar."

I forgot.

"I wait for your reminders," I grumble.

"This is also a reminder that you're helping me make the cookies."

I groan. "How many again?"

"Only two hundred. Lauren and her mom are making the other two hundred, and Shirley is making the pies."

"Jesus. We haven't done that many in a few years."

I nod. "Yep, so get ready."

One of Carolina's hobbies is hosting fundraisers. She's done countless silent auctions and dinners for people, organizations, or the church's needs. I love how much she loves helping others. I tag along, helping and allowing her to boss me around.

Her stomach growls again, and I hop off my bed.

"Let's get food in your belly."

CHAPTER SEVENTEEN

Carolina

"GOOD MORNING, LOVEBIRDS," Josh bursts out when we walk into the kitchen.

"Don't start," Rex warns.

Josh holds up his hands. "Hey, I'm happy for you! I've waited a long time for this moment. I'm a proud mama bear here."

"Waited for what moment?" I ask, diverting my attention into the kitchen.

He makes a sweeping gesture to Rex and me. "You two to bang."

Rex shoves his shoulder when he passes him. "We didn't bang."

Josh scoffs. "All right. I've waited a long time for you to *hook up*."

"Who says we hooked up?" Rex fires back.

"Your guilty-ass faces when I busted you in the living room." Josh raises his brows.

"We were playing video games," I explain, looking as guilty as he said we did last night.

What I'm wearing doesn't help our argument—Rex's tee, a pair of his sweats—and my hair resembles a rat's nest.

Josh opens his mouth to reply, but everyone's attention shoots to the tall blonde strolling into the kitchen, wearing a shirt that hits her knees.

She stands on her tiptoes and snags a mug from the cabinet before glancing at me, wearing an amused smile on her face. "You must be Carolina."

"Yes?" I answer in confusion.

She points at Rex. "He's in love with you."

"Told you!" Josh shouts.

"Every convo we've had, he's mentioned you." She tips her mug my way. "We order pizza; he tells us your favorite is chicken and pepperoni. We watch a show; he informs us how many episodes he's seen *with you*. Girl, I know enough about you that we could be best friends." Her smile grows. "I'm Angelica."

I offer a friendly wave. "I'm Carolina … although it seems you already know that."

The fridge shuts, and Josh holds up a carton of eggs.

"Is the happy couple hungry this morning?" he says. "I'm making French toast!"

"I'll never turn down French toast," I reply.

Josh starts pulling out ingredients while Angelica grabs a pan. Rex squeezes between them in the narrow space, snatches two mugs, and makes our coffee—adding the perfect amount of sugar and almond milk.

"I'm waiting for Rex to tell me that French toast is your favorite," Angelica jokes.

"Pancakes are her favorite," Rex inputs. "Extra syrup. Add bananas if possible."

He sets down a mug in front of me and winks, and my heart melts.

"I HAVE AN EXCELLENT IDEA," Rex says when we finish unloading groceries in my sister's kitchen. "You bake. I taste-test." He tips his head toward Tricia's kitchen table with a boyish smile beaming on his full lips. "I'll sit here, watch the master do her work, and then make sure they're scrumptious when finished."

I deposit the bags into the recycling bin. "Nice try, but no. You're the assistant baker today." I tug two aprons from the drawer and toss him a pink one printed with yellow rubber duckies.

"Can't blame a man for trying." He ties the apron around him with amusement. "I like this look."

After devouring Josh's French toast and evading questions from him and Angelica, we cleaned up and went to the grocery store for the cookie ingredients. Rex offered his kitchen, but room is limited there. Tricia's has more counter space and top-of-the-line appliances. We'll also be left alone since she and the family went away for the weekend.

It's been a while since I've baked this large of a batch. I'm a bit rusty and grateful Rex is helping.

"I will let you lick the bowl in reward for your help," I offer, strolling around the kitchen while gathering all the needed supplies.

He gives me a satisfied smile. "I love when you let me lick things."

The measuring cup slips out of my hand, crashing onto the floor, and I bend down to retrieve it. Normally, I'd roll my eyes and throw a dish towel at him—something along those lines—but his words hit a different spot. Not annoyance. Desire. He's right. *I do* love it when he licks things, but I'm too shy to tell him that.

When I rise, I replace the cup in my hand with an oven mitt and slap him on the side of the head, wishing desire weren't igniting through me. I'm supposed to be making cookies for my church fundraiser, and all I want to do is fall back onto my knees and taste-test him.

He exaggeratedly flinches with a satisfied smile on his face at flustering me.

"All right, what flavors are we baking up today, boss woman?" He scrubs his hands together.

I swoop my hand toward the ingredients. "Chocolate chip."

He snatches the bag of chocolate chips. "I call those."

"Oatmeal raisin."

He gags. "You can't do oatmeal raisin."

"What? Why?"

"People who make oatmeal raisin cookies deserve to be in prison." He stands taller. "Here us chocolate chip lovers are, minding our business and snagging a cookie, only to bite into it and discover it has wrinkled-ass grapes inside." He flicks the box of raisins along the island with his fingers. "And people wonder why I have trust issues."

"You have trust issues because you get too much in your head." I drag the raisins back and hold them up. "You're getting raisins. We need variety."

He scans the ingredients. "What are our other options? Peanut butter? Snickerdoodles?"

"None. Everyone has confirmed what they're bringing. I'm responsible for chocolate chip and oatmeal raisin."

"All right, but don't let anyone think I helped you with that disgrace of a cookie. I'm making the chocolate chip, and I will give you the honors of eating the nasty raisin dough."

"You're too overdramatic."

"I take my cookies very seriously, Lina. You know this."

"Yeah, yeah, yeah," I mutter.

"I'll be on sugar duty." He snags the sugar jar.

I pluck it out of his hand. "*I* will be on sugar duty." I set it on the other side of me on the counter, away from him, and waggle my finger in the air. "Remember last time I let you be on sugar duty?"

"Yes, they were heavenly."

"No, they weren't."

His palm goes to his heart. "You sure know how to hurt a man's baking ego."

"You put *way* too much sugar in them. They tasted horrible." I hand him the carton of eggs. "You're on batter-mixing duty."

"Well, if that isn't damn boring," he grumbles, opening the carton.

FOUR HOURS LATER, the house smells like a bakery, and the cookies are done.

I rub my hands together before turning around and washing them. "I need to shower and get ready."

Rex nods, and I swallow back my laughter at the flour handprint on his face from me tapping his cheek earlier. He tried to wipe it away with the back of his arm, and I was such a good friend and held back from telling him he missed it.

"Same," Rex says, throwing the last of our trash into the can. "Do you want me to pick you up or meet you there?"

"You can meet me there," I reply.

"Cool. I'll help load these into your car."

He carries most of the containers, and we stack them into my back seat before he kisses me on the cheek and says goodbye. I rush upstairs to shower egg yolk and flour off myself and start undressing when my phone beeps with a text.

James: Have dinner with me.

The high I've been riding from hanging out with Rex is wiped away, and the thought of having dinner with James makes me gag. I debate on not answering him, but like always, I do.

Me: Busy with a fundraiser tonight.

James: Can I come?

This time, I nearly heave up the few cookies I taste-tested.

Me: No. My parents will be there.

James: That's rude. Isn't it time to introduce me to your family?

I want to introduce him to my family like I want McDonald's to stop serving their fizzy Cokes.

Me: What do you want?

James: For you to stop hanging out with him. To stop fucking him.

Repulsion shakes through me. *Him* is Rex. I hate when James brings him into our mess.

Me: Stop. We're just friends.

James: Better be.

I toss my phone onto my bathroom counter with tears pricking my eyes. I can't ask Rex to make his Instagram private, or he'll question me. If I ask him to block James, he'll assume he's messing with me. My mouth will stay shut, my secrets hidden, and I'll keep dealing with James the best I can by pacifying him.

Eventually, he'll get tired of me.

Hopefully.

I ARRIVE at the church two hours early to set everything up.

The weather is on our side today, the sun shining bright with a slight breeze. The fundraiser is being held in the parking lot. My biggest goal during these events is to keep the kids entertained, so I made sure it was near the playground, I ordered a bounce house, and the elementary school principal agreed to attend dressed up as a clown.

Food and money have been donated, and from what I've seen on Facebook, the fundraiser should pull in a decent crowd, which is typical. Blue Beech citizens love their church, food, socializing … and *gossiping.*

The after-school program is a great cause. Years ago, my mother started it, and she runs it for free along with other volunteers. The church provides free childcare to children until parents can pick them up after work.

People are arriving, searching for seats while children run through the parking lot toward the bounce house.

"Hey," Rex says at the same time his arms wrap around my waist from behind.

His arms don't move as I turn around to face him.

"Hey." A hint of shyness is in my tone, surprising me since I'm always myself around him.

Then again, we've also never hung out in public the day after his face was between my legs.

He looks as hot as ever today with his black shirt and knee-length ripped black shorts with frayed ends. His hair is messy, per usual, and I can't stop myself from running a thumb over the stubble coating his jaw.

What happened last night exposed the attraction we'd hidden for too long. It's freeing now that everything is out in the open, and pride swells through me over the thought that he trusts me enough to take this step together.

My shoulders slump.

What is this step?

A quick speed bump of us hooking up, and that's all it'll ever lead to?

Tonight, I'm asking him. We've always been open and honest in our relationship. Even when we were holding back from anything physical, we knew the feelings were there—that there was so much love that it'd take a heavy chain saw to break it.

Only inches separate us, and his hands trail down my waist before tugging at the hem of my green dress. "I like this."

I peek up at him, biting the corner of my lip, wrapped in the zone of him. "Thank you."

He nuzzles his face into my neck. "I wish I could take it off."

That makes two of us.

I rub my thighs together, and he laughs when I push my body into him.

"Maybe later?"

The contagious grin on his face causes me to do the same when he pulls his head away, his hands still wrapped around my waist. "Are we having another sleepover tonight?"

Heat shoots up my neck. "If you want? Maybe we can play video games again?"

Excitement lines his features, and he chuckles before dragging me into his chest and pressing his lips to the top of my head. When he pulls back a bit, we stare at each other in hesitation, curious on our next move. Rex owns it by dipping his head down and pressing his lips against my mouth this time.

"I'd love another round of video games."

"Carolina!"

I jump back at the sound of my father's voice as he's stalking in our direction.

Shoot!

We were so wrapped up in our own world that I not only forgot there were other volunteers and my father here, but I was also close to making out with Rex at my church.

My dad will have a field day with this one.

A lecture is coming as soon as we're alone.

CHAPTER EIGHTEEN

Rex

PASTOR ADAMS IS POSITIVELY PUTTING a bad word in for me with God.

He's doing a sucky-ass job of hiding his frustration while strolling in our direction.

My kiss with Carolina was hardly a peck, but from his heated face, you'd think Carolina was straddling me, naked, on the teeter-totter.

While delivering my best face of innocence, I shove my hand out when he reaches us. "Pastor Adams. It's nice to see you again."

He shakes my hand, his firm tight, while his lips form an irritated frown. "Rex, I appreciate you coming."

"Anything I can do to help," I reply with a big, friendly smile.

Rick's gaze shifts to Carolina, and he jerks his chin toward the other side of the parking lot. "Your mom needs your help with the donation baskets."

Carolina's cheeks are as red as the roses I bought for her birthday this year. "Of course." She signals toward the tables. "Let me wrap this up, and I'll be right there."

"Nah, I got it," I say, waving my hand toward a table

covered in baskets. "Go help your mom."

"Thank you," Carolina says, shooting me an apprehensive glance before turning her attention back to her father.

The fundraiser reminds me of a mini carnival. A large pavilion is set up over the tables and chairs. The children have plenty to entertain them—playground, jump house, clown, and a DJ blasting kid shit. Carolina arranged a silent auction, and those entering the spaghetti cook-off are arranging their food placements. I raise a brow when I spot the dunk tank. Mr. Rogers, the old high school football coach, was the dunk tank dude, but he recently moved.

Who's taking his place?

I situate the tables and chairs exactly how Carolina does every time, and she returns minutes after I'm finished.

"Perfect timing. Show up right when the hard work is done," I joke.

"You're so hilarious." She rolls her eyes while walking away, waving me to follow her. "Come on, my favorite helper. I have the perfect job for you."

I follow her, having no shame in checking out her ass. "What's this job?"

"You'll see," she sing-songs.

"That's scary. Last time you said that, you auctioned me off for a date, forcing me to endure dinner with the town's cat lady."

"Ms. Gorgman is sweet." Her voice is full of sarcasm.

"She asked for her cake to go with the intention of me licking it off her later—verbatim." I shudder, reliving the moment in my head.

"Oh, please. I doubt it was the first time you licked food off a woman."

"Not cake, and most definitely not off a sixty-five-year-old woman who has the stench of cat piss."

"Lucky for you, it's not a date auction."

"Better not, or be prepared to drop your savings to buy a

date with your boy." I signal down my body. "You know this sells for big money."

She scoffs. "Calm down, Casanova. Your job is way better than paid dates."

When she stops, a groan leaves me.

"The dunk tank? Not fucking happening." I make a circle around my head. "Do you know how long it takes to perfect this look?"

"Five minutes," she deadpans.

Next argument point coming. "I don't have dry clothes to change into."

"You're covered. I brought some of yours from the loft."

"I love how well you planned this out without telling me." My finger moves to my chin, tapping it, as her face floods with delight. "If I recall correctly, whenever I ask for my clothes back, you say once they make it to your place, they're no longer mine. Sorry, babe, but I can't change into *your* clothes. It looks like you'll be sitting your pretty ass in that tank."

The thing looks like a death trap with the wire net around the tank and the red target on the bright yellow backstop.

It's her turn to signal to her hair. "It takes me a good hour to do this work of art." She grins, slapping my shoulder. "I win. Follow me, and I'll show you where to change and shower when you're done."

"Fine," I grumble. "I'm only doing this because I love your ass."

She grins wildly. "I know."

How does she always manage to talk me into this shit?

I'VE BEEN CHILLING in the dunk tank for a good thirty minutes, and I have yet to go underwater.

One reason might be that only kids have played.

I'm ninety percent sure that will change when Molly

hands Maliki the ball.

Shit.

"Dude," I blurt out, shifting in the uneasy wooden seat, the ice-cold water up to my knees. "Hand the ball back to the kid, and I'll buy you a round of beers." I pause to hold up four fingers. "Make that four rounds."

Today's goal is to not get wet.

Maliki turns his hat backward, throwing the ball up in the air and catching it. "Did you forget that I own a bar and get my beer for dirt cheap?"

"Fifty bucks then!"

He continues tossing the ball in the air.

"I'll give you permission to marry my sister."

"He doesn't need your permission," Sierra pipes in before throwing her attention to Maliki. "Dunk him."

"Why don't you allow me the honors?"

The crowd, filled with grown-ups and children, part as Rick comes through, all dramatic and shit. He stops in front of Maliki and holds out his hand. Maliki shoots me an apologetic look before passing the ball to Rick. My eyes widen when Rick faces me, and the serious expression on his face confirms he's determined to make this shot.

I'm unclear why Pastor Adams has a beef with me, but I thought after our breakfast, we were cool.

"Dad," Carolina warns, catching on to the tension.

"What?" Rick asks, acting clueless. "It's a game." His eyes flash my way, meeting mine. "Right, Rex?"

"Just a game," I repeat, hoping he's never been an avid baseball player. "Let him have at it."

Everyone's attention is on us as they watch my girlfriend's dad stretch his arm back as if he were throwing the winning pitch at the World Series and then chucks the ball toward the target. The crowd jumping up and down notifies me he's going to hit the target, and seconds later, my seat collapses, dropping me into the pit of freezing water.

"Holy shit," I can't stop from yelling as I come up for air before standing.

Rick doesn't pay me another glance while handing the ball to Maliki. "Your turn." Without waiting for his response, he spins around and walks away.

Aren't pastors supposed to be understanding, kind people?

That'd better have been a truce.

Maliki raises a brow in my direction as I shiver like a wet dog. "Seems you're bonding well with your future father-in-law."

"Never had a better relationship," I reply, my teeth chattering as I wrap my arms around my body.

"THANK you for getting wet for me."

Carolina is leaning against a wall in the hallway when I step out of the church restroom, wearing fresh, dry clothes.

Lucky for me, after being dunked by her father, my job ended. Carolina had a towel waiting for me when I jumped out of the tank, and I wrapped it around my body while rushing inside the church, barefoot. She was behind me, asking for a volunteer to be the next dunk tank victim, but no takers were speaking up. Not surprising. I doubt my fall looked enjoyable.

I drop the bag of clothes onto the floor and run my hands through my damp hair. "Next time, put me at the kissing booth."

She shakes her head, pushing off the wall. "Never happening, so don't get your hopes up."

"Why not?" I pick up the bag and throw it over my shoulder, walking in step with her. "Would you be jealous?"

We turn down a hall, passing volunteers, and my hand finds hers, weaving our fingers together.

Us doing this is more comfortable than I ever thought

it'd be.

It might be only holding hands, something we've done countless times, *but* it's more than platonic now.

She looks up at me with a radiant smile. "Absolutely, and you'd be the same if it were the other way around."

"Nah, I'd cut in line and buy all your kisses."

I grunt when I'm pulled down a vacant hallway and pushed into a dark room. While I wrap my head around what's happening, the door slams shut behind us, and Carolina's lips hit mine.

It's a sweet kiss.

Minimal tongue.

Lasts only seconds.

Her eyes search mine as she pulls her mouth away, but she doesn't move. "I've wanted to do that since you agreed to the dunk tank."

I lick my lips to taste her. "It was my pleasure."

She snorts. "It definitely wasn't."

"You're right." I kiss the tip of her nose and stare into her beautiful eyes. "You can make it up to me later."

"QUESTION."

My eyes sweep over to Carolina at her … question. She's sitting next to me in one of the two remaining chairs we left after cleanup. I'm in the other.

It's dark, nearly ten o'clock, and the fundraiser has ended. A group of people stayed behind and helped clean up, but it's only us now. Rick has dodged me since he dunked my ass, but I remind myself to reach out to him and figure out what's on his mind. My guess is, he's unhappy that Carolina and I are so serious yet not married. For as long as I've known Carolina, she's expressed her parents stress marriage and abstinence.

I'm tired, every muscle in my body aches, and I can't wait

to go home and collapse onto the couch.

"Answer," I reply, stretching my legs out in front of me.

"Can you clarify this?" She signals between us.

I raise a brow in confusion even though I'm not confused about shit. "Huh?"

"What's going on with us?" She delivers the words slowly, as if it'll take a moment for my brain to digest them.

This is what I've feared since day one.

The dreaded *what are we* talk.

It's not the first time I've been asked this question. Those discussions ended in awkwardness and me fleeing the scene.

I'm shit at expressing myself.

Shit at *clarifying* labels.

I clear my throat, scrubbing a hand over my now-sweaty forehead while gathering my thoughts before allowing them to fall from my mouth. Unlike with other women, there's no walking away from this conversation with Carolina. No matter how weird it gets, I'll have this talk with her. She deserves that.

"How about you clarify what you want us to be?" I finally say.

That's a good answer.

Whatever she wants to be, I'm game.

Her furrowed brows inform me I'm stupid, and that was not a good answer.

"Nope," she quips, shaking her head repeatedly. "We can't do that."

"Why not?" My mind races for the reasons we can do that.

She thrusts her finger into her chest. "*I* can't clarify what *you* want." Her finger points at me.

Valid point.

I want her, but I also need her help walking me through this so I don't fuck anything up.

I wrap my arm around her shoulders, and her chair rattles as I drag it closer to mine. I soften my voice as I say, "I want what you want."

Her head drops into the crook of my neck as she leans into me. "I can clarify what I want, Rex, but you're the only person who can speak for your heart, for where your head is."

"My heart is with you." The words come out effortlessly, but their meaning is massive.

I grin as she relaxes against me, and my hand strokes her arm.

"And your head?"

My hair rises on the back of my neck. It's not always the heart you have to fight. Sometimes, it's your goddamn head that fucks you up.

"My head is …" I release a heavy sigh. "I won't lie and say I know what I'm doing because I sure as hell don't. I can't promise to be perfect, but I can promise to give this everything I have."

She loses a breath when I turn her in her chair so we're facing each other, her features unreadable.

"Can you work with that?" I ask, fear storming through me.

Will that be enough for her?

A slow smile builds along her lips, settling my stomach, and her hands cup my face. "I can most definitely work with that."

"PERFECT TIMING!" Josh shouts when we walk into the apartment to find him and Angelica sitting on the couch while watching TV. "Looks like we're about to have our first double date! How was the fundraiser?"

"Good," Carolina answers around a yawn. "Long."

"You have any leftover cookies?" He raises his leg to nudge a closed pizza box on the table with his foot. "I'll share pizza."

"They're in the car," Carolina answers, thrusting a thumb toward the door. "You can go grab them if you want."

I followed Carolina home after we left the church to drop off her car. She made a pit stop into the loft and packed an overnight bag, and I drove us to my place.

Josh stands. "Be right back. You two make yourself comfortable, and everyone pick a movie." He snaps his fingers and does a circling motion around the three of us. "Make it a good one, so I don't pass out."

Angelica scoots over to give us enough room on the couch, and I collapse onto the other end. Carolina falls down next to me, her body halfway on top of mine.

The remote is in Angelica's hand as she glances over at us with a raised brow. "What kind of movies do you like?"

"I have a feeling I'll be outvoted, and we're bound to watch something romantic," I comment.

Carolina rolls her eyes while patting my thigh. "Honey, don't act like you didn't get emotional during *A Walk to Remember.*"

"Yes, because the girl reminded me of you!" I argue, throwing my right arm up in frustration before counting my reasoning with my fingers. "Preacher's daughter. Ugly-ass sweaters. The guy is the complete opposite of her. At the end, she dies." My attention briefly flicks to Angelica. "Spoiler alert."

A flash of understanding flashes in Carolina's eyes. "Oh shoot, I never thought about that."

"That entire week, I stressed, waiting for you to tell me you had a terminal illness and that the movie was a silent warning. Scared the shit out of me."

Angelica points at me with the remote. "You wait until you watch *The Notebook.*"

"Already seen it," I reply.

"*The Fault in Our Stars*?"

I nod.

"*The Vow*?"

I nod again.

"*P.S. I Love You*?"

Another nod.

Angelica looks back at Josh when he walks in. "You need to step your movie game up, babe. Rex has watched nearly every movie that I've cried over!"

Josh plops next to her with the container of cookies in his hand and whistles through his teeth. "Dude, quit making me look bad, or I'm not sharing the pizza *or* cookies."

"Don't get mad at me for being smart," I fire back.

He snatches a cookie and takes a large bite before gagging. "Jesus! What are these?"

"Oatmeal raisin," Carolina replies around a laugh.

He sticks out his tongue, gagging again, and tosses the cookie back into the container as if it were toxic. "Why would you do that to a man? I thought they were chocolate chip."

The three of us crack up in laughter.

"Told you," I say to Carolina. "Oatmeal cookies are blasphemous."

"And banned from our apartment," Josh adds.

"What about *Save the Last Dance*?" Angelica asks, flipping through the options.

"I love that movie." Carolina peeks up at me. "You haven't seen that one."

Angelica hits play.

The movie is actually pretty damn good.

JOSH AND ANGELICA are knocked out when the movie credits flash across the screen.

I'm spent as my eyes dart over to Carolina snuggled in my arms. "Another movie or bed?"

She yawns loudly, standing and stretching, and I do the same.

"Bed. Definitely bed." Her attention drifts to the snoring

couple. "Should we wake them?"

"Would you want to be woken up?"

"Probably." She nods. "That couch isn't very comfortable."

Josh's eyes pop open when I nudge his foot with mine.

"Hey, sleepyhead. It's bedtime."

He shakes Angelica awake, and they grumble a quick, "Good night," before sluggishly poking along down the hall. Carolina and I turn off the lights, moving to my bedroom in slow motion.

As soon as I close the bedroom door, Carolina rummages through my drawers, pulling out her favorite tee of mine. With her back to me and with no hesitation, she whips her dress over her head, causing my heart to nearly jolt out of my chest. Only seconds pass before she unsnaps her bra and slides the tee over her head. The shirt hits the top of her knees, and her nipples are poking through the thin fabric when she turns around and looks at me.

My mouth waters at the sight.

I gulp when the memory of us in the hotel room courses through my mind—of how similar the situation was and how I turned her down. I fight with myself on how to handle this. Sure, we hooked up last night, but we didn't take that final step.

No doubt that will happen if I touch her tonight.

She smiles back at me while walking to the bathroom, her hand brushing against my stomach when she passes me. I follow her, and Carolina snags the toothbrush I bought for the nights she stays over. My hand is nearly shaking as I brush mine. Her smile grows the second time she slips past me, and my knees nearly buckle when she hops into my bed and yanks the blanket up her body, stopping only inches underneath her neck.

My cock is obnoxiously hard, and there's no hiding it. The room is dead silent while I change into sweats, and the sheets are cold as I settle on my knees on the edge of the bed. She scoots over, giving me room, and I leave the bedside lamp on when I join her. My sheets still smell like her—a vanilla mixed with cherry scent.

She wastes no time in getting comfortable under my arm, resting on her hip, with her leg slung over mine.

Carolina is halfway straddling me, and I'm not freaking the fuck out.

It feels right.

Natural.

Where she belongs.

"Thank you again for everything," she says, rubbing her foot up and down my leg.

My arm swings around her waist. "Always."

I release a *hmph* when she pushes herself up to straddle me.

"I think you deserve a reward for all your hard work."

My hands settle on the tops of her thighs as I fight to control my breathing *and* not shift my hips. She's only wearing panties underneath that shirt, and her pussy covered with only panties would feel amazing against my cock.

"You normally reward me with cookies."

Yes. I'm suggesting she reward me with cookies rather than straddle me.

Fucking idiot.

She smirks, her pink lips full. "Would you rather have cookies?"

"I don't know."

Her smile wavers, confliction on her face as her gaze lowers to me, and my stomach twists at the sudden disappointment.

My hand leaves her thigh when I reach forward, pushing away a loose strand of hair away from her face. "Hey. What's up?"

She hesitates.

I slide my hand up and down her thigh in reassurance. "Come on, tell me."

Her face tightens, and she bites into her cheek. "I suck at this whole seduction thing."

A heaviness falls over me, and my voice is tender. "Trust me, babe, you don't suck at this."

She's not convinced. "You look like you'd rather me pluck your eyeballs out than be on top of you."

I tighten my grip on her to stop her from moving off me.

Here, I thought I was doing us a favor by holding back, and she thinks it's because I don't want her. As scared as I was that us being together would push her away, my constant rejection will do just as much damage, if not more.

I tilt my hips up, and she gasps when my erection presses against her core. "There's never been a question of *if* you turn me on. It's always been *if* this is a good idea."

Her eyes widen, understanding flickering on her face. "So, I *do* turn you on." The grin she was sporting minutes ago resurfaces.

The air grows thick, and I curl forward to cup the back of her head with my palm. Not a word leaves my mouth until our eyes are locked—hers with traces of every emotion.

Fear. Excitement. Love. Hurt.

We're so close that I feel her chest heaving underneath my shirt.

"I want this as much as you do, babe," I say, inches from her lips, not breaking our eye contact. "Hell, more than you do."

That gorgeous smile of hers grows larger than I've ever seen in all the years I've known her. "If I say something, do you promise not to throw me off your lap?"

Not going in the direction I thought this was going.

I arch a brow, my hands digging into her hair. "Sure?"

"I want you to take this step with me, Rex."

"Step?"

She blows out a long breath and lifts one of her hands, smoothing her palm over my face before settling it on my cheek. My mouth goes dry. Affection simmers in her eyes as we focus on nothing but each other, in our own little confused world.

Her words come out slow. Her tone soft. "Rex, you're capable of a relationship, and as someone who believes in you, who trusts you, I'm willing to put my heart on the line to prove it."

My hand covers hers resting on my cheek. "Carolina—"

She shoves my hand away to press a finger against my lips. "I'm not finished." Her finger leaves my lips and brushes my chin before she lowers her hand to my chest, tapping the spot over my heart. "This heart is capable of being a good friend, a good boyfriend, a good lover—"

"Is that what you want?" I cut in, my head spinning. "For me to be your boyfriend?" Just the thought sends a jolt of excitement through me.

Us together.

Boyfriend and girlfriend.

Lovers.

She nods. "More than anything." The serious look on her face morphs into a smirk. Her next words come out in a song, one sounding like a cheesy-ass car commercial, and she moves her shoulders from side to side in a dancing motion. "You know you want to."

She further proves her point by wiggling on top of me, rolling this romantic moment into a hungrier one filled with need for her.

"Let's do it then."

Her face brightens. "Really?"

My answer comes in the form of kissing her with everything I have.

We've lit the fuse, and I pray it doesn't burn everything we've built.

CHAPTER NINETEEN

Carolina

MY HEART THUDS against my chest.

Rex's tongue slides into my mouth, giving me the taste of toothpaste.

I grind against him in his lap while we make out, feeling his erection grow harder underneath me with every movement. My skin tingles at his excitement *for me … for us.*

"I want you," I whisper into his mouth.

He draws away, locking my eyes with his, and understanding dawns on his face.

This is it.

What we've been beating around our entire friendship.

Nervousness rocks through me as I grab the waistband of his sweats. I whip a leg over his, no longer straddling him, and am on my knees when I tug at his pants. I don't make much progress before his hand wraps around my wrist, his grip firm. Just as I'm about to argue, he flips me on my back and hovers over me.

"Swear to me, Carolina," he whispers. "Swear to me, this won't change us."

I shake my head, the pillow soft under my head. "It won't change anything. I swear."

All the reluctance he's been carrying splits into hunger, and his voice is thick as he speaks, "You want to fuck me?"

What does he think I've been trying to do for the past week? Play Yahtzee?

He leans down to whisper in my ear, "Do you remember the first time we had sex?"

His scruff rubs against my cheek, and I shiver when he pulls away.

I will until the day I die.

I nod. "Yes."

"God, I wanted to do so much more, starting with this."

Heat creeps up my spine when he pushes up my shirt, baring me to him, and palms my breast while lowering his body over mine.

"I love you in my shirts," he bites out, capturing my nipple in his fingers and lightly pinching it. "I wanted to suck on these." With the last word, he draws a nipple between his lips and sucks hard.

My hips tilt forward when he slides his tongue up and down my entire breast.

"My mouth watered to taste your pussy … to have it on my tongue, so I could taste you all night."

Unlike our first time, I stare down at him, not wanting to miss a second of what is happening, when he slides my panties down my legs. Our eyes are locked as he carefully spreads my legs. Then, my lips between my legs part, and he sticks his tongue inside me.

Holy mother-freaking crap!

"I wanted to set you on fire while I played with your pussy. Wishing I could suck on your clit."

He does just that, wrapping his lips around my most sensitive spot and slowly sucking it, circling his lips around it in the process.

Rex is a dirty talker during sex.

I love it.

Just as I'm wrapping my mind around his tongue being between my legs, he grips my thighs, pulling my butt off the bed, and drags me into his mouth, devouring me.

I'm dizzy.

I'm trying to keep up and watch, but when he loses his hold on a thigh and curves a single finger inside me, all eye contact is over.

I'm overtaken by tingles hitting every inch of my body, and my moans take over the room.

"There's that G-spot," he says with a chuckle.

I don't have to see him to know he's sporting a smirk.

With the few guys I've done this with, it maybe lasted a good ten minutes and resulted in no orgasm, but not with Rex … no. He's passionately kissing me between my legs, fingering me, and he rides me through one orgasm … then another. At this point, I'm doubting if he's going to have sex with me or just keep getting me off, using his tongue to appease me.

I'm not complaining, but I want more.

I want him inside me.

All of him.

I sigh at the loss of his mouth, and he stares up at me.

"You were so wet and tight when I got you ready for my cock," he groans out at the memory.

I writhe underneath him. "I remem—" I stop myself from finishing. "Actually, I don't. Please remind me."

He smirks, climbing over my body, and sweat lines his forehead when his mouth returns to mine. "Now, Carolina, a man will have a complex if you don't remember how good he filled you with his dick."

I taste myself when he briefly plunges his tongue between my lips before I lose him again.

He rubs a thumb over my bottom lip—that seems to be his thing. "You want to fuck me, Carolina?"

I nod repeatedly. "Yes … please … now." My voice is so strained; I hardly recognize it.

A yelp leaves me when he rolls us over—him on his back and me on top again, his hands firmly gripping my hips.

"Then, fuck me," he grounds out, tilting his head toward the nightstand. "Condom, top drawer."

I wriggle against him a few times, hearing him release a hiss, and then stretch along the bed to the nightstand. There's a box of condoms inside the drawer. It's nearly full, XL—not surprising since I've seen his cock a few times now. It was a struggle to take him all the way in my mouth last night.

I hesitate, taking in how he's having me do all the work, and build up the courage to appear as confident as I can.

He hisses as I drag his pants down, his cock springing free, and I fumble with ripping open the condom wrapper. It's the first time a guy has asked me to do the honors.

His muscles tense when I stroke him once before rolling the condom onto his thick cock.

"Is that good?" Stupidity hits me at my question, but it's important.

Homegirl is not getting preggers over here.

My parents would really shit.

I scrub a hand over my forehead.

Why am I thinking about my parents right before having premarital sex?

"Is everything okay?" Rex asks, rising on his elbows at the change in my mood.

I nod. "Mmhmm. *More* than okay."

"Take off your shirt, so I can see all of you."

I whip it off and throw it across the room. Our moans fill the room when I align myself with his cock and slowly ease my way down, as he fills every inch of me. It's been a while since I've had sex, so there's a slight pain, and I still for a moment.

"Holy fuck," he hisses, biting hard into his lower lip. "You're tight."

I only nod while adjusting to his size.

"You good?" Rex asks.

I'm grateful he's not rushing this, that he's giving me time.

I nod again. "I'm perfect."

His hand rises, rubbing circles over my clit, making me wetter.

Turning me on even more.

Well ... that's a way to get my mind off the twinge of pain.

"This will be better than the last time, I promise." I buck forward as he slows his movements on my clit.

"Every time is perfect with you, babe." His hand locks around my hip before his jerk forward.

A burst of pleasure barrels through me, my ache of pain turning into an ache of needing more of him, and I slowly grind against him.

He stays still, allowing me to take charge.

At the rotation of my hips, his rise, matching my tempo.

It doesn't take us long to find the perfect rhythm.

Sex with Rex is amazing.

Perfection.

Better than what I imagined.

I fall forward, unable to support my weight, and rest my hand onto his chest, knowing I'm close to my brink.

That slow tempo speeds up until we're going wild, all the years of sexual tension bleeding through us. My hand moves from his chest to the headboard as he drills his hips into me, his hand on my waist tighter to keep me from flying off him, and I collapse against him, moaning out my release, not caring who hears.

He thrusts violently underneath me, losing every ounce of gentle control he's ever had for me, and I gasp when he rolls us over again. As soon as I fall to my stomach, he props my hips up, his hand sliding down my back, and I level myself on my elbows, peeking back at him.

Hunger fills his face.

Need in his eyes.

Not wasting a moment of not being inside me, he fills me again, pounding into me hard and fast.

I smile as another orgasm approaches.

I'm not getting a fake Rex.

This is real.

All him.

How he is in bed.

How he likes it.

He's giving me all of him, showing me all of him.

"You feel so good, Carolina," he moans. "Do you feel how hard I am inside you?"

I gasp, fighting to control my breathing … to speak. "Yes." It's a struggle to release even that word.

"I'm going to come so hard inside you."

I slump against the bed, my body trembling as soon as my stomach hits the warm sheets, and I grin at the splotches of sweat on them.

From us being together.

I shudder as I release my orgasm, saying his name in a low whisper.

He gives me a few more thrusts before slamming into me one last time, holding me in place, and releasing a low groan, my name leaving his lips louder than his did mine.

Seconds later, he pulls out and collapses on his back next to me.

Sweat covers our bodies, the scent of sex in the room, as our chests heave in and out.

The door to our friendship has been closed and locked, the key thrown away.

There's no returning.

We're somewhere new.

Hopefully, this *new* won't ruin us.

———

WE DID IT.

Rex and I finally had sex.

Amazing, *out of this world, will never be better with anyone else* sex.

We're tangled up in his sheets, naked, after another round this morning.

It was different than last night.

It was slow.

Every hair on my body rose, and I orgasmed in minutes as he whispered sweet things into my ear.

"You're beautiful."

"I love being inside you."

"Love how we fit together perfectly."

"You own every inch of me."

Not only is Rex a dirty talker in the bedroom, but he can also be a sweet one.

Rex props himself up on his elbow, me on my back, as he stares down at me. "What are you up to today?" He tucks a strand of hair behind my ear, and even though his eyes are tired, they're crinkled at the corners as a smile takes over his gorgeous face.

My smile is shy in return. "Working and then nothing really."

Other than regaining some energy after the workouts you've given me.

Screw a gym membership. All I need is good sex from Rex.

Sex with him is the equivalent to one week of cardio.

"Working and then hanging out with me?" he corrects.

"Duh." I groan at the sound of Bob Marley playing from the kitchen.

"Josh is up." Rex chuckles.

"At least we'll get fed well."

Reggae means Josh is cooking one of his infamous breakfasts. Sure, loud music first thing in the morning is annoying, but he makes up for it with his kitchen skills. My stomach grumbles, just thinking about it.

"We need it after last night."

"Do you think he heard us?" A blush runs over my skin.

"I'm positive all of Blue Beech heard us. You'll be getting calls about your bad behavior later." He tickles my side, causing me to burst out in laughter. "You made me work up an appetite this morning. Let's hope Josh is making pancakes."

AFTER ENDURING an hour of dating questions from Josh and Angelica—their smug expressions confirming they most definitely heard us last night—we trek back to Rex's bedroom.

Rex hops in the shower, and I fall onto his bed, resting my back against his headboard. I capture my phone from the nightstand.

As badly as I wanted to join him, my legs feel like noodles.

My vagina needs a break.

My stomach drops when I pull up my notifications.

James: We need to talk.

I need to talk to him like I need to grow antlers out of my head.

The text was sent at one this morning, and I debate whether to answer.

He could've been in one of his moods.

Stupidly, I reply.

Me: No, we don't. Kick rocks.

Seconds later, my phone rings.

James calling.

My heart rages against my chest. He normally doesn't call. He prefers to type out his threats, so I don't miss them.

I decline the call.

It rings again.

Decline.

I cast a glance at the bathroom when it rings again, hearing the shower running, and my hands are shaking when I answer.

"What?" I hiss into the speaker. "Leave me alone!"

"Who is this? Why are you texting my boyfriend?"

My hand tightens around the phone at the sound of her voice.

Margie's voice, releasing in a nasty snarl.

I clear my throat and lower my tone, attempting for it to sound masculine. "Sorry. Wrong number."

Click.

The phone rings again.

James calling.

The best morning of my life—waking up, wrapped in Rex's arms—has been ruined by him. Tears slip down my cheeks, and I quickly push them away with my arm, ridding the evidence for when Rex comes back.

"Everything okay?"

The phone falls from my hand when Rex walks into the room, a towel around his waist, water droplets on his chest.

"You look like you saw a ghost," he adds, concern on his face.

I shake my head and hate myself for lying to him. "It's just Margie."

Technically, it isn't a full lie.

It was Margie.

"Still blowing her off?" He drops the towel, and my mind momentarily forgets my issues at the sight of him naked. I frown when he pulls a pair of gray sweatpants on. "Don't you think it'd be right to clear the air and tell her everything? She deserves that."

I flick my phone farther away from me on the bed as if it were poisonous. "I'm not blowing her off. I'm keeping my distance." *Same thing, but it sounds better.*

He swipes a shirt from a drawer, pulling it over his head. "It's not fair to her."

"Life isn't fair sometimes." I cross my arms. "I'm not opening that can of worms. It's better for her to think I hate her than for her to hate me."

"She wouldn't hate you."

"She called me a skank-ass ho."

"Technically, she didn't call *you* a skank-ass ho."

"Close to it."

"Not even close."

"Look, I'll reach out when I feel comfortable." I jump up from the bed with a frown on my face. "I need to get ready for work."

CHAPTER TWENTY

Rex

I BROKE the cardinal rule of our friendship.

I fucked Carolina.

And I have no regrets.

My heart feels closer to hers, our connection stronger, and I'm pissed I didn't take this step forever ago. It'd sure have saved us from a lot of troubles.

Fear creeps in as I doubt that we can stay this way.

There's no way in hell I'd ever hurt her, so I hope to God she doesn't stomp on my heart.

THE ONLY DAYS I'm a morning person is when I wake up early to visit Carolina at work—less people to steal her attention away from me.

Today, I'm visiting her during the lunch shift.

I want to see my girl.

As usual, the diner is packed when I walk in. Shirley's is known for its kick-ass lunch specials. Her sandwiches are to die for.

I spot Kyle and Gage seated at Kyle's regular booth, wearing their blue uniforms. They're partners on the police force and often stop by for a quick bite while on duty. I walk down the aisle and head straight to my usual booth. I texted Carolina, asking her to keep it open for me. My plan was to surprise her, but I didn't want to lose my chance to sit in her section.

"Shirley!" I greet, stepping up to the bar. "Mind if my girl takes a lunch break?"

Shirley pinches my cheeks. "As much as I love this cute face of yours, no. We're slammed. She'll have a break in an hour after the rush dies down."

"Have lunch with us," Kyle calls out, waving me over. "She's our waitress, so you'll still be able to make googly eyes at her."

"I'm going to need that table anyway, sweetie," Shirley says. "Carolina can make some extra cash, too."

I smile, failing to mention that I'd give her a tip far larger than anyone who'll sit in that booth, and walk over to Kyle's booth. He slides over to make room for me to sit next to him. Carolina grins when she spots me and slides the guys' plates on the table in front of them.

Her attention swings to me as she wipes her forehead with the back of her arm. "Hey. I didn't think we'd be so packed today. Sorry for Shirley giving your table away, but you know it's hard to say no to her. I planned to text you when I got a sec."

"It's cool, babe." I don't bother picking up a menu and glance at the guys' plates.

Gage has the buffalo chicken.

Kyle has the grilled tenderloin.

I nod toward Gage's plate. "I'll have that. Shoestring fries. Water."

"Got it." She tucks her pen behind her ear and scurries off to the kitchen.

"You two are cute," Kyle says, grabbing the bottle of ketchup.

"Mmhmm," Gage adds, thrusting a hand through his dark hair.

Gage isn't much for conversation. He's the quiet one, and his fiancée, Lauren, is loud enough for the both of them.

We chat for a while.

Gage says he and Lauren are trying for another baby.

Kyle tells me the sale on Chloe's house fell through.

"Is it still available?" I ask, perking up in my seat. "No backup offers?"

"Still available," Kyle replies. "Know anyone who'd be interested?"

"Me."

"You want to buy her house?" Kyle draws out.

I shrug. "Why not? My lease ends in a few months. I have money saved up for a down payment."

"Look into it," Kyle says. "I'll talk to Chloe and see if there's anything we can do to help."

It'd be cool as hell to live next door to them. I wasn't close with Kyle growing up, since he was so much older, but as he's settled down, our relationship has grown stronger.

Our conversation stops when a voice comes through their police radio, telling them there's a family of raccoons stuck in a dumpster.

"Serious business," I comment as they take their last bites and wipe their mouths.

"I'd rather have that than the other," Kyle states. A wave of sadness spreads along his face as he digs his wallet from his pocket. There will never be a day Kyle doesn't remember the scene he walked into that changed his life and how he had to break the news to Chloe of her loss.

I stop him. "I got it. Go help those little critters."

Kyle nods. "Thanks, brother."

Gage slides out of the booth. "I got you next time I see you at Down Home then."

They say good-bye, and I stack their plates up before sliding them to the other side of the table. Crumpling up the napkins, I pile them on top of the plates, wanting to clean up the table as much as I can so Carolina will have less work to do.

Pulling up a book on my phone, I kick back in the booth and read until Carolina arrives with my food, setting it in front of me.

"You need anything else?" she asks.

I slide my napkin toward her. "Your number, hot waitress."

She laughs, shaking her head. "Sorry, I'm spoken for by my wonderful boyfriend."

"Lucky man." I wink.

"What he doesn't know won't hurt him, though."

"Oh, really?" I raise a brow.

She snags her pen from behind her ear, snatches the napkin, and writes something on it. Folding it up, she slides it to me. I can't stop myself from doubling over laughing when she waggles her eyebrows and then skips away in that cute little uniform of hers.

My cock stirs as I read her note.

I can't wait to get you naked tonight.

Xoxo

I shake my head and tuck the note into my pocket.

CHAPTER TWENTY-ONE

Carolina

"CAN WE TRY SOMETHING?" I ask, wrapping my arms around Rex's neck.

"Sure?" He tips his head down, and the water from the shower blurs my view of him.

I unclasp my arms, dropping them to grab his hand and slide it between our naked bodies. His breaths turn harsh, his back straightening, when I close our fingers over his already-hard cock and move them up and down the length of him.

"You want to watch me jerk off?" he hisses through his teeth.

"Yes."

My heart gives a nervous jolt when I fall back a small step, creating a narrow space between our bodies, giving me a perfect view of us working his erection. A gasp leaves me when he tightens his hold on his dick, causing me to do the same, and his head falls back in ecstasy.

There's no taking my eyes off this … off him.

His soaked abs are strained, and the muscles in his arms tense with each movement. His thick hand, which has made me orgasm countless times, grips his cock, pumping up and down. Tingles sweep through me at the memory of the sounds he made that day.

This is it.

What I wanted to see so desperately that morning.

"Confession," I whisper, my eyes not leaving our connection.

He bows his head, his eyes fixing on me, his breathing ragged. "Let me hear it."

Our pace slows as we speak.

"When you were in the hotel …" I start before stopping in hesitation. "Before the wedding, I saw you in the shower."

Understanding dawns on his face. "You watched me jack off?"

I nod, putting more space between us.

"Fuck," he groans before sweeping his eyes up and down my body.

Thrill powers through my veins.

I want him again.

Need him.

It's never *just sex* with me and Rex.

It's love.

Mutual respect.

Feelings out of this world.

I push my wet hair away from my face to gain an unobstructed view of him.

"Tell me," he demands. "Tell me what you saw."

"Your hand on your cock." I squeeze my hand over his, feeling his thickness.

His eyes slam shut, his pace the same. "Did you wish it were yours?"

"Oh God, yes." *I've never been more turned on in my life.*

"Did you wish you could join me?"

"Yes."

"Do you like it better up close?"

"Yes," I whimper, as if the only thing functioning in my

body were my hormones, and my brain can't come up with another word.

He stifles back a deep groan. "Is that why you wanted us to shower that night?"

"Yes," I whimper again, the word leaving my lips more strangled.

"Come here."

I'm not given the chance to move on my own when he grabs my waist and tugs me to him, his hands roaming to my ass cheeks to lift me up.

"I'm not finishing on the shower floor. I'm finishing in you," he grumbles.

My legs instinctively wrap around him as he pushes me against the wall at the same time his lips crash against mine, his tongue immediately sweeping into my mouth. It doesn't take long until we're messily making out, grinding against each other.

"Fuck," he groans, his forehead meeting mine.

"What?" I ask, unable to stop my hips from grinding against him, feeling his hardness rub against me—*so close* to my core that it's driving me wild.

His head doesn't move. "I'm about to freeze my ass off to get a condom."

When he starts to separate us, I tighten my legs around his hips.

"I'm on the pill," I blurt out, my nails digging into his back.

His face is turned on and anxious as he stares down at me. "You sure?"

"Positive. Now, get inside me." I slightly lift my hips, giving him the perfect angle.

My back arches when he thrusts inside and pushes me harder into the wall.

Our mouths stay connected as we steal each other's breaths, and he screws me against the cold tiles of the shower.

"DO you know how perfect you are?" Rex asks, standing naked in front of me while drying me off from our shower.

I shiver in his arms, looking up at him while combing my fingers through my hair. "Nope, so you can go ahead and tell me."

He chuckles, his eyes soft as I lift mine to meet his. "That doesn't surprise me." He snatches one of his shirts from the bathroom vanity. "Arms."

I swing my arms up, and he tugs the shirt over my head. It's white, my nipples showing as my soaked hair drips onto it. "You know I love it when you pump up my ego."

He runs his cold finger down my cheek, stroking it, giving me goose bumps I don't care about. "How's this? Here's all the reasons I love you—"

My heart nearly stops when I interrupt him, "Did you … did you just say, you *love me*?"

He raises a dark brow. "Uh … yes."

"You love me?" A smile lights up my face.

A smirk flickers across his lips. "Uh … yes."

My head is spinning. "Like … you're in love with me?"

"Uh … yes."

My hand flies to my mouth as my heart bursts with joy.

His eyes brighten at my reaction. "Has that not been obvious to you for, I don't know, *years*?"

It has.

I just thought I'd never hear him say it.

That he loves me like I love him.

"It's amazing to hear you say it out loud," I explain.

"Is it now?" His smirk grows. "I'll remember that whenever I want to make you smile."

A gasp leaves my throat when he drops the towel from my body, hauls me over his shoulder, and rushes into the bedroom. I bounce on the bed after he tosses me onto it and crawls up it seconds later, in the space between my legs.

He caresses my hair while staring down at me, his forehead still beaded with water. "I should have said that a long time ago, huh?"

"Yes, definitely." I curl my legs around his hips, drawing him closer. "Same goes for me. I should've told you how much I love you."

His lips curl into a smile before he slowly kisses me.

We're wet against the sheets as he makes love to me just as slow, whispering he loves me with every thrust.

My life was empty until I met Rex.

He filled me with light.

Then, when that light began to fade, he lifted me up.

No matter what I've gone through, he's always been by my side.

My dark times are always brightened with the lightness he brings to me.

I stare up at him, watching his face flood with love and desire as he makes love to me.

I know what I need to do.

I have to fix what could break us.

EVENTUALLY, Rex has to shower by himself.

I don't join him. It'd probably end up with wet, sloppy sex again.

My grip on the phone is so tight that I'm shocked my fingers aren't crushing it.

This has to end.

Rex has opened up his heart to me, giving me his all.

I owe him the same.

If he were to ever find out my secrets, it'd damage our trust.

Would he hate me if I told him? Probably not.

Would he try to fix it? Yes.

Would he hate me when I told him not to? Yes.

It hurts my heart to know I'm hiding this, but he can't know.

A chill crawls up my spine, and I take a deep, steadying breath when I hit *his* name.

Me: This has to end.

It takes him less than a minute to respond.

James: No. We're not ready.

Me: I AM READY.

James: Too bad. I'm not.

I blink away tears.

Me: WHY? This is ridiculous!

James: What's ridiculous is you leaving me when I told you not to.

My anger spirals out of control as I hold myself back from throwing my phone across the room. *Screw him.*

Me: Are you kidding me? You know why I left!

I have no idea why I'm arguing. My goal is to make him happy so he leaves me alone.

James: You never gave me the time to explain myself.

Oh, he explained himself aplenty.

He texts again before I reply.

James: Meet me, and we'll talk.

Me: I'm not meeting you!

James: It's meet me or nothing.

Horror flows through me.

Meet him.

Rex will for sure ask me what's going on if I tell him I'm meeting James, but seeing him might be my final way out of this.

Me: Fine. Where?

James: Tomorrow. My place. Noon.

Oh, hell no.

Me: I'm not going to your house.

James: The bistro off-campus?

Me: Too public.

James: Public is anywhere but my house.

Me: I'll be there at noon.

James: Love you.

There's no stopping me from texting him back with my precious endearment.

Me: Go screw yourself.

James: I liked it better when you screwed me.

I throw my phone down on the bed.

I hate him so damn much, and I know he won't make it easy on me tomorrow, but I have to attempt to play nice with him. All I need is for him to sign a document.

If only it were that simple.

I've never lied to Rex before.

I've omitted the truth, yes, but never flat-out lied.

That'll change tomorrow.

CHAPTER TWENTY-TWO

Rex

"HEY, babe, what are you up to today?"

Carolina whips around at my question, giving me her back when she opens a cabinet and takes forever finding her mug of choice.

"Hanging out with my mom and Tricia," she replies, twirling around in her socks with two mugs. "We're having lunch. Shopping. Girl time. Should be done before dinner." She glances down at the floor as she makes the few steps to the coffeepot. "You?"

I shrug. "Might go for a run and then work on the game."

"Want to stay in or go out for dinner later?"

"Whatever you want."

We eat a quick breakfast, and after she kisses me good-bye, I change into my running clothes. The sun is out, a nice breeze flowing, when I run through Town Square. I'm interrupted by a good fifteen people with questions about my mother and Carolina.

Before heading back to the apartment, I make a pit stop at the local doughnut shop that has a kick-ass smoothie menu. Something with coffee in it sounds damn good. My sleep has been shit lately, and I have a long day of working on my game. Not that I'm complaining since the lack of sleep is from all the sex I've been having with Carolina. We're like two teenagers who just discovered orgasms.

I walk into the small shop, the smell of fresh baked dough and sugar smacking my face, and I stand in the busy line. People are seated around small pub tables, snacking and drinking.

"Rex! Hey, Mom! Rex is here!"

Henry comes running over to me, a doughnut in his hand and chocolate frosting on his face. Tricia is struggling to keep up with him as she pushes the stroller with Addy in it while carrying a pink smoothie in her hand.

Henry pops the final bite of his doughnut into his mouth, not muttering another word as he chews it up when Tricia reaches us.

"Hi, Rex," she greets, thrusting a napkin into Henry's hand.

"Hey, guys." I ruffle my hand through Henry's hair before turning my attention to Tricia with a polite smile.

"Can I come over and play video games today?" Henry bursts out.

"If it's okay with your mom."

Carolina brings Henry over when she babysits sometimes. He loves my video games. Plus, I feed him junk food.

Speaking of Carolina …

My eyes sweep over the shop before returning to Tricia. "Is Carolina with you?"

She shakes her head, her answer drawing out in confusion, "No … is she supposed to be?" Her eyes widen, showing the regret of asking me that question.

"She said she was hanging out with you and your mom." I step out of line when my turn comes up, losing my place, but I don't want to miss talking to Tricia for answers.

"Uh …" Tricia fumbles for words. "Maybe she and my mom had plans and forgot to tell me."

I nod. "I'll call her."

Shock and apology flood her face before passing into worry.

Carolina isn't someone who lies.

The only times she hasn't been truthful with me is when it's about *him.*

I say bye, no longer giving a shit about the smoothie, and fish my phone from my pocket as I speed-walk toward my apartment.

When I hit her name, I get no answer.

I try again.

Rings until it hits voicemail.

And again.

Not trying to be on the line of stalker shit, but what the hell is happening?

Is she hurt?

I'd think it was an emergency had she not lied about being with her sister.

She's hiding something from me.

My mind twists and turns with possible scenarios.

I shove my phone back into my shorts pocket and sprint home. I'm nearly out of breath when I get there and rush up the stairs while calling her again. Her phone is ringing when I walk into the living room.

"Dude, that thing has been ringing nonstop," Josh complains when I come into his view. "I'm half-tempted to throw it out the window."

"Is Lina here?" I rush out, searching the room how I did at the doughnut shop.

"I woke up fifteen minutes ago, but I haven't seen or heard her."

She'd have also answered her phone if she were.

Her phone rings again, the call not from me, and I find it on the nightstand when I walk into my bedroom, following the noise.

Tricia calling flashes across the screen.

The call ends before I get the chance to answer. Snatching the phone, I see tons of text messages on her screen. All of them from James.

The fuck?

I try four different passwords before succeeding in unlocking her phone. I'm an asshole for this, but she's been missing, and a bad guy from her past is texting her.

Something is up.

James is at the top of the list when I open her texts.

James: You still coming over today?

Carolina: I'll be there.

James: Wear something sexy.

I clutch the phone, ready to throw it across the room, but I stop myself since it's not mine.

It's a jackass move, but I read through their few texts. Most of the texts have been deleted, although I'm certain they're similar. I'm capable of hacking into her phone and reading them, but the thought makes me sick to my stomach.

My head spins so hard that I can hardly think straight as I continue reading the texts she sent at ten this morning.

Carolina: Leaving now. Be there in 2 hours.

James: Can't wait.

She left twenty minutes after sending that message, and an hour and a half has passed.

How has she not realized she forgot her phone?

The phone beeps with another text.

James: Where are you?

I debate on answering when another text comes.

James: I made us lunch. How far away are you?

James: Baby, answer me, so I know you're still coming.

I nearly puke at him calling her baby.

I want to throw the phone into the toilet and flush the fucker.

I hit his name to get the contact information and grab my laptop, doing a search on his phone number even though I already know who this *James* is. She broke down and told me that night she cried in my arms.

My suspicion is verified.

James Cordry.

Professor James Cordry.

Motherfucking asshole.

Why is Carolina talking to him again?

All I can do now is wait for answers.

FOUR HOURS LATER, Carolina comes barging into the apartment.

Uneasiness lines her soft features as the lies start falling from her lips. "I'm sorry if you tried calling. I lost my phone." Her eyes are red when she looks at me. "Can you use the Find My Phone feature you did last time this happened?"

My eyes darken on her, my pulse hammering in my throat as I take her in and stay seated on the couch, her phone gripped in my palm.

She's fighting to look cool, calm, and collected.

Too bad I know her well enough that she's far from that.

Guilt screams along every feature of her beautiful, lying face.

I hold the phone up. "Found it."

She releases a sigh of relief. "Thank God. I didn't want to buy a new one."

This is a shitty situation, and I feel like a shitty person.

An insecure guy who's interrogating his girlfriend about cheating.

My hand clenches around the phone, dread sinking through my veins of where this will lead. Hesitation hits me before I reply, and I take in every inch of her, searching for differences.

Her lips look plumper than when she left.

Did they kiss?

Her face is more flushed.

Did they have sex?

She barely pays me a look when she grabs the phone. "Thank you." Her tone is polite—her *church* voice is what I call it. "I'm going to change into something more comfortable."

I nod my head, my voice bitter. "By the way, how was hanging out with Professor Cordry?"

She freezes mid-turn, gaping at me. "W-what?"

My teeth grit. "You weren't with your mom and sister today."

"What are you talking about?" She grips her throat, rubbing it, catching the truth to replace it with lies.

"I ran into Tricia earlier, and you were nowhere to be found." I snap my fingers. "She didn't even know you had *plans*. Words of advice: get your story straight if you're going to lie."

"What?" she repeats, as if that were the only word she knew.

Her phone beeps, and pain flicks along her face when she glances at the screen.

I raise a brow, releasing a harsh laugh. "Is that a text from … what is the professor to you?"

My asshole is coming through, but I don't care.

Why the hell did she push us to be more than friends so much if she was still seeing him?

Was I her rebound until they got back together?

"Rex." Her lower lip trembles, and the phone drops from her hand to the floor. "It's not what it looks like."

"Explain it then," I spit. "It sure *looks like* you lied to me and went to him." I spread my legs, leaning forward, and rest my elbows onto my knees, shaking my head and feeling like a fucking fool. "You deleted most of your texts with him … out of what? Guilt? Secrecy?" I tap my temple. "Only liars have to delete shit from their phones."

"James and I … we have history." She clutches her arms around her body.

"And we fucking don't?" I burst out.

"You know what I mean, Rex."

I stand and thrust my thumb into my chest. "I was the one who held you in my arms when you were crying *over him*!" I shake my head with a snarl. "Now what, huh? You still have feelings for him? He decided he was done sticking his dick in other women and wants you back?"

"We … we needed to talk," she stammers, her face turning red.

"In person? You drove two hours to talk instead of a phone call?" I throw my arms out. "Or even a text—you know, how you've been communicating with him behind my back?"

"No." She squeezes her eyes shut. "He'd only talk to me in person." When she opens them, she blinks back tears, causing me to soften my tone.

"To do what?"

"End things."

"Didn't you end things months ago? Have you been talking to him behind my back this entire time?" The anger returns. I'm burning with so many questions.

"No …" Her eyes drop. "Sometimes."

"Jesus!" My voice is thick as it rises. "This is why I didn't want us to cross that line! I wish I'd never touched you!"

"Don't say that," she whispers, tears falling down her cheeks. "It's complicated."

"Damn it, Carolina, I can do complicated."

She looks away from me.

I pinch the bridge of my nose before moving in front of her. "What's going on? Why are you talking to him? Seeing him?"

"Because he won't give me a divorce!"

CHAPTER TWENTY-THREE

Carolina

Six Months Earlier

THE TEXT on my phone has me grinning like a child on Christmas.

James: I love you, my wife. Come over.

Wife!

That grin overtakes my face at the endearment.

Me: I thought you were busy tonight?

I asked him to have dinner at his place, but he told me he had a business dinner to attend.

James: Change of plans.

Me: Just got to my dorm. Give me an hour, and I'll be there.

James: Turn around and come see me. I miss you, baby.

Me: Fine. Twenty minutes.

James: Is your roommate there?

Weird question.

Me: IDK?

James: Have you talked to her today?

Me: This morning. Why?

James: No reason. Hurry up and bring your cute ass here.

My dorm room door is unlocked, and I hear sobbing as soon as I walk in. Margie is collapsed on the floor, her back slumped against her bed, and her face is red and puffy when she peeks up at me.

"Margie?" I drop my bag and fall onto my knees next to her. "Are you okay?" Stupid question on my part considering she's a crying mess.

She sniffles, mascara running down her cheeks. "Yes …" *Sniffles.* "No."

My stomach flip-flops as bad thoughts rush my mind. "Did someone hurt you?"

She shakes her head.

"What then?"

She rubs at her eyes, smearing her makeup more, and blinks away tears. "Promise you won't judge."

I reach forward and squeeze her hand. "Promise not to judge."

She inhales a breath of courage. "I'm sleeping with a professor."

Oh, man.

That confession hits close to home.

"I take it that fell apart?" I ask in concern.

"I didn't know he was married!" she shrieks, the tears reemerging. "I was over at his house earlier and went through his phone." Her voice rises. "He was texting someone he called *My Wife*. He got married in Vegas last weekend!" She snags a flip-flop from the floor and throws it across the room. "I'm so fucking stupid!"

My body stiffens, ice chilling my veins. "What?"

"He's been sleeping with some other slut and married her," she seethes, the words spewing out like venom. She slams her palm against her chest, her cries louder. "Why wouldn't he marry me? Why'd he pick some skank-ass ho over me?"

I dread the answer before I ask the question, "Which professor?"

"It doesn't matter." She pulls her knees to her chest, resting her chin on them.

"Come on," I push. "I won't tell anyone."

Her nostrils flare, her sadness swirling into anger. "Professor Cordry. Asshole of Psychology."

My head spins, and I suck in my cheeks to hoard in my anger … my pain.

The name is a slap in the face.

My voice is thick as the words slowly leave my mouth. "I didn't know you were taking his class."

"I'm not," she replies. "We met at the coffee shop on campus. He asked me out, and my dumbass said yes."

"How long have you been seeing each other?"

"Two months."

It takes everything I have not to break down next to her.

Call it a heartbreak party.

If I lose it, she'll know everything.

I have to get out of here.

I snatch my phone and fake getting a text message before jumping to my feet. "I have to go."

I should hug her, give her a kiss on the cheek, and tell her everything is okay.

But it's not.

Nothing is okay.

There's no way I can spew out that bullshit without breaking down.

I have to see him.

I need to kick him in the balls … scream at him … and … *divorce him.*

"YOU CHEATING, LYING SCUM!" I explode as soon as James answers his front door, throwing the diamond ring in his face.

The ring I only wear when we're together.

Never in public.

Not counting when we got hitched in Vegas and spent the weekend there.

Hot tears swell in my eyes.

I cried and cursed him the entire ride here.

I hate myself for how stupid I am.

"What the hell?" he asks.

He knows why I'm angry.

That's why he told me not to go to the dorm.

Why he asked if she was there.

"You're sleeping with Margie!" I shout.

"Who?" He rubs his chin, playing stupid while standing in the doorway.

I sweep my arms out, and my voice cracks. "My roommate! You're screwing her!"

"Keep your fucking voice down," he hisses.

"Screw you!"

The door swings open wider seconds before he clasps his hand around my elbow and tugs me inside, slamming the door behind us.

"Why would you do this to me?" I shriek, jerking out of his hold. "To us?"

My hands are shaking. My chin is trembling. My mind is racing.

James moves, standing tall in front of me, and shoves his hands into the pockets of his pants. "Baby, I don't know what you're talking about."

No sign of guilt or regret is on his face.

No sign of him feeling apologetic for ripping my heart out of my chest and stomping on it.

No longer do I see the man I fell for.

Now, I see a man with slicked-back dark hair, wearing an expensive button-up and black pants and a phony smile on his face.

James Cordry is a good-looking man in his thirties.

He's a smooth talker. Successful. Intelligent. A liar.

The perfect storm for a naïve woman searching for love.

I loved him. Opened up to him. Changed myself and broke my values for him.

Did things I'd never thought I'd do—all in the name of love.

I was younger, inexperienced, and allowed him to lead every step in our relationship.

I shove him away when he reaches out and attempts to take my shaking hand in his. "Don't touch me!"

"Carolina," he says sharply. "Calm down. Why are you acting so distraught?"

"Why did you tell me you were busier earlier?" I question. "Is it because you were with her?"

"I had a business meeting. It got canceled. I texted you because I wanted to be with the woman I love. The woman who said *I do* to spending the rest of her life with me."

"Liar!" I scream, slapping his hand away when he tries to touch me again. My heart knocks against my chest, breaking into pieces, and it takes everything I have in me not to fall apart in front of him. "Just tell me the truth. That's all I want from you."

He shrugs. "There's nothing to tell."

"Tell me! Be honest!"

He drags his hand through his hair. "Nothing to tell, so stop your bitching. I've had a long day, and the last thing I need is you coming in, acting like a lunatic." He shakes his head, his face burning. "Here I thought, I was in love with a grown woman, not a dramatic brat."

"I'd rather be a dramatic brat than a cheater." I glare at him in disgust. "We're done."

He stares at me, sure of himself, and laughs coldly. "Oh, Carolina, that's where you're wrong, baby. We're not done until I say we're done."

"No, James, that's where *you're* wrong," I argue with a scowl. "I'll be filing an annulment first thing in the morning."

A venomous smile crosses his face. "You do that, and I'll let everyone on campus and your *preacher father* know what a whore you are."

I inch forward and smack him across the face.

He winces, rubbing his jaw, but doesn't back away. "Don't do that again. That's your only warning."

"We're over."

He shakes his head. "You're mine."

"I was until you cheated on me." I scoff. "I'm sure she's not the only one you've been with either. I don't even want to know how many women you've screwed behind my back."

"Nah, she's the only one, and it's your fault it happened."

Startled, I stumble back a step. "Excuse me?"

"You ditched me for your little high school fuck boy. I saw Margie at the coffee shop. I didn't know she was your roommate until we fucked and she talked about you."

"Yet you kept screwing her," I seethe.

He shrugs. "She was good in bed."

I move forward to smack him again, but he catches my wrist, tightly gripping it so I'm unable to pull away.

"I told you not to do that again," he growls out.

I'm not strong enough to break his hold. "*I told you* I want a divorce. Go be with someone else."

He snorts. "I don't want someone else."

I fight him as he pulls me into his living room and shoves me onto his couch. As soon as my butt hits the cushions, I bounce up to leave, but he shoves me back down.

"Please stop," I whimper. "Let me leave."

This is a stranger to me—not the James I fell in love with.

My first boyfriend is a wolf in sheep's clothing.

"Why do you even care if we're together?" I cry out. "You can find a new girlfriend tonight!"

"You're different than the others," he says slowly ... gently. "You were made for me. The other women, they wanted the thrill of *sleeping with a professor.*" He snaps his fingers and points at me, moving his finger up and down over and over again. "You, on the other hand?" He steps in closer, his feet hitting mine as I fight to control my breathing underneath him. "You love me for *me.*"

"Loved," I correct. "I'll figure out a way to forget that stupid marriage ever happened."

I go to stand again, but he pushes me back down.

"Want to know why we're not done?"

I break down when he tells me.

TEARS. Arguing. Threats.

I spent three hours at James's house, experiencing all of the above until I promised to keep my mouth shut and he let me leave.

He's broken me in every way imaginable.

I don't even know who I am anymore.

As I grew closer with him, I became distant with Rex.

Ignored my parents' phone calls.

Skipped a few classes.

Tears return at the realization of how dumb I've been.

How blind.

As soon as I get into my car, I pull out my phone and find a text from Margie, asking when I'm coming back to the dorm.

I ignore it.

How do I explain this to her?

Tell her we've been sleeping with the same man ... and I'm his wife?

James made it clear that telling anyone, especially Margie, was a big no-no.

"She's angry, and she'll get me in trouble," was what he said.

"Good," was my response.

"She spills information; I spill information," he fired back.

No telling Margie for me.

Putting my car into drive, I go to the only person who can fix me.

Regret barrels through me. If only I'd confessed to Rex during the dozens of times he begged me to tell him who I was dating, he'd have told me I was being stupid, being used, and to leave him.

Maybe I would've listened to him.

Too late now.

When James found out Rex was the hack master, he bought me a separate phone to talk to him on in case Rex wanted to look into who I was communicating with. I was betraying Rex in every way imaginable.

I'm sobbing hysterically when I call him in the dead of the night and say I'm outside his dorm.

His voice is sleepy when he tells me he's coming.

My sobs grow louder, harder, as I run through the rain to the entrance of the dorm, waiting for him … for his comfort.

The door flies open, and Rex's eyes widen, his lips snarling when he sees me.

Not wasting a second, I run into the arms of my security blanket, of the person who's been there for me and I know will never break me.

Into the arms of the person I should've trusted.

The only man I'll trust ever again.

My mind is blank as he walks me inside, and I cry in his arms.

"What's going on?" His chin is trembling in anger. "What

the fuck happened? Did someone hurt you?" The arms around me tighten at his last question.

"Not here," I whisper, burying my face into his neck.

He lifts me, and I wrap my legs around his waist while he walks us up the stairs to his floor. The hallway is empty—*thank God*—and the light stays off when we land in his dorm room.

His questions start as soon as he drops me onto his bed. "Lina babe, what's going on?" His voice hardens as he asks the same question he did earlier, "Did someone hurt you?"

"Yes," I say into the darkness.

"What?"

The air grows heavy, an anger I've never seen from Rex surfacing.

"It's not like that," I rush out. "No one ... *hurt me*, hurt me." I cover my face with my hands. "This is embarrassing."

He falls to his knees and removes my hands, one by one. "I can take embarrassing." He runs his finger along my jaw, wiping away drops of rain and tears. "Tell me."

I sniffle, unable to look at him, to see the disgust on his face when I tell him. "You have to promise not to judge me ... or get mad."

"Lina, you know I'll never judge you for shit. I'll have your back, no matter what."

I inhale a deep breath, and my words come out exactly how they did when Margie made her confession with a few word tweaks. "I'm dating a professor."

"What?" he asks. Even though I can't make out his face all that well, I can hear the shock in his voice. "Who?"

"Professor Cordry."

"That motherfucker," he hisses. "I'm going to kick his ass."

"No, you can't," I sob.

"I can. He took advantage of you."

Leave it to Rex to think it was all James's fault, as if I had no play in it.

Everyone sees me as this perfect woman who makes smart decisions. Maybe I am smart, except when it comes to love … to men.

I shake my head. "No … he didn't. I'm a grown woman."

"You're a naïve college student who's never broken out of her shell," he fires back. "Big damn difference."

"We're the same age—"

He cuts me off, "It's different." He rises to his feet, grabs dry clothes, and hands me a shirt. "Get out of those wet clothes."

I pull my shirt over my head while sniffling before giving it to his hand he has held out. "Oh my God, I'm getting your bed wet." The realization hits me.

"You're cool." He hands me the bottoms next.

I undress underneath the blanket, changing into the dry clothes, and he slides into bed when I'm finished. Some of my sadness wears down when he wraps his arms around me and kisses the top of my head.

"Everything is okay. You'll be okay. You're strong."

I whisper my confessions to him.

How I met James.

How we hit it off and secretly dated.

How I found out he had been doing the same with Margie.

I don't tell him about us getting married … or how James will always have the upper hand with me.

I DROP OUT OF COLLEGE.

No one, except Rex, knows why.

I'm terrified of my parents' reaction.

Rex and Josh moved my things out of the dorm, and I haven't talked to Margie since the day she told me she was sleeping with James. I feel terrible, but I can't be around her without feeling guilt, without getting us in trouble.

He has dirt on us both.

I poured bleach on the phone James had bought me and then tossed it in the trash can.

All of this to get rid of him.

It's not that easy.

He knows my regular phone number. It's what we talked on until things grew serious.

I move back home to get as far away from James as possible.

There will be space between us, and maybe he'll forget about me and find someone new.

James thinks I'll come back to him because if I don't, he can ruin me.

CHAPTER TWENTY-FOUR

Rex

"CAN YOU REPEAT THAT?" I ask, unsure I heard her correctly as my jaw falls slack. "Did you say, you're *married* to that asshole?"

My head is spinning as I digest her words.

Her gaze drops to the floor when she nods.

Certain I'm mistaken, I ask again, "You married him?"

"I did," she whispers, failing to lift her eyes.

Questions hurl through my mind so fast that I struggle to grasp one to throw at her.

"How?" I seethe. "When?"

A heavy, unrecognizable tension consumes the room, and for a moment, I'm not sure she'll answer.

She blows out a stressed breath, and her eyes are cold and teary when she raises them. I ache to stand and comfort her, wrap her in my arms, but her betrayal stops me. I need answers.

"It was a week before I broke things off with him," she explains, taking slow steps before collapsing onto the chair next to the couch, her shoulders slumping. "He took me to Vegas for a weekend, and we went clubbing with his friends. I drank a lot, and somehow, marriage came up. It sounded like a good idea at the time. I was alcohol-and love-drunk and thought we'd be together forever."

"If you were drunk, you can get an annulment. Problem solved."

She clutches her arms around her chest, and our eye contact is wiped out again when she stares at the floor, releasing a heavy sigh. "I can't do that."

"Why not?"

"It's complicated."

"Carolina, look at me, damn it," I snarl, the ache to console her returning. "You file. Sign the papers. It's done."

My job as her best friend is to be her rock.

I've taken on that role. Loved that role.

I can't be her rock if she's hurting me.

My fear of our friendship being ruined has become a reality.

"He threatened to tell my parents," is her ridiculous reply.

I scoff. "Did you think no one would find out about your marital bliss? Why'd you tie the knot if you had to keep it a secret?"

"Our plan was to wait until he was no longer my professor. Until then, we kept it low-key."

"That's the stupidest shit I've ever heard."

Those beautiful, deceitful eyes of hers widen. "Wow. Really, Rex?"

"Yes, really." I scrub my hand over my face. "Why do you care about your parents? You won't be the first person to divorce someone. They won't like it, but they'll get over it."

"He …" She hesitates. "He said he'd grant me a divorce if …"

I wait for her to finish but get silence. "If what?"

She swallows a few times. "If I stay away from you for a year and try to work things out with him."

"Are you kidding me?" I shake my head, anger burning through me. "Scratch my earlier statement. *That's* the stupidest shit I've ever heard." My temples throb. "Are you *considering* it?"

A sharp pain runs through me at her lack of response. Even with what my father put our family through, I've never been so hurt.

"I don't know what I'm considering!" she cries out. "All of this has just been thrown at me! I need to get my head straight. I just need time!"

"Time?" I fire back. "How long? A *year*, like he's asking?"

"I never said that's what I want," she chokes out. "I said, he *gave* me that option."

"Fuck this." I stand and pull my keys from my pocket. "Someone needs to set this asshole straight."

That someone being me.

I should've done this a long time ago.

"No!" she shrieks, jumping up from the chair and scurrying behind me, grabbing my elbow and attempting to pull me back into the living room.

I jerk out of her hold. "I'll fix this for you. I promise."

"Don't threaten him," she whimpers around her plea. "*Please* leave him alone. We can act like he doesn't exist, and eventually, he'll get tired of me and go about his way."

I blow out a frustrated breath. "If he doesn't? Will you stay married to him?"

Nothing makes sense.

Why does she give so many fucks about divorcing him?

I need answers.

Carolina won't give them to me; therefore, I'll get them from James.

I'll fix this.

She dashes in front of me when I start walking again, blocks me from the door, and takes my face in her hands.

"Don't leave me." Her lips tenderly brush mine. "I need you with me, Rex."

"I'll be back in a few hours," I grind out against her mouth, my teeth catching on to her lower lip.

"Please," she begs, pulling away an inch before rubbing her thumb over my lips. "Do whatever you want tomorrow, but tonight, I need *you.* The man who'll never turn his back on me. *You*—your love, your security, your arms around me."

Tears slip down her cheeks, hitting her thumb and my lip.

"Okay," I whisper, putting my anger aside at the sight of her pain. "I'll stay."

CAROLINA PROMISED to give me answers tonight before she left for work.

Last night, it was too fresh—my anger, her pain.

Neither of us knew what to do or where this would lead for our future.

It was like we were too scared to discuss it, to change everything between us.

There's more to this story.

Carolina's parents being disappointed isn't what's stopping her from divorcing James. She's always been scared of disappointing them, but she failed when she dropped out of school.

I'm pissed the entire drive to the university, and the lecture hall is empty when I walk in.

Exactly what I planned after pulling up his class schedule.

Professor Asshole is gathering up papers and shoving them into a brown leather briefcase. He halts, papers fluttering to the floor, when he notices me walking toward him.

He speaks before I get the chance to, his tone cool and collected, "Let me guess … you're here because of Carolina?" He whistles. "Gotta say, I'm shocked she told you."

Other than looking up his pictures the next morning after Carolina came to my dorm, crying, this is my first time I've taken a good look at him. I understand his appeal. He's tall, fit, and on the younger side. His good looks, expensive clothes, and smooth-talking personality are what draw women to him.

I don't speak until I'm standing in front of his desk, nearly in his face. "Quit playing games and give her a goddamn divorce."

A bold smirk crosses his face, and he falls back a step. "Don't tell me what to do with *my wife*."

My wife.

Those words send a spiral of anger through me.

"Wife?" I clench my jaw, my pulse skyrocketing. "Not for long."

"Oh, really?" He draws himself up to his full height, thrusting his chest out and tensing his muscles—a lame attempt at appearing intimidating. "Is that what she said? That she planned to *divorce me*? It wasn't the tune she was singing yesterday when she came to *my house*."

His house.

Dude knows how to piss another guy off; that's for sure.

What did Carolina see in this douche bag?

My ribs tighten as I hold myself back from jumping over the desk and pummeling his face in. "Yes, that's *exactly* what she said—that you won't give her a divorce and are playing mind games."

He shakes his head, a laughter filled with edge coming from him. "I don't play mind games with *my wife*."

If this motherfucker says wife *one more time, Carolina will become a widow.*

"What do you have on her?" I ask, getting straight to the point.

"None of your business. This is between me and *my wife*, so stay away from her."

My nails bite into my palms as I clench my fists. "Listen, creep—"

He cuts me off, "How does it feel, screwing a married woman, *Rex*?"

"She doesn't want to be married to you," I fire back.

"Do you plan to date her if we divorce?"

"Yes."

"Marry her?"

"Yes."

He smiles deviously while fishing out a phone from his pocket. "Tell me something then, how would you feel … how would your *mayor father* feel if your new girlfriend's pictures were posted online?"

I blink, and it takes my eyes a second to adjust to the screen when he shoves the phone in my face—answering all the questions I came here for.

This is why she won't leave him.

This sneaky motherfucker.

I jerk the phone from his grimy fingers, throw it on the floor, and stomp on it, shattering it to pieces underneath my Chuck Taylor.

"Are you sure you want to date my wife *now*?"

My crushing his phone doesn't seem to faze him.

Phone down.

His face to go.

I circle around the desk faster than I've ever moved in my life, grab him by his scrawny-ass throat, and slam him against the wall, pinning him into it. "You motherfucker!"

"Ah … so she didn't tell you everything."

He gasps when I tighten my hold on his neck, and it takes everything I have not to keep choking him when his face starts turning purple.

I came here to scare him.

Not to kill him.

Even though I thought of dozens of ways I wanted to kill him on the drive here.

He bends at the waist when I release, his hands resting on his knees as he inhales deep breaths, nearly choking on them when I pull away.

"Sign the divorce papers when they're delivered to you," I demand, wiping my hands down my pants and turning to leave.

He snorts coldly. "You don't think there's more where that came from?" A smug smile takes over his face. "I have plenty of pictures of her." He tips his head toward the phone. "You might've broken my phone, but I still have them *everywhere.*"

I circle his desk and snatch his iPad from it.

It breaks when I stomp on it next.

"Two devices down," he says. "*So many more* to go. I have them saved *everywhere,* waiting for Carolina to make the wrong move. If she decides to leave me for you, there will be repercussions. She belongs with me—someone mature—not a little video game–playing college kid. I might've made a few mistakes with Carolina, but she's mine."

"I don't know if Carolina has told you what I'm capable of. I will not only kick your ass, but I'll also hack into everything with your name on it—phones, computers, emails, your fucking preschool records if I have to. Every-motherfucking-thing."

"You don't think Carolina has told me how you can hack into accounts?" He rubs at his red throat. "Which, by the way, is illegal, and I'd definitely turn you in for whatever you did."

"Good luck proving it. You might be a sloppy motherfucker, but let me promise you, I'm not." Pointing at him, I narrow my eyes. "Delete every picture and leave her the fuck alone. Find another student to bang since they seem to be your type, you fucking creep."

"Or what?"

"Like I said, I'll search through everything you own."

"Are you threatening me?"

"Nope. Only telling you what I'll do. I won't stop digging into every move you make until you leave her alone."

"Fuck you," he spits.

"Prepare for me to know your every secret, Professor." I grab his briefcase, slide out the laptop inside, and hold it up. "I'll smash this up as soon as I'm finished with it."

CHAPTER TWENTY-FIVE

Carolina

REX TEXTED me two hours ago, asking if he could stop by the loft.

Considering all the text messages I've received, I have a hunch I know what him coming over means. We've hardly spoken since this morning, and even then, there was an uncomfortable silence as I got ready for work at his apartment.

Maybe he needs space to decide if he still wants to date me after he found out about James.

Stupid—that's what I was for thinking I could hide my marriage from him. Then again, I didn't expect Rex to open up his heart to me like he has and take the leap with me I'd wanted for years.

I never told Rex because I thought being with him wasn't an option. All this time, I've waited for us, only to hit a roadblock—a block I have no idea when it'll open.

I've shifted in twenty-five different positions on the couch trying to get comfortable. My head throbs, my heart ready to dive out of my chest.

Honestly, I'd have no problem with that.

I'd hand it over to Rex—a promise that, no matter what, he has it.

Not James.

Not anyone else.

Him.

It'll always be his.

Right now, even though I love him, I want to kick his ass.

"Are you nuts?" I screech when he walks through the front door with his computer bag, anger on his face. "James said you went to his lecture hall and threatened him."

His visit to James shouldn't surprise me. Even after the lies, Rex will always protect me. It's what he's done our entire friendship—with my cousins, with anyone who gave me shit, and now, with James. Rex would destroy anything in the world than see me in pain.

The cold glare aimed in my direction confirms I'm not the only mad person in the room.

"Sure did," he snaps.

"Rex," I say carefully. "Please don't get involved in this. I asked you to leave it alone, and I'll figure it out."

"Figure it out?" he shouts, his eyes not leaving me. "What is your plan on *figuring it out*?"

I chew on my lower lip. "I don't exactly know that yet."

His anger heightens. Even last night, he wasn't this upset. Dread takes over my body as I wait for him to throw whatever he's pissed about at me.

James told him something.

The question is, *What did he tell him?*

"When did you plan to tell me the reason you won't divorce him is because he's blackmailing you with nude pictures?"

Good thing I'm sitting, or my knees would've given out, and I'd be crying on the floor. I'd love nothing more than to sink into these cushions and disappear. The pie I ate at work earlier is threatening to make an appearance in this argument … talk … whatever it is.

He told him.

I want to slice and dice James right now.

Go Lorena Bobbitt on him.

It takes me a moment to find my voice and not die in front of him. "He … he told you?"

"He fucking showed me," he hisses through clenched teeth. "I wanted to kill the bastard."

I close my eyes as they burn with tears and choke out my answer, "He's been holding it over my head since the night we broke up."

Rex will never look at me the same way again.

"Are you shitting me?" he screams. "You've just been letting him threaten you all this time? What the hell, Carolina?"

"I didn't know what to do!" I sob.

That's right.

I was stupid and sent James naked pictures of myself.

I was even *stupider* because I didn't even cut off my face in those pictures.

James knows he has me right where he wants me—the preacher's daughter whose reputation means so much. All he's done since we broke up is threaten me with them.

"Gee, I don't know," he argues. "Ask your best fucking friend for help! That's what you could've done!"

"I knew what your *help* would be."

"I would've fixed this problem for you months ago. You wouldn't be dealing with this jackass."

I violently shake my head, swiping away tears in the process. "It won't solve it. You can't hack into every device he owns. You don't know where he has them or if he's printed them off or stored them on a random drive."

"I'll find wherever he has them."

"What if you can't?"

"I'll take matters into my own hands. I've managed to snag his IP addresses, passwords, and looked through his laptop before trashing it."

"You *stole* his laptop?"

"Borrowed it," he corrects.

"So … you're giving it back?"

"Accidentally broke it while borrowing it." He shrugs. "I'm clumsy sometimes."

"I bet." I sigh heavily. "I appreciate you wanting to help, but all I can do is ride this out until he decides he's done with me. I thought him dating Margie would help, but she broke up with him again."

He arches a brow. "He and Margie are dating again?"

I nod.

"Even after she found out he was married?"

"Apparently so. When I texted him the other day, asking for a divorce, she had his phone. I thought maybe if they'd worked things out, he'd let me off the hook. I was wrong."

Yesterday, James blamed me for their breakup since it was over my text. Annoyingly, he still has me under *My Wife*, so she doesn't know it's me.

I wish I could tell Margie everything.

As the tears come faster, I cover my face with my hands. "God, this is embarrassing."

Rex plops down next to me on the couch, grabs my shoulders so I'm facing him, and plucks my hands off, one by one. "What's embarrassing is you not trusting me enough to tell me. You know everything about me. Every secret. You'd for sure know if I got married."

The hurt is clear on his face.

Rex's problem isn't that I made a mistake.

It's that I kept it from him.

That I didn't trust him with my secret.

I gulp, my eyes meeting his. "I'm sorry."

He nods, an inch of forgiveness in his features. "Why

haven't you gone to the university and reported him? You don't even have to tell them about the pictures. He'd get in trouble for marrying you; I have no doubt about that."

"You think getting him fired from his job will convince him not to revenge-porn me? It'd give him more incentive because he'd have nothing to lose."

Rex grabs his laptop from the case. "To work I go then."

I snatch it from his hands. "You can get in trouble for that. You don't think I told James you'd do that? He'll report you, especially if it's any emails from his university account."

"You have no idea of the lengths I'd go to protect you." He snags the laptop back from me. "I'll risk it all."

He opens the computer, powers it on, and starts hitting keys.

I thrust a hand through my messy hair. "Do you … are you … are we …?" My voice is low and shaky.

He glances up from the computer. "Are we what?"

"Do you hate me?"

"Nope," he answers with no hesitation. "Am I pissed as fuck at you right now? Yes. I'd never hate you for making a mistake—unless it's cheating on me." This time, he does hesitate. "Which you haven't done, correct?"

"I'd never," I rush out around a gasp. "I'd never let another man touch me. There's no way I'm ruining the one thing I've wanted for years—the person who means everything to me. That is something you'll *never* have to worry about."

He shuts his eyes. "It's killing me you're married to another man and that there's nothing I can do to convince you to change that."

"I'll figure it out, I swear."

He thrusts his thumb toward me, the expression on his face breaking from frustration to a slight smile. "Which brings me to my next point. No dick until you're no longer a married woman."

I wince. "What?"

"It'll give you more incentive to change this situation … and allow me to break some laws." He rests his palm on his chest. "As I've said before, your boy is a man of morals."

I roll my eyes. "Pfft, whatever." I shake my head, my tears starting to dry as his anger calms. I throw my head back in a groan. "I can't believe he showed you pictures of me."

He taps my thigh before leaving his hand to rest there. "Yeah, no offense, but not very smart, babe."

"So, no girl has ever sent you nudes?"

"I'm feeling it's not a good idea to answer that question."

My Rex is resurfacing. No matter how upset he is with me or how dumb my choice was, he'll never stop having my back … never fail to put a smile on my face, even in the shittiest of situations.

"Come here," he says, waving me to him, and I scoot closer. The tip of his finger lifts my chin, and his lips slowly brush mine. He speaks against them, "Never be embarrassed with me, okay? No matter what, I'll be by your side, fighting with you."

I nod, resting my hand on his cheek. "Thank you."

He kisses my lips, my cheek, the tip of my nose, and then my forehead before pulling back. "Now, turn on one of those stupid-ass romance shows you like to get your mind off the bullshit, and I'll be busy at work over here."

Tension leaves my body. "Busy hacking into James's files?"

"Files, photos, emails, text, phone calls …" He shrugs as if it's no big deal.

"That's scary you know how to do all that. You should get a job with the FBI."

"Thought about it once, but I'm not one to follow rules."

———

MY EYES ARE SLEEPY, and I rub at them as Rex carries me to bed in his strong arms. I yawn loudly as he flips on my bedroom light and attentively drops my sleepy self onto the comfy bed.

He sits down on the edge of it, peering down at me as I lie on my back, and runs a finger along my cheek, slowly stroking it. "Everything will be okay, babe. All I need is honesty."

I close my eyes, relaxing at his touch, at his presence. "Nine billion percent honesty from now on. I swear it."

"Sorry, I'm going to need nine billion and one percent to be happy."

A lazy laugh escapes me. "*Fine.* Nine billion and one percent." I reach forward and slide my hand up and down his arm. "Will you stay with me tonight?"

Being in his arms is the only way I'll be able to get a wink of sleep.

His arms are my comfort blanket I never want to give up.

"Will your sister care?"

Rex has never spent the night here. Our sleepovers always happen at his place.

I shake my head in response.

"You sure?"

"Eh …"

Definitely not sure but willing to risk it.

Willing to risk anything to keep him here with me … in my bed … in my life forever.

"We can say you slept on the couch."

Scooting over, I flip the covers up to allow him enough room to join me. Realizing I'm wearing a dress, I rise to my knees and pull it over my head, now wearing only a bra and boy shorts.

Rex lifts from the bed, panic ensuing me.

He's leaving.

My hands shake as I wrap my arms around my body, my eyes glued to him as he walks to my closet.

He snags a shirt and tosses it to me. "If we're sharing a bed, put this on, please and thank you."

I raise a brow. "I'm not wearing that to bed."

"You're also not going to seduce me in your bra and panties."

"Get over it." I roll my eyes, bunch the shirt up in my hand, and toss it onto the floor before patting the bed. "It's cold, so get in here before the panties come off next."

He throws his head back. "Fuck, you kill me."

I grin mischievously.

"Get in bed. I'll be right back."

Not giving me the chance to ask what he's doing, he leaves the room. Minutes later, he returns with his laptop. Setting it on the bed, he pulls off his shirt and then his jeans, showing off his semi-erection.

I lick my lips, my mouth watering.

"Nope," he groans out, snapping his fingers before pointing at my mouth. "Keep your lip-licking and eye-fucking to yourself tonight. Not happening."

"You suck," I grumble, dramatically falling back on the bed.

He collapses next to me, pulling his computer on his lap, and rests his back against the headboard. "Yeah, yeah, yeah."

"You can take a break, you know," I comment, rising up onto my elbows and focusing on him.

His eyes go to the laptop. "I want to get as much work in as I can. This shit is time-consuming. Also, you can bet your ass, James is frantically clearing his shit right now. I need to get to everything before he does."

Guilt crashes through me as I frown. "You're taking time away from your game. That's not fair."

"I'm okay."

"What if you don't find anything?"

He shrugs, rubbing the back of his neck, kneading away

his tension before going back to work. "I'll plant something on his computer then."

"Are you serious?"

"Yes," he answers sharply, not giving any more explanation.

"Rex," I start, stress in my tone. "I don't want to do this shady."

"You're not doing shit; it's me."

With that, he goes back to his work.

My eyes get heavy, all energy for an argument gone, and just before I fall asleep, what I need to do to make this right hits me.

I don't deserve this.

Rex doesn't.

Margie doesn't.

Any other girl who James has manipulated doesn't.

It's time I stand up for myself.

"HAVE YOU EVEN SLEPT?" I ask the question as my eyes slowly open to find Rex in the same spot he was in my bed last night, the computer still on his lap.

An easy smile hits my lips.

All this time, I was scared he'd leave me after finding out about James, about the photos, but he's here, by my side and ready to fight this out with me.

I've always loved my relationship with Rex, but now, it's so much more. My heart bursts with so much passion for this man.

I loved him in high school.

I tried fighting my attraction in college.

Now, there's no doubt, no fighting. This is the only man who will own my heart.

He stole my heart the day he tried bribing me to write a damn Shakespeare paper.

"Morning, sunshine," he says, paying me a quick glance, his eyes sleepy, before going back to work on the computer. "I got a few hours."

Guilt consumes me.

He's losing time to work on his video game.

Losing sleep.

All for my stupidity.

I should be the one going through James's shit. Sure, I'd need to figure out how to hack and all, but it's not fair to Rex.

I'm sitting, pulling the sheet up my chest, when he speaks again, "You know, Iowa has a law criminalizing revenge porn." He moves his gaze my way, finally giving me his full attention. "If he posts intimate or sexually graphic pictures without your knowledge, he can be criminally charged for it."

"So what? We wait until he posts the photos? We can't get him in trouble for threatening to post them?"

"I'm still looking into that, but I wanted you to know that if he does do anything with them, he can get in big trouble. We need to bring that to his attention if he doesn't already know and make it clear you will press charges against him."

"If I were to press charges … my parents would find out."

"Yes, probably." He frowns, going back to work. "Until then, we find more blackmail."

"What if I have an idea?" I ask around a gulp.

He raises a brow, his typing paused. "Shoot."

MARGIE STARES at me from across the table. "I was shocked when you texted me since you've been dodging me for months."

Same, Margie. Same.

It's what needed to be done.

No more running scared from James.

No more allowing him to control me.

He needs to go down, and unless someone steps up, he'll do it again … and again … and again to innocent women. I've decided to take on the job of breaking that cycle—or at least attempting to. First things first. I need to apologize to Margie, and then I need to ask her for a favor.

After telling Rex my plan, I texted Margie, asking her to meet with me. Whether she'd reply, I had no idea. Thankfully, she did, and three hours later, here we are, sitting at a table in the park, having coffee.

It's strange, seeing her after everything that's happened.

Neither one of us is the same as we were before James stormed into our lives.

The happiness that took permanent residence on her face when we lived together has dimmed. James stole some of her light, and I want to punch him in the face for it.

We'd cluelessly slept with the same man.

Whether she knows that, I'm not sure.

I'm taking a risk by being here. Last time we talked was when she had James's phone, and I don't know the status of their relationship. Even though James said they broke up, he could've manipulated her into getting back together. She could tell James everything I say.

I take a sip of my caramel macchiato, wishing it contained something stronger for liquid courage. "I apologize for being distant. I'm truly sorry."

Gripping her iced coffee, she leans back in her chair, focusing her blue eyes on me. "What happened, Carolina? I was so confused. I confessed a huge secret to you, I was heartbroken, and then I never saw you again."

Here goes nothing.

I'm struggling to find the right words even though I rehearsed them so many times on the drive here.

"That night"—I close my eyes, pulling in a calming breath

—"when you told me about sleeping with Professor Cordry . . ."

"Yes?" She raises a brow, sadness spreading over her face.

"That other girl he was seeing—*his wife*—that's me."

She gapes at me, her mouth dropping open. "Wait, what?"

"We'd been sneaking around for six months and stupidly gotten married a week before you found out." The memory tears a hole in my chest. "I had no idea he'd been dating you, too. When you told me, a wave of shock hit me, and I freaked out. When I ran off, it was to confront him about the cheating."

"Wow." She cringes, resting her coffee on the table. "Did he know we were roommates?"

"He said he didn't when you met, but I don't believe anything that leaves that man's mouth." I blow out a deep breath. "We got in a fight over Rex texting me at one in the morning and didn't talk for days. I think that's when he met you."

She releases a spiteful laugh. "God, I was so flattered at the time. I was used to dating stupid frat boys, and here was this guy, making me dinner at his house instead of inviting me to parties where he did keg stands." She throws her arms out. "Why didn't you tell me?"

"When I confronted him, he threatened me with—"

"Let me guess," she cuts in. "Pictures?"

"You, too?"

She nods. "Yep. He begged me to get back together after the whole wife thing, saying they had a quick fling in Vegas and everything was over. Since then, we've been off and on—off every time I catch him with someone else. A few days ago, I found he'd been talking to women on some stupid secret app and receiving naked pictures of them, and I finally left him."

"According to Rex, he has quite the collection of nudes."

When I asked Rex if any of the photos were of Margie or

other women we knew, he shook his head, saying he didn't know because he wasn't going to look through them.

"How'd Rex know?"

"He hacked into James's accounts to find information to stop him from blackmailing me."

"Oh, good old Rex," she says with a smile. "The man who'd do anything for you."

I grin at the truth in her words.

"Tell me that grin means you two finally got your heads out of your asses and admitted you're in love with each other."

I nod. "Sure did."

A genuine smile crosses her face. "I'm so happy for you, Lina!" She pauses for a moment. "I'm also sorry for calling you a skank-ass ho."

A laugh escapes me. "Since you didn't know I was the wife, I totally understand. I would've thought the same thing."

"Those words would've never left your mouth."

"I said, I would've *thought* the same thing." I blow out a breath and frown at the subject change I'm about to throw out. "So, you and James are done? You're no longer dating him?"

She shakes her head. "Dating? No. Talking? Unfortunately. He won't leave me the hell alone."

"He likes the power," I say matter-of-factly.

She nods in agreement. "The asshole sure does."

"He said if I told you what a piece of crap he was, he'd also release pictures you'd sent him." I'm unable to meet her gaze for a moment as my stomach turns. "It was a reason I was scared to tell you, but I can't keep letting him do this to women."

"I understand." She reaches forward and settles her hand over mine before giving it a tight squeeze. "His threats are brutal. It's scary, hearing them and knowing it might jeopardize my future career."

Margie's majoring in communications and journalism. With her goal of being a news anchor, a public figure, nude pictures of her online would demolish any job opportunities.

We separate when I pull away to take a long sip of my coffee. The fear of James retaliating against Margie for me exposing him terrifies me, making me question my plan. I need Margie's permission before I make any decisions. She deserves that respect from me.

"We need to band together," I say, sitting up straight in my chair. "Rex spent last night reading through James's texts and emails. There were more women he was threatening, and Rex managed to get their contact information. Legally, we have nothing on him since he hasn't gone through with his threats—"

"That we know of," she adds.

"That we know of," I repeat, my eyes meeting hers. "What we do have on our side is his profession. We can report him to the university. There's no way, if we step forward and expose him, the university will overlook it. James will get in trouble. The more women, the more they'll have to listen to us."

"What if the university doesn't do anything?"

"Rex's brother's girlfriend is a journalist." I shrug. "I'll have her write an exposé on him."

"Another problem."

I raise a brow, fully aware there can be a million problems with this plan of mine.

"If we do this, it'll piss him off more. Who's to say he won't release them out of spite?"

That's a question I've contemplated a million times.

"It's a risk we have to take," I explain around a nervous sigh. "Before I meet with the dean, who we have a meeting with in a few hours, I'll text James a web link that tells him the legal repercussions. Let's pray it works."

With Rex's parents being who they are, he had his mother reach out to the dean and schedule a meeting for us. All of this is happening so fast, and I don't know how my head isn't spinning. Not only did I contact Margie, but I've also reached out to the other women on campus.

Margie sits across from me, eyes wide and speechless as she drags her fingers through her hair—her nervous tic.

"You don't have to come," I whisper, fighting to keep my voice strong as I tap my chest. "But I'm done with being his puppet."

It takes her a moment as she sucks in a few long breaths before replying, "What's the next step?"

"We have to talk to the other women," I say, dragging my phone from my crossbody bag. "Two have already agreed to meet with me, and I'm waiting on responses from the other two. I don't know if James has pictures of them since Rex isn't a creep, but he did send them threatening texts."

I pull myself up from the chair, lean forward, and rest my palms on the table. "You in?"

Margie abruptly smiles. "I'm in. Fuck Professor Cordry."

CHAPTER TWENTY-SIX

Rex

A LONG YAWN escapes me as I trudge into my apartment.

The exhaustion of being up all night, searching through James's shit, is hitting me.

Breaking into his phone was child's play, and it turned out, it was all I needed to discover sufficient evidence for him to get in trouble with the university.

He's made a game out of exploiting female students for the past four years. He'd meet them, date them, gain their trust, and then ask for nudes. When they declined, he'd assure them the photos were safe with him and other bullshit lines. My stomach curled, vomit pushing its way up my throat, when I read the threatening messages he'd sent to them when they attempted to break up with him. It looked like Carolina was the only one who'd gone far enough to marry him.

He's a womanizer.

A creep.

A fucking predator.

Men like him remind me of my father—manipulative and power-hungry.

Carolina is taking a risk by turning him into the university, and I'm so damn proud of her for showing that asshole her resilience.

James underestimated Carolina and the people who had her back. His manipulation might've worked on other women, but Lina has someone who'll kill for her, die for her, break every bone in someone's body to protect her.

I can't wait for that fucker to go down.

THE IDEA of catching up on sleep rolls through me, but I stop myself. I've been on standby since Carolina left this morning, and my phone has been glued to my side as I wait for an update.

I'm pouring my sixth cup of coffee when Carolina calls.

"Hey, babe," I answer. "How's it going?"

"Margie and I spoke to the other girls James harassed, and the six of us are going to the dean," she replies with hope in her voice.

Good.

Let him get what he deserves.

The hopefulness in her voice changes into worry. "We're doing this."

"I'm proud of you, babe." I wish I were there, at her side, wrapping her in my arms.

"Fingers crossed and pray to every saint that James doesn't retaliate."

Let him fucking try.

"You sure you don't want me to come with you?"

"As much as I'd love that, this is something us girls need to do together."

"I understand." I open the fridge and grab the leftover box of pizza. "I'm here if you need anything. Call. Text. Send a raven."

Her voice turns gentle. "I know, and that's why I love you so much."

It's heaven, hearing her say those words.

Sure, we've shared *I love yous* plenty of times, but it hits different when it's more than friendship.

Never did I think we'd be as intimate as we are now.

"Keep me updated." I plop down on the couch and take a bite of the cold pizza.

"I will," she says in almost a whisper.

"When are you coming home?"

"I'm going to stay at Margie's tonight, so we can catch up and be there for each other."

Even though her staying with Margie means she won't be with me, I smile. Carolina has never had many girlfriends and was thrilled when she and Margie became close. It broke her, losing that.

I nod even though she can't see me. "Good luck, baby. I love you."

"I love you, and thank you for having my back."

My hand goes to my heart. "Always."

I PAUSE MY GAME, tossing the controller onto the floor, when my phone rings.

Two hours have passed since I last heard from Carolina. I've refrained from calling or texting, waiting for her even though it's been killing me.

It's a dick move for frowning when it's Kyle's name on the screen, not hers.

I hit answer. "Yo."

"Hey, brother," he says. "I have good news for you."

Leaning back on the couch, I kick my feet onto the table. "I hit the lottery?"

"Even better. You can become my neighbor."

I straighten. "Really?"

"Really. I talked to Chloe, and she's willing to work with whatever you need. I'm going to text you a contact we have from the bank, so we can get you a loan."

The first thought that comes to my mind is Carolina.

Living with Carolina.

Sharing a house with her.

Letting her decorate it with all her girlie shit … but demanding she allow a few video game touches throughout the place.

It's perfect timing. My lease expires in two months, and Josh's girlfriend has been up his ass about him moving in with her.

Kyle goes on to give me price details and his contacts, and in the background, I hear Chloe say she'd love to have me as her neighbor.

There's no stopping me from chuckling. "Looks like she's more open to being my neighbor than she was with you when you moved in."

Chloe hated Kyle then, and he took great pleasure in annoying her. He'd greet her with a cheerful morning every day, and she'd respond with either a, "Fuck you," or the middle finger.

I love how she gave him so much shit and also how she managed to calm my brother down.

He needed someone to do that for him.

Like I need Carolina to be the calm to my chaos.

Us Lane boys tend to give our hearts to women nothing like us, who put us in our place and make it their mission to make us better men.

Excitement beams through me when we hang up.

Look at me.

Becoming a fucking grown-up.

CHAPTER TWENTY-SEVEN

Carolina

TODAY HAS BEEN the hardest day of my life.

We sat in the dean's office and shared our stories, exposing the scars James cut into us. I go last, tears at my eyes from listening to the stories, and break down harder at the reveal of my intimate life.

Never have I been flooded with so many emotions.

Anger. Sadness. Shame.

For so long, my fear circled around being judged, but the dean, she isn't disgusted with me.

She's disgusted with James.

Two hours later, she apologizes for James's behavior and thanks us for our honesty. Asking what she planned to do with James is on the tip of my tongue, but I bite it back, letting it go for now.

I'm not sure anyone knows the answer to that yet.

"We did it," Margie says with a low sigh when we walk out of the building.

"We did it," I repeat, matching her sigh.

If you'd told me a week ago that I'd be here with Margie, giving James what he deserves, I would've said you were as nuts as him.

Rex, his love, brought out that strength in me.

I've always had it. I just needed the nudge to build it.

We leave the university and load into Margie's car.

Where else do you go after you've told on your creep of a professor who's also your husband? The store for wine, junk food, and frozen pizza.

We veg out in front of the TV, watching Netflix, and when I finally go to sleep, it's with a smile on my face because I have my friend back.

CHAPTER TWENTY-EIGHT

Rex

TWO DAYS HAVE PASSED since Carolina exposed James to the dean of the university.

No one has heard from him, nor do we know whether he's been fired.

It's a waiting game.

If the university fails to make shit right, I'll take it to Chloe. She loves exposing assholes.

To get Carolina's mind off the drama, I'm taking her out tonight. I rented a hotel suite and booked a dinner reservation at Clayton's, the nicest restaurant outside of Blue Beech.

I'm showering when my phone rings, and since freezing my dick off to answer it doesn't sound fun, I ignore it.

Seconds later, it rings again.

I rinse the soap off my body, acting like I hear nothing.

The third time it fires off, I open the shower door, snag a towel, and am shivering when I grab my phone. My stomach twists when I see the name flashing across the screen, and I nearly drop it from answering so quickly.

"Hello?"

"Rex, it's Tricia," she shouts, alarm etched in her tone. "There's a man in the loft, arguing with Carolina. George is at work. I locked the kids in the house and am going in now. I thought you should know … to come here."

A chill colder than the one I had when I jumped out of the shower sweeps through my veins. "What's he driving?" Dropping my towel, I pull on clothes, not caring what they are. The phone is balanced between my shoulder and ear, and I struggle to tug on my shoes while running out of the house.

"Blue BMW."

Fucking James.

A blue BMW was registered to his name two years ago.

A deep breath leaves Tricia. "Going in now."

"Stay on the phone with me."

"Shoot!" Her voice trails off, becoming distant. "My dad is calling."

"Wait!"

The call ends.

I jump into my car, grip the steering wheel, and gun the gas. Heads turn in my direction as I speed through town.

I'll kill James if he lays a hand on her.

I'm only minutes away from Tricia's when I call Kyle.

"You at work?" I rush out when he answers.

"Yeah. What's up?"

"Carolina's crazy-ass ex showed up at her place."

"Shit. She's staying at Tricia's, right?"

"Yes."

He fills Gage in. "We're on our way."

Fingers crossed Kyle coming doesn't piss Carolina off, but he's a cop. If James pulls anything dumb, Carolina can file a police report, providing further evidence of his harassment. The drawback, though, is there'll also be evidence if I kick his ass.

I cut the wheel into Tricia's driveway, arriving before Kyle and Gage. I sprint up the stairs, hearing arguing from the loft, and burst inside without knocking.

Everyone's attention swings to me while I take in the

scene. Sure enough, James is here. Carolina is standing across from him, her hands clutched to her hips, and fury covers her face. Tricia is next to her, glancing around and searching for answers.

James's bitter eyes shoot to me, a sinister smile on his lips. "Oh, look," he spits. "Your little boyfriend came to the rescue, bitch."

Not a thought stops me from rushing to him, clutching the collar of his shirt, and Tricia gasps when I punch him in the face. Last time, I was nice, only choking him a bit, but James needs to learn a bigger lesson this time.

He shuffles back a few steps, his hand curling around his nose to stop the blood from my blow. "You broke my nose, you little shit!"

I stand in front of him, blocking his view of Carolina and Tricia, and my knuckles ball into fists as I wait for his retaliation.

"James!" Carolina shrieks. "You need to get out of here."

"No, *wife*," James barks, lifting his hand from his nose, blood now dropping onto the carpet. "I'm only getting started. How dare you go to the dean and pull that shit, you stupid fucking whore!"

His insult pushes me to advance his way again. He stumbles backward, attempting to dodge me, but I'm faster. A rough grunt leaves him when my hand wraps around his neck, and I pin him against the wall—the same way I did in his classroom.

Apparently, this is how we communicate best.

For someone who delivers threats to women like he's a mailman, he sucks ass at sticking up for himself *with men.*

He flails, gasping, and the pain he put Carolina through consumes my thoughts, causing me to tighten my hold. It isn't until Carolina tugs at my arm, sobbing my name, that I relax my grip.

"Carolina, go outside and wait for Kyle to get here," I hiss.

"We're here!" Kyle shouts.

When I glance over my shoulder, not only do I see Kyle and Gage, but Rick is also next to them.

Just great.

"Rex," Kyle draws my name out in caution. "Let him go. He'd be dumb to pull anything in front of the police."

Carolina continues to pull at my arm.

"Go to them, and I'll let him go," I tell her through gritted teeth. Never in my life has so much anger surged through me.

She nods, scurrying backward, and stops next to Kyle.

James's blood is on my arm when I release him, and he bends at the waist, panting. Not trusting him, I stand to his side, my eyes glued to him, in case he tries or says something stupid.

I've placed Kyle in a shitty situation. He's a police officer on duty, and I nearly choked a man to death in front of him. If he arrests me, I'll understand and accept the punishment. James had better be in that car next to me, though.

"What's going on here?"

My attention leaves James and cuts to Rick at the sound of his voice.

Rick's eyes darken as they level on James. "Who are you?"

"James Cordry," he answers through harsh pants, pointing at Carolina. "Her husband."

It takes everything in me not to knock his ass out.

Rick's attention darts to Carolina. "*Your husband*?"

The air turns dead, no one wanting to be the first to speak, until Tricia steps up.

"You're *married* to him?"

"She sure is," James replies with a smirk, which is blocked seconds later when he rubs his arm underneath his nose, catching drops of blood. "And she's cheating on me with this asshole." He tips his head my way.

Carolina's eyes shoot to me like an SOS signal for help.

"Their marriage is bullshit," I explain. "He's blackmailing her into staying with him."

Regret hits me at my words.

How will we explain his blackmailing without mentioning the pictures?

The loft is crowded with people, but my only concern is Carolina … and James making a stupid decision behind me.

"I'm so lost," Tricia mutters.

"That makes two of us," Rick snaps, his gaze bouncing among the three of us in this fucked-up love triangle. He throws his hand out toward Carolina. "It seems your sister is married to this man … *this stranger* … and is having an affair with Rex."

"That's right," James answers, stroking the red marks on his neck.

"I don't want to be married to you!" Carolina screams.

"How did you end up married?" Tricia asks.

"You see—"

Carolina speaks over James. "It's a long story that doesn't need to be told right now."

"A long story you had no problem telling the dean," James snarls.

"She deserved to know what kind of man you truly are!" Carolina screams.

The walls shake, everyone stopping, when Rick slams the door shut.

"That's enough," he yells. "I want answers."

"I'll give you answers," James says. "After these officers get this man away from me and arrest him."

"Rex," Kyle says, waving me over. "Move away, so he feels safe."

"Fuck him," I growl. "He doesn't deserve to feel safe."

"We don't care about him, man," Gage comments. "We'd prefer not to arrest you."

"You'd better arrest him!" James shrieks. "You witnessed him assaulting me!"

Gage looks over at Kyle. "I didn't see anything. Did you?"

Kyle shakes his head. "Must've been before we showed up."

James points at his nose. "Evidence!"

"He ran into a wall before he came in," I explain with a shrug.

"I hate when that happens," Gage says. "Now, get over here, Rex."

I shoot James a warning glare before moving, and everyone stares at him as if he were on trial.

"Dad," Carolina says, "this needs to be a private conversation."

"No need to talk in private," James blurts out. "It's quite simple, sir. Your daughter married me and now wants a divorce. Since I won't sign the papers, she's blackmailing me, lying to the dean so I'll lose my job." His eyes narrow on Carolina. "Retract your statement and tell them you lied. I'll sign the divorce papers, let your little boyfriend clear my devices, and be on my way." His voice shifts into a plea. "*Please.* I can't lose my job over this."

Carolina shakes her head. "No. I won't do that to the other women who stood strong with me to expose you. Your behavior needs stopped before you put another woman through hell."

"*Please*," James pleads. "If you don't, I'll ruin your life just as much. Don't forget, all I need to do is hit a simple button—"

Kyle grabs my shirt, stopping me from lunging at James.

"You do that, and not only will you be fired from the university, but you'll also be prosecuted," Carolina states matter-of-factly. "No longer will I allow you to threaten me. Do it, and you'll go to jail."

Defeat crosses James's face. "Please," he begs.

"Leave before I have them arrest you for being here," Carolina tells him, her voice strong and firm, before she holds a finger up. "Actually, I'll be right back."

James mutters, "Shit," under his breath while Carolina darts to her bedroom, returning seconds later with papers, a pen, and a Kleenex in her hand. I tense when she approaches him and shoves a Kleenex in his hand.

"Here," she says. "Don't want you to get blood on these."

Everyone watches her in confusion, and James wipes his nose, balling up the Kleenex in his fist when he's finished.

"Divorce papers," Carolina says, waving them in the air before shoving them into James's chest. "Sign them, or I'll have these kind officers make a police report. I'm sure you'd *really* lose your job if the university found out you came here and threatened me."

We wait for his next move, and time slows while Carolina and James have a staredown. The hate Carolina feels for the man who has put her through hell is clear on her face. Finally, James nods, snatches the pen, and walks around her to the coffee table. Bending, he signs his name.

"There you go," he says, slamming down the pen and leaving the papers on the table before adjusting his attention back to Carolina. "Happy now?"

She nods, and her voice is stone cold as she says, "Very."

"Thanks for ruining my life," he spits, his face tightening into a grimace. "I'm out of here."

I step in front of him, standing tall and cutting him off on his way to the door. "Remember what she said. Do anything stupid, and she'll press charges."

"Got it," he bites out, maneuvering around me.

Everyone shuffles out of his way, and he keeps his head down while storming out of the loft. Not a word is muttered until the door slams shut behind him.

"Well," Kyle says around clearing his throat, "looks like our work here is done."

"Yep," Gage agrees, rubbing his hands together. "We'll make sure"—his voice trails off as he gets his words straight—"that guy leaves, and then we'll be on our way."

Kyle throws me a wary look. "Let me know if you need anything or if he comes back."

"We will," I say.

They say their good-byes to everyone, and as soon as they leave, Tricia asks, "Are we talking about this now or later?"

"Later," Carolina and Rick answer at the same time.

Rick wears an unreadable expression as he pushes his hands into the pockets of his slacks and focuses on Carolina. "Please stop by the church when you have a minute."

Carolina's response comes out in a whisper. "Okay."

Rick tips his head in my direction. "Rex."

Tricia follows Rick as they leave.

Thank fuck.

Carolina needs time to process everything.

She places her palm on her chest, her hand now shaking, and her eyes glaze over. She composed her emotions, but now that everyone is gone, they're releasing. "Did that happen?" Her gaze pings around the room as if she imagined everything. "Did James really come here and tell everyone I was his wife?" She rushes over to grab the papers and holds them up. "And he … he signed the divorce papers. How was it that easy? He's been giving me hell for months, and all of a sudden, it's—*bam!*—here you go?"

I stand behind her, wrapping my arms around her waist, and kiss her neck. "Depends on what you think *easy* is. Your dad now knows about your marriage to James."

Her shoulders slump, and she drops the papers. "It was bound to come out sometime."

"I'm shocked he gave in so easily."

"He was cornered and hadn't expected an audience, hadn't expected *the cops* to show up." She turns, and when she wraps her arms around my neck, her unease fades. "He doesn't like his secrets exposed, and a room full of people found out he'd had a relationship with me—more evidence that could get him in trouble."

My eyes meet hers. "Does that mean you're not mad at me for calling Kyle?"

"Am I embarrassed? Absolutely. Did it help my situation? Yes." She nudges her nose against mine before drawing back a few inches. "So, thank you."

"You never told me you had divorce papers."

"I had them drawn up, waiting for when he'd finally agree to sign." She groans, tilting her head back. "Gosh, I wish it hadn't happened in front of everyone. I wanted to melt right into the carpet and disappear."

I run my hands up and down her arms. "I can help with that."

She arches a brow. "Huh? Did you turn into Harry Potter?"

"No, we can disappear from town tonight. Pack a bag."

"YOU'RE RIGHT," Carolina says. "Getting out of town has helped clear my head."

"Glad I could help." I fold my arms behind my head, resting them against the headboard of the bed, and stare at her as I'm spread out along the soft hotel sheets.

Carolina had a bag packed within ten minutes after James's dramatic visit. We stopped at my apartment for mine and drove to the city. Our dinner was bomb, and even though we had chocolate mousse at the restaurant, we ordered chocolate covered strawberries and champagne from room service.

Cliché? Yes.

Who cares?

All that matters is, my girl likes it.

As our relationship has grown more serious, we haven't done too many *date* things together. My goal is to change that.

She eats the last strawberry, licking chocolate from her fingers, and my dick twitches when she crawls up the bed on her hands and knees, wearing the same teddy she had the night at the hotel of Faye's wedding.

"Is it bad that I thought it was hot when you punched James?" She straddles my lap, a flirtatious smile on her plump lips.

Moving my arms, I rest my hands on her thighs. "Oh, really?"

Goose bumps travel up her skin when I run my fingers across it and push the teddy up to her waist.

"Yes, really." She tips her head down and separates her next words between kisses. "I think you deserve a reward."

I moan, bucking my hips up. "You love rewarding me."

"I definitely love rewarding you."

I pull the teddy over her head, throwing it across the room, and flip her over onto her back. When I slide into her, it's slow and gentle; it's *making love.*

"You're all mine," I moan into her mouth. "Say it."

"All yours," she gasps as I suck on her neck.

"Forever."

"Forever."

CHAPTER TWENTY-NINE

Rex

TWO MONTHS **Later**

I shake out my hands, an attempt to stop my palms from sweating, and take a calming breath before opening the door.

I've never been so nervous, walking into a church.

My nose wrinkles at the scent of wood polish as I walk down the aisle separating the pews. Rick is standing on the pulpit at the head of the room. His attention moves from the Bible on the lectern to me as I grow closer.

"Pastor Adams," I greet, sliding those sweaty palms down my jeans.

I've never been a flustered person.

Nervousness isn't the norm for me.

"Rex," he says, sliding his glasses off his nose and setting them down next to the Bible. "This is quite the surprise."

Yesterday, Carolina's divorce was finalized. James had been fired from the university two weeks after Carolina talked to the dean. His story hit the news outlets, so everyone knows what a scumbag he is now. Carolina considered returning to school but ultimately decided to take online classes, unsure of her career dreams now.

"I want to marry Carolina," I blurt out before the nerves get the best of me and I pass out.

He blinks, as if he's unsure he heard me correctly. "Excuse me?"

I stand tall, straightening my shoulders. "I'm in love with your daughter, sir, and I would love nothing more than for her to be my wife."

It's old-fashioned as fuck, asking for Rick's blessing, but I want the guy to like me. My anxiousness is the fear of him saying no since he's never been a fan of mine. Sure, it'd look bad if I proposed without asking for permission … but it'll look real damn bad if I do so after he didn't give me his blessing.

Him saying no won't stop me from asking her to be my wife.

Call me an asshole.

I give no fucks.

He stares at me, his eyes unreadable, before gesturing for me to follow him. Neither of us mutters a word as we walk down a narrow hall and land in a small office. Clearing his throat, he perches on the edge of the old wooden desk, his stern eyes pinned to me, and he clasps his hands together in front of him.

"My daughter's relationship with you has always concerned me," he states.

So far, not going so well.

"I didn't like it," he continues. "With your reputation, I worried you'd hurt her or be a negative influence, but you've proven me wrong."

Shock smacks into me.

Not where I thought this convo was headed.

I stand there, not saying a word, as he keeps speaking. "You've been a pillar of strength for her, and I appreciate that." His hands unclasp, and he throws them out my way. "I apologize for judging you, for doubting your intentions, but hopefully, you understand my concern."

I only nod.

Is this a yes?

I nearly fall on my ass when he stands to hold out his hand.

"I'd love nothing more than to welcome you into our family."

Hell to the motherfucking yes.

I shake his hand, unable to contain the smile taking over my face.

CHAPTER THIRTY

Carolina

"I CAN'T BELIEVE we're moving into our own house!" I squeal, jumping up and down with the new set of keys in my hand. "We're going to decorate, and I'm going to have nine million bookshelves and a great kitchen to bake in!"

Rex's game took off, breaking nearly eight hundred million in sales *in the first week*, and there's already talks for a second one. To say I'm proud is an understatement.

A few weeks ago, he asked what I thought about us moving into Chloe's house.

Living together.

Him and me.

I was ready to start packing as soon as he asked.

Today's the big day, and lucky for us, we have a team of helpers. Maliki, Kyle, and Gage are here to assist us with the heavy loading. Also helping is Rex's half-brother, Trey, and Lauren's brothers, Dallas and Hudson. Chloe and Lauren are here, and they dragged Lauren's sisters-in-laws, Willow and Stella, here to be Team Unpack.

Before moving in, we had the walls freshly painted and new flooring installed. The new furniture we'd purchased was delivered and assembled three days ago, so all we need to do is unpack and relax in our new place.

"Man, am I going to miss my old bedroom," Trey says, standing in the doorway of the guest room before walking in and falling back onto the full-size bed.

Trey lived here with Chloe before they moved in with Kyle.

"You can spend the night here whenever you want," Rex says, patting Trey on the back when he stands.

I dodge Maliki carrying a box down the hallway and stop at the empty room that once belonged to Chloe's niece. Resting against the doorframe, I imagine the possibilities. My thoughts are broken by Rex's voice.

"Pizza is here!" he yells, paying the deliveryman and grabbing the stack of pizza boxes from him.

We move, unpack, eat pizzas, and drink beer, and six hours later, the gang leaves. It's been an exhausting day, but it was worth it.

"Have you decided what to do with the spare bedroom?" Rex asks while helping me clean up the kitchen. "I'm thinking"—a smirk passes over his face—"game room?"

I dry my hands off on a dish towel and shut the dishwasher. "I have something else in mind."

He raises a brow. "What do you mean?"

"I have a surprise for you."

"I love your surprises."

"Why?" I laugh, shaking my head. "Because they normally end up with us naked?"

He snaps his fingers, a boyish smile on his lips. "Exactly why I love them, babe."

"Hopefully, you'll like this one." I gulp before moving around him and grab my phone from the counter. Unlocking the screen, I pull up the photo I found on Pinterest. My eyes stay fixed on his face as I wait for his response, afraid to miss an expression that crosses it.

He scratches his head. "Uh …" His eyes dart from the phone to me, back to the phone, and then to me. "A baby room?"

"A *nursery*," I correct, dragging the phone away from his puzzled face and setting it down.

His dark eyes widen. "Is this you saying you want to be my baby mama?"

I nod.

That boyish smile of his lights up as if he's on top of the world. "Seriously?"

I play with my hands, a shyness hitting me. "I know we haven't been dating that long."

Rex reaches out, grabbing my face, and runs his hand along my chin. "Are you serious, babe? We've pretty much been dating since high school."

"You're okay with us having kids?"

"Fucking ecstatic. I say we start now."

"That might not be my only surprise," I whisper.

"Two surprises? I like this."

His hand falls when I pull away. My heart gives a twist in my chest when I grab my purse and retrieve the small box I shoved in there earlier.

"Whoa," he says, his eyes zeroed in on the long stick I pull from the box. "Is that what I think it is?"

I nod again, the pregnancy test in my hand, afraid to speak as color stains my cheeks.

He advances a step, staring at me, speechless for a moment as his eyes widen. "Holy fuck … we're going to be parents?"

"We're going to be parents," I confirm.

An intoxicating grin lights up his face as he grabs mine.

There's no stopping my smile from matching his.

I've always wanted to be a wife and have children.

It'll be even better when my best friend, the man I love, is by my side.

Our eyes meet, his gleaming with excitement, and his thumb strokes my cheek. "You know what this means, right?"

"What?" I don't tell him I know exactly what it means—*me gaining weight, crankiness, spending thousands of dollars on baby stuff, having our entire lives change.*

"Your parents already think I'm corrupting you—"

I interrupt him, "They do not."

He snorts. "Wait until they find out I knocked you up out of wedlock."

"They'll get over it," I grumble, scowling.

His hands leave my face, and he gives me a quick peck on the lips before turning around.

My eyes narrow as he leaves the kitchen, disappears down the hall, and then returns with nothing.

Okay, maybe he returns with nothing physical, but his mood has shifted. Even though his excitement is clear, a wave of nervousness pours from him.

He clears his throat, and the way he's staring at me—full of affection, adoration, *love*—gives me goose bumps. "I want to return the surprise."

"Okay," I draw out.

Seconds later, when he drops down to one knee, my hand flies to my mouth, and I nearly fall on my ass. I peer down at him, taking in the man I've loved since high school—who brought me out of my shell, who made me believe I was more than just the quiet preacher's daughter—and I know that I never want to lose him.

"First comes love." There's a slight tremble in his words. "Then comes marriage … and then comes a baby in a baby carriage." He reaches up, his palm spreading out along my stomach, and rubs it.

My heart nearly explodes out of my chest when he fishes a jewelry box from his pocket.

The tremble in his voice is gone, replaced with a confidence that is full Rex. "Carolina Adams, the girl who stole my heart, who let me corrupt her with tequila the first day we hung out, and the woman who made me want to be a better man. I wouldn't be where I am now had you not been by my side every step of the way, being my biggest cheerleader and putting up with my shit. We have the love. Now, will you give me marriage before we put our baby in a carriage?"

Tears are in my eyes, my hand going back to my mouth, and this time, it's my voice that's trembling. "You have such a way with words, babe."

He grins that grin I love. "Gotta give a man credit. Now, what do you say? You're scaring the shit out of me down here."

I gesture for him to stand, then swing my arms around him as soon as he's on his feet and kiss every inch of his face, the word, "Yes," leaving my lips between each of them.

He rubs his thumb over his bottom lip when we separate. "Damn, it was easier for you to agree to be my wife than to write a Shakespeare paper."

EPILOGUE

Carolina

Six Years Later

I'M SHAKING MY HEAD, trying my hardest to act annoyed, as we walk into Sierra's backyard. "You spoil her *way* too much."

"What?" Rex asks, raising a brow.

I nod toward the sparkly pink unicorn cake in his hands. There was only supposed to be one birthday cake at the party, but Esme insisted she wanted a unicorn one.

What Esme wants, her daddy gives her.

"And River isn't spoiled?" he asks, tipping his head toward the Power Ranger cake I'm holding.

"Eh, good point," I mutter.

Like Esme, River tends to get what he wants.

"I wonder how many times this will happen," Rex says.

"This is only the beginning," I sing-song.

"Oh, the perks of having twins."

That's right.

We have twins.

I nearly fell off the ultrasound table when the tech told us. I had her check it again, just in case she'd forgotten how to count, but nope, two babies were inside me. No wonder I'd been eating so many bags of Peanut M&M's. I was eating for three, and that required a lot of M&M's … and ice cream … and carrots dipped in salsa.

Rex gagged every time I ate the carrots.

Who would've thought the two go well together?

Pregnant Carolina—that's who.

Even though I was a terrified mess, knowing Rex would be by my side put me at ease. No matter what, together, we make a great team.

The twins are already in the backyard in their swimsuits, waiting for us to give them the go-ahead to get into the pool. We do when we notice Willow sitting at the edge of the pool with her feet in the water. She gives us a wave while she plays lifeguard. Dallas is next to her, watching the other side of the pool as the kids splash each other.

"Oh, look, another cake," Sierra comments when I set mine down on the table. Next to it is a tall three-tier cake with a dump truck on it.

"Next year, we're sharing *one cake*. I don't care how many tears are shed," Maliki says. Walking over to us, he's shaking his head, while Molly is behind him, counting down the reasons she needs an iPhone.

"Have fun convincing Rex of the one-cake rule," I comment as Rex slides a stack of plates down the table to make room for the unicorn cake.

"I'm cool with that," Rex says. "Just make sure the boys are okay with a pink cake."

"I never said it couldn't be the one that my son picks out, which it will be. I said, *one*," Maliki corrects.

"Of course," Sierra mutters with an eye roll.

A baby boom hit Blue Beech. The same day I planned to announce my pregnancy, Sierra did, too—neither one of us knowing about the other. Four days after I gave birth to Esme and River, Sierra had her baby boy, Jax. He's a mini Maliki, exactly like his daddy with dark hair and his laid-back attitude.

That same year, another three baby girls came into the Blue Beech world. Kyle and Chloe adopted Callie. The sweetest in the bunch—*sorry, Esme*—who always shares her snacks and doesn't mind being last in line. Gage and Lauren had their little girl, Ava, who's as outspoken as her mother. Then Mia came, Stella and Hudson's glamour girl, who's already a fan of makeup and handbags. Dallas and Willow's son, Easton, was also born that year. While Callie is the sweetest girl, Easton is the sweetest little boy.

Our nights out have turned into playdates. We make them fun, and it helps that Sierra created the perfect backyard oasis. They had a pool installed and a massive custom play set built, and they have a roomy outdoor grill area. The kiddos love the pool, and since there are so many of us, each couple takes one-hour shifts, watching them swim.

"Dad!" Molly whines, interrupting us. "My birthday is in two months. Let's call it an early birthday gift."

Maliki shakes his head. "I'm not buying you a phone to text Noah all night."

"That's her *boyfriend*," Jax says, running over to us in his swim trunks, Scooby-Doo floaties wrapped around him.

"Ugh, he's not my boyfriend," Molly yelps.

"But she wants him to be her boyfriend," Maven, Dallas's daughter and Molly's best friend, cuts in.

Molly shoots her a dirty look.

"I think it's cute," Sierra says, sitting down at the table. "Maliki's daughter dating his best friend's son."

"She's not dating anyone," Maliki growls.

I grab a soda and sit down next to Sierra. "Noah is Cohen's son, right?"

She nods. "He's such a sweetheart. Cohen got him a phone, and he loves texting Molly." She glares at Maliki. "He texts her on *my phone*, which means Molly always wants it." She holds her arm up. "I vote yes to the phone."

Molly jumps up and down, clapping her hands. "Yay!"

"I need to talk to Cohen about this," Maliki grumbles. "No way am I having my daughter date a kid who hits on all the waitresses at his dad's bar."

Sierra rolls his eyes. "He's a preteen."

"Preteen or not, I don't give a shit."

Rex collapses in the chair next to me with a bottle of water in his hand, and I tune out Molly, who's still presenting her cell phone argument.

I relax in my seat, watching them play in the pool. "Can you believe they're five years old?"

"Time has flown." Rex reaches out and squeezes my thigh. "I say, we make another."

"TIME FOR BED," I call out.

Esme yawns, tipping her head back to look at me with sleepy eyes from where she's sitting on the floor between my legs. "But, Mommy, I'm not tired." Another yawn.

"Honey, you can barely keep your eyes open." I wrap the hair tie around her braid before kissing her forehead.

She loves when I braid her hair before going to bed, and then I undo it in the morning since she got her mama's hair—thick and dark.

"Hey! I'm not tired!" River shouts, running into the living room, clad in a Power Ranger costume.

River also inherited my thick, dark hair, but he got his height from Rex. Esme, on the other hand, is small like me.

"I wonder why you're not tired," Rex says, walking into the living room in gray sweats and a tee. "Is it because you snuck an extra slice of cake?"

"Maybe." River grins before pushing the Power Ranger

mask over his face.

"There is absolutely no doubt he's your son." I laugh, shaking my head.

Rex rushes over to River, playfully throwing him over his shoulder. "This Power Ranger needs his energy to fight crime tomorrow!"

River bursts out laughing as Rex carries him to his Power Ranger–themed bedroom.

"Your turn, sweetie," I say, helping Esme to her feet.

We hold hands while walking down the hallway into the pink bedroom Rex had professionally painted with unicorns and castles. I read her a short story, kiss her good night, and turn her night-light on before leaving the room. Rex comes out of River's room at the same time, and we cross paths—me going to River's room to kiss him good night and Rex doing the same with Esme. It's our nightly routine, but we switch every night, so each one gets quality time with us alone.

We're in the same home we bought years ago, but we've talked about building a new house since Rex's games have been so successful. We've saved enough money to pay for it with cash and not have to worry about bills constantly. If we decide to expand our family, we'll definitely need more room. It'll be sad, leaving Chloe and Kyle. We've grown so close, and Esme and Callie have become close friends.

I'm in my bra and panties, my pajamas in my hand, when Rex walks into the bedroom. My mouth waters when he softly shuts the door and takes his shirt off. We heard all the *marriage changes sex* talks when we were engaged, but we're the same Rex and Carolina as we were before we said our vows. The sight of my husband never fails to turn me on.

"Stop," he demands.

I pause, raising a brow. "Huh?"

"Don't waste your time with putting those on." He erases the distance between us, wrapping his arms around my waist. "We're about to make another baby."

KEEP UP WITH THE BLUE BEECH SERIES

All books can be read as standalones

Just A Fling
(Hudson and Stella's story)
Just One Night
(Dallas and Willow's story)
Just Exes
(Gage and Lauren's story)
Just Neighbors
(Kyle and Chloe's story)
Just Roommates
(Maliki and Sierra's story)
Just Friends
(Rex and Carolina's story)

ALSO BY CHARITY FERRELL

BLUE BEECH SERIES

(each book can be read as a standalone)

Just A Fling

Just One Night

Just Exes

Just Neighbors

Just Roommates

Just Friends

TWISTED FOX SERIES

Stirred

Shaken

Straight Up

Chaser

Last Round

STANDALONES

Bad For You

Beneath Our Faults

Pop Rock

Pretty and Reckless

Revive Me

Wild Thoughts

RISKY DUET

Risky

Worth The Risk

ACKNOWLEDGMENTS

Thank you so much to the following people:

You, my fabulous, wonderful readers for picking up my books and taking chance on me—for reading my words.

Jill McManamon, Jennifer Mirabelli and the Wildfire Team, Brooke Cumberland, Jovana Shirley, Jenny Sims, Mark Simion, my Street Team, Bloggers, Bookstagrammers, Give Me Books Promotions, and LJ with Mayhem Cover Creations,

.

I am forever grateful.

ABOUT THE AUTHOR

Charity Ferrell resides in Indianapolis, Indiana with her boyfriend and two dogs. She grew up riding her bicycle to her small town's public library and reading everything she could get her hands on. She's been known to read while waiting on stoplights to turn green.

CPSIA information can be obtained
at www.ICGtesting.com
Printed in the USA
BVHW031137050921
616108BV00008B/439